CONTENTS

Chapter 1 - The Hidden Cave.	7
Chapter 2 - The Land of Trymyll.	23
Chapter 3 - A day's journey from here......	29
Chapter 4 - Llewel the Elder	37
Chapter 5 - Trymyll.	44
Chapter 6 - Asmodeus the Dark Elder.	50
Chapter 7 - The Wand Tree.	57
Chapter 8 - The Road to Castell y Blaenoraid (and more lessons)...	67
Chapter 9 - A night to remember....	75
Chapter 10 - A detour and a trap.	83
Chapter 11 - Teaching Tom.	91
Chapter 10½ - Meanwhile, back at the cottage...	101
Chapter 11½ - Let the training commence...	108
Chapter 12 - Flying Lessons.	116
Chapter 14 - Arrival at Castell y Blaenoraid.	129
Chapter 15 - Castell y Blaenoraid, the tale continues....	139
Chapter 16 - Jon & Tom partner up.	144
Chapter 17 - To the Dragonlands.	157
Chapter 18 - The Council of Blaenoraid.	168
Chapter 19 - Llewel's Revenge.	180

Chapter 20. Llewel the Loser.	188
Chapter 21 - The Plot Thickens.	203
Chapter 22 - Between a Rock and a Hard Place.	216
Chapter 23 - Llewel at the Council of Blaenoraid.	222
Chapter 24 - Wizards Robes.	230
Chapter 25 - Return to the Dragonlands.	237
Chapter 26 - Get to know your Dragon.	248
Chapter 26½ - Tom and Ren.	257
Chapter 27 - How to get your magic back.	262
Chapter 28. The Master returns.	276
Chapter 29 - Order is Restored.	285
The End – Or is it?	290
Glossary of names, places, and magical things.	291

The Tales of Trymyll
Book One

Thomas, Wizard's Son.

Joseph R. Mason

JOSEPH R. MASON

Copyright

©Joseph R. Mason 2020. Except as provided by The Copyright Act 1956 UK,

No part of this publication may be reproduced, stored in a retrieval system, or transmitted in any form or by any means without the prior written permission of the publisher.

This novel's story and characters are fictitious. Certain long-standing institutions, agencies, and public offices are mentioned, but the characters involved are wholly imaginary.

All rights reserved.

ISBN: 9798570931572

Dedication

To my parents

Joseph Walter Mason

28th January 1908 - 24th March 1985

Alethea Ann Mason

29th February 1916 - 16th February 1952

who died when I was 4 days old.

To my wife Julia.

....and all who said: "He'll never do it."

CHAPTER 1 - THE HIDDEN CAVE.

In the village where Tom lived, not much happened, in the county where Tom lived, not much more happened. In fact, in the whole of the country of Wales, in Tom's eyes at least, nothing ever happened. As he walked out towards the small mountain at the back of his village, he pondered that thought. Life was dull. But that was about to change.

Tom was thirteen. He came from a small village in Wales, it doesn't matter which one, for that is neither important nor relevant. For those who do not know, Wales is a principality of the United Kingdom.

Now Wales is actually a great place to be. But in Tom's eyes, as a country, it stank, actually, it wowed. It had mountains, forests, rapid streams, gold, caves, and caverns to explore and snow in winter. It was a land of magic and mystery, dragons and wizardry, adventure, and even great danger; at least it is like that in the eyes of the storyteller.

However, Tom lived in an ex-mining village, "ex" because the coal mine closed in 1985 after the miners' strike. Now, many very odd years later I would like to say what a prosperous area it now is with industry all around and everyone happy in their jobs. But of course, that's not true, only four out of ten adults had proper jobs, the rest had little. Somehow, despite having so little to live on, most of the adults still smoked and the men still went to the so-called "Working Men's Club" and got drunk on a Friday night, got even worse on a Saturday night.....and then went to chapel on Sunday, for the forgiveness of their sins! 'Working Men's Club,' thought Tom as he strode by, more like a dosser's paradise! Even at his age, he could not understand why. Not his thoughts, of course, he had heard his foster parents, the Hadley-Smythes, say it many times before.

The Hadley-Smythes had moved to South Wales from Oxfordshire a couple of years ago to retire 'near their roots' with some vague claim on Welshness. Apart from the fact that neither of them were Welsh, had no relatives in Wales, neither had a Welsh name nor could they speak a word of the Welsh language, they were indeed very Welsh, well at least they lived there anyway. In reality, Tom didn't know anyone who spoke Welsh in South Wales, but that was not the point.

They had both been university professors at one of the universities in Oxford. They were never clear about which one nor did they ever manage to say what they lectured on. All Tom knew was that they spoke in a very funny manner, pronouncing every letter and syllable. They couldn't pronounce some simple words, to them a house was 'a hise', they would never say bike, always bicycle. They drunk only the best red wine, or red wane as they called it and referred to fizzy wine as champers, always followed by a "haw, haw, haw," which was their version of a laugh. Anyway, Tom was stuck with them, despite what he thought about them and adults in general, they had always been kind to him and only lived a few doors down from his mum's house in an end-terrace with quite a nice garden. Why people so grand lived in a miner's cottage was a mystery to Tom, but somehow their cottage seemed much bigger on the inside, they had a grand piano in the front room and a huge candelabra hung in the centre of the room. They had always welcomed his friends and seemed to be able to produce fantastic cakes and sweets for him and his mates out of thin air. He had been with them for a couple of years, they arrived just after Howl, a small Jack Russel terrier which had sort of adopted Tom but then moved into his mother's house.

Tom went to the local comprehensive school; it was a small affair with less than four hundred pupils. Every few years, the council would try to close it and merge with a couple of other schools in neighbouring villages, but they kept protesting and marching on the council offices, so the council would back down and let it lie for another couple of years. Tom didn't really like school, not helped by Mrs Glynn, his form tutor, who was, in Tom's eyes, a tyrant and a bully. Tom could not see that she was hard on some of them because she cared for them and wanted them to succeed. In many ways, Tom could only see the worst in grown-ups, he judged them all the same as his father who had left him, deserted him, and didn't care at all.

The only good thing about school was his mates and rugby. He loved rugby, he didn't exactly have the build of a prop forward, but Tom was a good scrum half, he was quick and almost seemed to run between the legs of the opposition. His long red hair looking like a human torch as he ran, his bright blue eyes flashing left and right, looking for an opening. Tom was a popular lad and was always picked for the school under fifteens rugby team.

Tom and his mates used to love the countryside, and at weekends they would explore the small mountains that surrounded the village. They used to pretend to be spies, sent to find out about a secret hideout somewhere in the village, they would run across the fields, hide behind the dry-stone walls shooting pretend rifles, build bases inside the mouths of the many caves, watching the village below through old loo rolls which they pretended were binoculars. But those days were past now, they were teenagers, full of anxiety and torment, rebelling against an unjust world and of course playing computer games instead.

Tom was no worse off than some but far worse off than many. In fact, Tom was remarkably close to the bottom of the heap. He only had a Mum and didn't know where his dad was; he had left when Tom was a week old and took his only brother with him. His brother Jon would be about fifteen now; he had never seen him, if he had, he couldn't remember him, and his mother never spoke much of either of them. So, neither did he. All he knew was that his brother had the same flame-red hair and piercing blue eyes that he did. All he had to remember his dad by was a small gold signet ring. The ring was made of pure Welsh gold with a black onyx stone with the emblem of a dragon carved into the face. It just fitted onto his right-hand ring finger, he had never thought much about it, he had worn it for as long as he could remember. It was small and difficult to come over his knuckle, otherwise, he was sure his mum would have taken it away and pawned it by now. His mum was ill, in a wheelchair, crippled by life she used to say, she had trouble breathing and had an oxygen bottle strapped to the wheelchair. The only visitor his mum ever had was Father Seamus O'Reilly, a Roman Catholic priest, strangely, they weren't even catholic.

However, some days he preferred his own company, sometimes he liked to walk out onto the mountain at the back of the village to a cave about halfway up, sit in the entrance and look out over the valley to the village below with its tiny little people all rushing about their dull lives, Tom didn't know why they hurried so, most had nothing to do and nowhere to go.

Tom believed in his own mind that he was the only person who knew of the cave, none of his friends ever mentioned it, he never saw anyone else near it and there were none of the normal signs of human activity, cigarette ends, empty beer cans, discarded bottles of cheap cider, and used instant bar-b-ques. There were several caves around here; all had the signs of human detritus and waste, but not this one. It was named Dragon's Hole, Tom didn't know why; no one believed in dragons, this was the twenty-first century after all. But Dragons Hole it was, always had been and probably always would be. The fact it had a name meant that others knew it was there, it was on the maps and everything, you could even see the entrance on Google Earth, but no one ever came up here, except Tom.

Tom had now reached the edge of the village and proceeded

up the road to the stile which bridged the dry-stone wall. He crossed the field of sheep climbed another wall and started up the steep path to the cave. He never wondered why, if no one ever came here, why was there was a path? He never worked out the reason why none of the local youth came here for their illicit smoking, underage drinking, and stuff....

He had come up the rough path to the cave many times and sat at the cave entrance to look and think but had never ventured any further in than the few feet or so that the entrance light allowed. Inside it was dark, very dark, very, very dark! Today he felt adventurous and had brought a torch. He had thought about this quite hard, did he want to go further in than the light allowed? What if there was someone in there? A mass murder escaped from prison hiding there, bats, ghosts, witches, or a huge snake. But no, he was Tom, he feared nothing and did not believe in ghosts or witches or anything scary, in Britain we did not have poisonous cave snakes. Bats could do you no harm at all and if there was a mass murderer on the loose, he would have seen it on the TV.

He gingerly ventured in, scrambling across rocks until the light was just behind him. He could hear dripping water as it seeped through the rocks and from the ceiling. He could feel his heart pounding inside his chest. Torch time he thought, the light penetrated the darkness so quickly it seemed the darkness retreated into the rocks. Tom climbed across a couple more boulders and to his surprise found that, once he was a few feet in, the scattered rocks were behind him and there was quite a flat path ahead. The small torch threw up huge shadows as he moved, shapes formed and dissolved on the walls of the cave like ever changing fast moving clouds. He could make out a huge spire in the distance, but soon realised it was the shadow of a rather small stalagmite, or was it a stalactite? Never could remember which was up and which was down.

"Now, what was the memory jogger?" he said to himself, "stalactites have to hold on tight!"

So, he was right. He saw the shapes of monsters, dinosaurs, trees, towers, all for a fleeting moment before their form dissolved to another shape. Tom ventured on, deep into the cave. Then he saw two green orbs floating just in front of him a good eighteen inches apart, it gave him quite a start and he stopped in his tracks. For some reason, he did not turn and run, for an even less explicable reason he was not even that scared. As his eyes focused, he could see they were eyes, big eyes, several inches across, pearlescent green with long vertical slits to let the light in. In front of them, he could make out a couple of nostrils at the end of an exceedingly long nose. What on earth was a cow doing this far back in the cave he thought, albeit a big cow he thought, he even verbalised his thought.

"What are you doing here then cow?" Tom said in his best Welsh accent.

"Cow?" a voice came back, but this time with a perfect, crisp and clipped Oxford accent, "who in the Makers name are you referring to as a cow?"

Beads of sweat instantly formed on Tom's brow and the blood drained from his face. Tom dropped the torch, which of course went out......

"Hadley-Smiff! What are you doing here?"

"Hadley-Smythe is the correct pronunciation, however, I am not he."

"Mass murderer then?"

"No, No my dear boy, it is I Howel," the voice replied.

"Howl the talking cow?"

"NO! Not Howel the talking cow for crying out loud! Oh alright," there was a small 'pop' and the eyes and nose joined up to what appeared to be an enormous purple dragon. He must have been forty, fifty, maybe sixty feet long, scales, long neck, and huge teeth, in fact, all the normal mythical creature features! But purple? He just looked so the wrong colour! More caricature than reality.

"Don't be stupid!" Tom said, "dragons don't exist, especially not purple ones."

"Well," said the dragon, "if I had a penny for every time someone said that to me, I'd have enough money now for a cup of tea and a small Welsh cake."

"How can I see you in the dark?" Tom said.

"Simple, it's called dragon light," the dragon said in a matter of fact sort of way.

"Not going to eat me, are you?" Tom didn't quite know where that question came from but was somehow glad he had got it in early.

"No dear boy, I am not going to eat you..........unless of course..... no, no, dragon humour, take no notice."

"Are you magic then?" Tom asked.

"Of course," Howel said, "otherwise you would not be able to see me, it is after all pitch black in here."

"Don't believe in magic," Tom said.

"Oh super, now I have enough money for a cucumber sandwich as well," he replied irritably.

"I've got a dog at home; his name is Howl. We call him that because that's what he does when we don't take notice of him. He howls."

"Enchanting, and what sort of dog is this Howl?" Howell asked, even though he knew the answer.

"He's a Jack Russell we think. We've had him a couple of years. He is quite cute, though rather bad-tempered though. Dunno where he came from, just turned up and stayed one day. Anyway, how come you speak English then?" Tom didn't know why he was telling a dragon about his dog, nerves he suspected.

"Because dear boy, if I spoke Welsh you wouldn't understand a word I said!" There was now an even bigger hint of irritation in his voice.

"So, you can speak Welsh then?"

"I can, I speak over one hundred languages, fluently!"

"Latin?" Tom asked.

"Yes, Latin as well, we speak it more and more nowadays to sound authentic," he said, more for effect than anything else and with more than a hint of sarcasm.

" Okay," Tom replied, "and there's no need for sarcasm."

"Whatever!" said the dragon with a wearisome sigh, sounding more like a post-pubescent teenager than a sixty-foot dragon.

"So then, why are you here? In this cave like?" Tom said, again in his best Welsh accent.

"I am the keeper of the gate to the Land of Trymyll," he replied with a certain amount of pride.

"So, you have to stay in this old cave all the time then?" asked Tom.

"No, every Tuesday, Thursday and alternate Saturdays," he replied, again sarcastically, "Of course I don't, but it is a full-time job, have you never seen the advert in the corner shop 'part timekeeper of the gate required, enquire within'?" The dragon calmed, "Sorry about that, life can be a little tiresome, I have been the gatekeeper for a little under five hundred years and you are only the thirteenth different person who has come through the gate."

"Five hundred years don't be daft, no one lives that long," Tom said.

Howel ignored the interruption and continued, "I am the gatekeeper, but the cave is locked and invisible to all unless I or my master opens it up, only then do I need to be here in this horrid, damp little hole."

Then in reply to Tom's earlier statement, Howel continued without drawing breath...

"Maybe humans do not live for five hundred years but dragons do, anything up to two or three thousand years for most of us, some, red dragons, even longer. Anyway," he continued, "My time here is almost ended, I will be gone quite soon."

"You going to die or something then?"

"No dear boy, contract runs out in five years, then I'm off to the Himalayas for a holiday before returning to Trymyll," he then said as an afterthought, "Are you saying I look old? I'll have you know I am barely six hundred years old and in my prime, at least another millennium and a half left in me if not two! Even more if I eat well!"

"Sorry," Tom said semi-apologetically, "lights not too good in here."

"Anyway," Howel continued, "Tom?" almost as a question, "may I call you Tom?"

"Well yes," Tom replied warily, "How do you know my name?

"Because, my dear boy, I have been watching you since the day of your birth and calling you for the last two months."

"Calling me?"

"Yes, calling you. Why else do you think you are here?"

"But I am always here, I come here all the time."

"You don't, you have only been coming here for the last eight weeks, you only think you have been coming here forever. Have you never wondered why you always come here alone?" Howel did not wait for an answer but continued, "It is because this place only exists for you. No one else can see it or find it."

"But I can see it on maps and Google Earth and stuff."

"Yes, I know you can, but no one else can."

"But I've shown it to my mates on the computer."

"Yes, I know that as well, but as soon as they turn away, they forget what they have seen, children have such short spans of concentration."

"What about the path?"

"Only you."

"The stile?"

"Only you."

"The mountain?"

"Now we are being silly. Of course, the mountain is there. But people can only see what I let them see. Now we must get on, there is much to do."

"Sorry mate, you might have lots to do, but I have to get back for my tea."

"Oh contraire," Howel replied, "we have lots to do and you dear boy are going nowhere."

"But the Hadley-Smiffs are expecting me."

"No we're not, not tonight anyway," Howel replied.

"What do you mean by that?"

"Oops, slip of the tongue dear boy, forgot to mention, the Hadley-Smythes are just a figment of our imaginations and other people's imagination. Now they are as if they never existed, which of course they didn't. So, as I said, we must push on."

"Hang on, hang on, you don't get away with it that easily, I've been stuck with those two phony Welsh people for two years, I get one sentence of a very bad explanation and you say, we must push on?"

"Well," Howel said, "there's not that much to say, they did exist, sort of, but they were sort of magicked up by Llewellyn the Brave and me in the imaginations of all who met them. Oh, and you only think you've been with them for two years, it was actually only two months, it just seemed longer," he paused, "for both of us."

"But they were real, solid, there," Tom said frustrated, "I saw them with my own eyes, not with my imagination," he stopped short, "what do you mean only two months? I was with them for two long years!" His voice lifting to a slight screech.

"It is so difficult to explain to a non-magical person, yes they were there, without a doubt, but then again, they weren't there at all. If that makes sense. Anyway, they're gone now and no one in the village will remember them."

They started to go along the cave's path further and further from the entrance, further and further into the darkness.

"I still remember them."

"Well of course you do," Howel continued, "that is because without knowing, you helped form both the illusion and the reality, their images were woven into your thought patterns in a far more intricate way which one day soon you will hopefully understand."

"What about my mum?"

"Oh no, she is real, very real."

"That's not what I meant, and you know it," Tom said irritably.

"She remains on the other side. She knows you are here; she knows you are in safe hands."

"I wish I did."

"Oh! Dear boy. You can be so hurtful, of course you are in safe hands, if you were not, I would have probably eaten you by now," he said with a chuckle, "and not only are children so tasty, they add years to one's existence."

"Why am I here? Cos I'm not going nowhere till I know," Tom said while still walking.

"My dear boy, you really are in the safest of hands," Howel said again, but this time in a concerned, almost warm voice, "The reason for your being here is simple, it is, in fact, the reason for your very being, it is your destiny dear boy, your raison-d'être."

"Is that Latin?"

"No, ...French."

"Meaning what?"

"Meaning, the most important reason or purpose for your very existence. All will be revealed in good time. My job is just to get you over the threshold and one day's journey in, and then you will be met by Llewel the Elder who will take you on from there."

"What if I don't want to go, what if I decide to turn back and run back to the village?"

"You can't, and you know it. You are so like your brother; he is petulant as well."

"You know my brother?"

"Yes, and your father too, both have trod this path before you. Many, many times."

"But Jon was only two when he and me dad disappeared."

"Maybe, but he and your father came this way and have been back and forth many times."

Tom continued in silence, he might meet his dad and brother; that was a good enough reason to go on if he ever needed one. But what if he did? What would he say? How would he feel? How would they feel? They deserted him after all. Would he love them? Should he love them? Could he love them?

"Painful thoughts," said Howel, "and ones I cannot answer, questions only you can sort out if and when you meet them. Oh, excuse me! Did I mention dragons can pick up thoughts?"

"So, you can read my mind?"

"No, your thoughts, not your mind. There is a difference, a thought is just a suggestion of what is going on in your head, I can only get the thought."

If and when, thought Tom. Forget the 'if' word, just think about 'when'. He continued to walk silently but now with more purpose.

Tom had never met a dragon before, he still wasn't sure if he believed in them, he had much to learn about them. He never imagined them to be purple, did not know they could talk and did not realise they were so camp!

"...and I heard that thought! I am not camp, I am cultured, well-bred and well brought up ......and I still might eat you," he added as an afterthought to make himself sound harder.

"And I don't believe you will eat me because," he was interrupted by Howel mid-sentence.

"And what brings you to that epic conclusion?"

"......because if you have been watching me since I was a baby and have gone to all the effort with the Hadley-Smythes and the cave and all that, you would have wasted a lot of time and trouble for such a small snack. Especially if you have a close look at me, I'm just skin and bone, there's more meat on a butcher's apron!"

"Oh, brother! Another one of those clichés that you humans use to try and buy time before my dinner. Don't eat me, I have a fat friend. They all whine the same pathetic line or a variation of it!"

"What! You do eat people then?"

"Well yes," the dragon replied with a slight awkwardness, "but not all the time and always with good reason."

"Good reason?" Tom more squeaked it than articulated the statement.

"Yes, good reason," Howel replied, "you see, some consider it a sport to hunt and kill dragons, and it can be done if you know what you are doing, the only way is with an enchanted sword, spear or arrow of cold iron. Oh, and you have to know where to stab me."

"Where's that then?"

"That dear boy is very privileged information. Anyway," he continued, "it inevitably ends in them being eaten. Now, this is the interesting bit, every time a dragon eats a human, four things happen. As I am sure you know a human's life is three score years and ten. When you eat one, every year they are under the age of seventy is then added to the dragon's life and every year older is deducted by the same amount. Fortunately, all these knights are young and foolish, so we often put on a few dozen years every time. Plus, when you eat them you gain all their knowledge plus their language, and if from a wizard family, their magic powers as well. So, it's win, win, win, win, win!"

"That's five wins and only four points," Tom said.

"Oh yes, the fifth win is, they do taste so good!" Howel said this with a definite smile and a wink.

He and Tom continued their walk through the cave, it seemed like miles to Tom, the fact was, it was linking his world to a parallel world on the other side of the universe, so miles didn't come into it, it was light years! Howel started to talk......

"There are things you need to know, and I will teach you some as we walk. First, as we have already started, let us continue to talk of dragons, obviously my most expert subject, but I excel in so many. Dragons come in many shapes and sizes, but what matters is their colour. Golden dragons are the most magically powerful, and if you can align yourself with a Golden Dragon, you will share their powers. Golden Dragons are always for good and never evil. They can change their size and shape, their normal 'disguise' is a sparrow-hawk, but they can metamorphose to any shape they wish, even take on the form of a human if desired. Queen of the Golden Dragons is a graceful female called Máthair. I doubt that you would ever meet HRH Máthair, Queen of the Golden Dragons, but if you do, always best behaviour, and watch your manners.

Red dragons are to be sought after as a companion; they are very magical, faithful, trustworthy and have longer lives than any other dragons. Unfortunately, their metamorphic other is a hen or cockerel according to their gender. They are also, in many ways, quite mad. Their queen, Aelwyd, Queen of the Red Dragons, is, completely bonkers. But please don't tell her I said that should you ever meet her. Unlikely as that is.

Purple dragons are of course the most cultured, intelligent, good looking and modest of all dragons and grossly underrated in my opinion. Our alternative shape is a most undignified and unhappy affair, that of a small dog of an indeterminate breed but akin to a Jack Russel. Oh why, oh why could it have not been something more magnificent, a golden eagle, or at least a beautiful pure-bred dog. A proud Weimaraner, a noble Doberman or even a loving Labrador?" his voice trailing off whimsically at the end.

"You mean you're a mongrel then."

Howel ignored the remark and continued....

"Blue Dragons are the most dangerous, they have no scruples and will eat you as soon as look at you. They normally disguise as black cats, so never trust a Blue Dragon, and never trust a black cat. They are not very magical and can only hold their alter-ego shapes for a few minutes before reverting to a dragon again, the little magic they have is dark, very dark. They also tend to be very stupid. Above all, treat all dragons with suspicion, as many are both able to change their shapes and some their colour if they have the right magic. So, before you approach any dragon, make sure you know their true colours."

By the time Howel had finished his long instruction, and there was much, much more which was not recorded here, they had reached the end of the tunnel, the exit was tiny, just big enough for Tom's skinny little thirteen-year-old body to squeeze through. A very welcome light pierced into the darkness.

"Well, I suppose this is goodbye for now," Tom said.

"And why do you say that my young child?"

"Well, for a start, you are about 20 foot too fat for a hole that's about one-foot across," Tom said rudely.

"I'm so glad you listened to my lesson on dragons," Howel said wearily. There was an audible 'pop' and when the smoke cleared the 60-foot dragon reappeared about the size of a small dog. In fact, he was a small dog, albeit a purple one. Tom laughed at such a sight but tried to hide it as a cough, Howel looked as scornfully as he could at Tom, (being a purple dog did not help him look angry at all). Tom laughed even more at the scowl and headed for the open air. Howel shook and settled into a white, black, and tan patched Jack Russell.

"Quickly though the hole. Thankfully, I can hold this shape for a quite a while, long periods if I must, but it is so undignified."

They scurried through into the light and emerged atop a huge wooded valley.

"What! You look just like Howl!"

Another 'pop' and the dragon was back.

"Of course I do, that is because, I am he."

CHAPTER 2 - THE LAND OF TRYMYLL.

No sooner were they through the small cave exit when 'Pop' and the small dog returned to his natural form of a dragon, a sixty-foot Purple Dragon. Now Howel looked completely different, the huge dragon looked, well, like a dragon instead of a cartoon character, Howel was still purple, but now it was an iridescent purple, shimmering in the light, ever-changing hues and colours, now Tom could see scales, huge purple scales reminiscent of plated armour. Massive wings with horned spikes like sharpened spears at each joint in the wing, a massive head with teeth, row upon row of sharp, no, incredibly sharp teeth and a red glow in his chest where his fire cavity was. Tom stood there awestruck, of course, he had never seen a dragon before and had nothing to compare, but he was breath-taking. A sixty-foot magical talking dragon. This was beyond wow!

"Welcome to the Land of Trymyll," Howel announced.

"So, where's Howl then?"

"As I said, I am Howl, as you would say, actually my name is Howel. H.o.w.e.l," he spelt out to make sure Tom understood the difference.

"Yes, but where's me dog gone?"

"I, Howel the Purple Dragon and Howl, as you call him, are the same. Look, never mind for now. You obviously heard nothing of my lesson on dragons. I'll try again later. But for now, we must move on."

He still sounded like Hadley-Smyth, so not at all frightening.

"So, as I said earlier, welcome to the land of Trymyll."

"Looks like Wales to me," Tom said with a disappointed voice, "all valleys and mountains, I was expecting something different; I don't know what mind you, just different."

"Well, this is as different as it gets. But don't worry dear boy, Trymyll is different, quite different."

As he looked out over the valley, Tom could see some differences, but they were not huge, but then, as he thought, what was he expecting? Well, he was not expecting anything, because he had not anticipated any of what had happened today.

He could see mountains and forests, way into the distance he could see smoke rising in the furthest mountains, he assumed this must be volcanoes, but these were the Dragonlands. The smoke was from the dragons which lived in that part of Trymyll. A place he would have to venture to one day, but not something he either had to worry about or have knowledge of now. In another direction he could see vast flat countryside disappearing off into the distance, there were wooded areas, rivers, and small villages, he could see quite a large town some miles away. Another turn and he saw a vast lake, and he meant vast, it must have been twenty miles long and ten miles wide, it was massive. It still didn't look much different from Wales mind you; Tom was just about to say that again when.....

A huge eagle swooped down; in his talons, he held a basket. He landed next to them and to Toms surprise spoke to Howel.

"The master has sent food and drink for the boy."

"Thank you, Griff," Howel replied. Before Tom could even think what was happening, the eagle was gone.

"Different enough?" enquired Howel.

"Different enough," replied Tom with a grin.

Tom opened the basket, he was surprised to see its contents, again he did not know what to expect, but somehow, this took him by surprise. There were his favourite cheese and chutney sandwiches, thick white bread, crusts on. Cheese and onion crisps, a chocolate bar, a couple of cans of lemonade and an apple.

"Well, what were you expecting?" said Howel "Stuffed quail and a flagon of ale?" he paused and then continued, "The master has such a sense of humour, conjuring such food for you. Don't get too used to it though; next time it might be the quail and ale dinner!"

"I hope not," Tom said, "beer does funny things to people, where I come from, in Wales that is, the men drink beer on a Friday night and fall over in the street. Disgusting behaviour if you ask me."

"You forget so quickly. I do know these things; I was living in your grubby little town for some time."

"It's not grubby, it's a proper Welsh mining town and we are a proud people."

"Proud of what I have no idea," Howel muttered under his breath.

Tom tucked into his lunch, the lemonade was warm, not the best way to drink lemonade he thought. Howel picked up his thought and spoke.

"If you don't like warm lemonade, cool it down a little."

"And how am I supposed to do that? I seem to have forgotten to pack a fridge!" Tom retorted.

"Simple magic. Even a human can do it if they try, it is just a simple cantrip. A little lesson in physics combined with a little lesson in magic. Physics first. Your lemonade is made up of billions of molecules," Howel said with a sigh like a bored teacher at school, "when a liquid is heated, these molecules move around at an ever-increasing rate until they eventually break apart and form steam. When a liquid cools, they move around slower and slower until they eventually stop altogether and form ice. So, we focus on the can, imagine the molecules inside all rushing about frantically, then we visualise them slowing down and slowing down and slowing down," his voice became slower and softer as he spoke as if he was demonstrating what he was saying, "any questions?"

"Yes. What's a can trip?"

"A cantrip, my dear boy is a very minor spell, taught to an acolyte to build his confidence. Many humans can perform a cantrip. These include cooling water, lighting a candle, or calling a pet over without speaking. Any more questions?"

"What's an ac-o-lite?" Tom said the word vowel by vowel as he had never heard it before.

"An acolyte is in wizarding terms, an assistant to a wizard who is learning magic, a sort of apprentice. You will be an acolyte once your training begins."

"What training? Who says I want to be a wizard anyway? I don't even believe in magic. No such thing as a wizard." Tom stopped short. He had seen magic in the last hour which had amazed and shocked him. This morning he didn't believe in dragons, especially not purple ones. Even if he had believed in dragons, which he didn't, he wasn't expecting a sixty-foot one to turn into a small dog to scrabble through tiny cave exit. He didn't believe that an eagle could talk, but he heard one. He still didn't believe in wizards anyway.

"Anyway, I've got to get back."

Howell ignored him and continued, "Oh my, oh my. You Tom will meet a wizard by the end of today and another in the morning. One day Tom, you will be a very great wizard indeed."

Tom tried not to think it, but he thought it anyway. 'This dragon has definitely lost his marbles now'.

"Rude," said Howel, "very rude indeed."

Tom looked down at his can of lemonade. Condensation was running down the outside of the tin, the can was very cold, very cold indeed.

"Did I do that?"

"No dear boy, I did."

They paused while Tom finished off his lunch and put the second can of lemonade in his pack.

"Right, we really must get on, we have to be somewhere before the sun goes down and it is quite a hike from here. Luckily for you, it's mostly downhill."

"Why are we walking?" asked Tom.

"What would you suggest, we wait for a bus or hail a taxi?"

"Well," Tom said gingerly, "could I not ride on your back and fly through the air?"

"No." Howel replied sternly, "It takes great skill to fly on a dragon's back. It's not as easy as you think and the ones you see at the cinema are not real dragons, they are computer-generated images."

"I knew that," Tom retorted, "cos dragons don't exist."

As soon as he said it, he felt stupid, after all, he was saying it to an actual dragon.

"Anyway, it would draw too much attention to your coming. Others also await your arrival, but they are not so friendly."

"What do you mean? Who? And why not so friendly?" Tom asked slightly worried.

"Llewel the Elder will reveal all to you when he is ready."

"Anyway, who is this bloke Llewel the Elder? Why is he so important that only he can tell me what's going on?"

"Llewel the Elder is important; very important, especially in his own mind, he is one of the seven High Elders of the council which govern the land of Trymyll, and you must be important as well if they send one of their own to help take you safely to the capital, Blaenoraid."

"What do you mean? Why am I important? Why am I here?"

"I have already said too much. You must trust me. No more questions please."

Howell sounded so pathetic; Tom decided to drop the subject.

And so, they continued their walk silently down the mountain and into the valley, a thirteen-year-old boy, who didn't believe in magic or dragons, and a sixty-foot purple dragon who did magic. No contradictions there then.

CHAPTER 3 - A DAY'S JOURNEY FROM HERE……

Tom and Howel started down the mountain and into the valley. The path was steep and at times quite slippery, near the top, the trees were small and stunted the vegetation coarse and scratchy, mainly heather and gorse. Lots of rock and shale underfoot making the going quite slow at times. As they moved down the mountainside the trees became bolder in appearance the shrubs greener and other foliage grew, making it softer underfoot. This made walking easier but no less tiring, after several hours of walking, stumbling and the occasional fall by Tom, they found themselves in what could only be described as a forest at the bottom of the valley. Here the trees were tall, every hue of green, some almost yellow in appearance and the odd copper beech tree interspersed amongst pines, yews, and other evergreens. It was very wild. It looked as if he may have been the first-ever person to set foot in here. Totally undisturbed virgin forest.

There was a sudden crack and a pop, Howel had turned back into Howl and Tom was left standing there. Ahead he could see an old man of Afro-Caribbean origin, walking through the woods. He had a staff in his hand which he leaned on heavily to walk and over one shoulder hung several dead rabbits which were freshly caught, and a brace of pheasant. On the other shoulder hung a bow. He walked slowly and steadily as if with purpose but with a distinct limp, he had the pain of age carved into his face.

Tom froze as he didn't know whether this was one of the "less friendly" people Howel had spoken of. Suddenly, behind the old man, Tom saw what can only be described as a hideous creature silently creeping up behind him. The 'thing" walked upright like a man but had scales like a fish, flaming red hair and terrible looking teeth, brown and sharp like barbed ivory thorns, long claw-like nails at the end of sinuous fingers and a look of cold hate on its face.

"Look out!" Tom shouted.

Before the word 'look' had even left his lips the creature sprang, as he did the old man, he turned with unusual agility for a man of his age............and then the most amazing thing happened, without seeming to move, the man appeared beside Tom, bow stretched, arrow already loosed and flying, as if in slow motion towards the thing. His aim was true and just before it struck its heart, the hideous monster turned to fire, then smoke and then vanished in the wind.

"What on earth was that!" exclaimed Tom in a highly agitated and squeaky voice.

"Thank you," the old man said, "must be losing my touch, he almost got me that time, and I almost got him. That dear boy was a trygall," said the old man.

"What do you mean by almost got him? I saw the arrow hit him and he disappeared in a puff of smoke," said Tom, "don't tell me you missed him, and he's still out there."

"Oh, don't worry about Tryg, he does that all the time."

"All the time!" exclaimed Tom, his voice getting higher with each word.

As he spoke, the smoke reformed and the trygall appeared next to them, this time, however, he was different, still ugly, pug ugly in fact, but with a sense of peace about his face and an 'almost' smile on his face.

"Allow me to introduce, this is Tryg, my personal trygall, I am Flintock the Elder, and you are? ...."

"Tom....., Tom Jones," he said with some trepidation.

"And what are you doing wandering in the woods all alone young Tom?" Flintock said in a teasing sort of voice.

"Err. Walking my dog?" Tom replied, raising his intonation at the end of the sentence which turned it into a question.

"Yes of course you are," said Flintock replied with sceptical voice, "and where is your dog?"

"Well here," Tom replied pointing at Howel in Jack Russell mode.

"Call that a dog?"

"Yes," Tom said sheepishly

"What's his name then?"

"Err…. Howl?" He said, again sounding more like a question than an answer.

"Well I've never met a dog with a name like Howl," he said, "a big purple dragon called Howel, however, that's a different matter."

There was a pop and there stood Howel, all sixty foot of purple dragon with a slightly embarrassed look on his face.

"How did you know?" Tom asked.

"Well, I am a great wizard, I have sight beyond sight, I understand things you have never heard of or dreamed of, I have power beyond power and knowledge beyond knowledge, but mainly….," he paused for dramatic effect, "I saw you coming," he laughed.

"Hi Flintock, how are you, and how's Tryg?" asked Howel.

"We are both well, thank you. I saw you coming so I caught us all some supper, you both must be hungry after your journey. There is a hut I have prepared just through this thicket where we can safely stay the night, I have placed many enchantments around it so no one and no thing can find it or see it."

Tom didn't mind the no one, but the no thing bit was a little unnerving.

"Oh, and by the way, the limping old man thing is just a ruse until I was sure who was coming."

As he spoke, Flintock morphed into a much younger man, his skin was almost ebony black, but he was tall, upright, strongly built and Tom could see that he had quite a handsome face with high cheek bones and two symmetrically cut scars on each cheek, "and I'm sorry about the little game Tryg and I play, it keeps us both on our toes you understand."

Tom didn't like to say so, but no, he didn't understand. They all walked deeper into the woods, there was a small clearing, and in the clearing, there stood a hut, or at least the remains of a hut. It was small, no bigger than a garden shed, it was tatty, run-down, broken, overgrown with ivy and had a hole in the roof.

"How are we going to sleep in that? It's too small, we won't all fit in," Tom declared.

Flintock cut him short.

"Oh, it's not that bad, looks can be deceiving, it might be quite nice inside,"

"I don't somehow think so," Tom muttered under his breath as he walked all around the outside of the 'garden shed' before going back to the front.

The door swung open and they entered in, Howel now in doggy mode for obvious reasons. The door closed behind, it was very dark, but there they were, one boy, one wizard, one trygall and a 60-foot dragon, now the size of a small dog.

As Tom's eyes became accustomed to the gloom and as torches, candles and candelabra were magically lit, he could not believe his eyes. They now all stood in a great hall with doors on all sides, a vaulted ceiling with windows all around to let in the light, a huge table in the middle, comfortable chairs, sofas and cushions all around the room and a massive fire burning in an enormous inglenook fireplace at the far end of the room. It seemed as big as a football pitch, and yet he knew that they had entered a small hut. Tom at once exited the building, ran around the shack and back into the front door.

"Like I was saying, it looks a bit rough on the outside, but once you're in, it can be quite comfortable."

For once Tom didn't know what to say. His thoughts were racing, his heart was pounding, but he was silent. He wanted to say something, but he was so overwhelmed, so excited that he just couldn't find the words.

Flintock broke the silence, "come, let us eat, Tryg, make yourself useful and get the dinner on."

He threw the rabbits and pheasant to the trygall who then bounded down the hall to the far end to prepare food.

"He can cook then?" Tom asked, finding his tongue again.

"Oh yes, trygalls are very fine cooks, they have an instinctive knowledge of herbs and spices, they can forage for nuts and roots and from very little produce a very fine feast indeed."

"What else can they do?"

"Well, magically little. As far as magical powers, they are a bit of a one-trick pony. They are firemasters."

"Firemasters?" questioned Tom.

"They can, as you saw earlier, disappear into smoke, reappear out of the smoke, they can also turn into a fiery torch and can control fire in any way they want, raining fire onto their enemies, moving fire around or even bringing any fire into themselves thus removing it from whatever is burning. Trygalls are powerful friends but fearsome enemies, it was Tryg who lit all the torches and candles when we entered."

"Why is he called Tryg?"

"They all are," answered Flintock.

"How come?"

"They just are....... No imagination I suppose."

There was a small cough from the other side of the table, it was Howel.

"Excuse me for mentioning this but is it not rather impolite to talk about someone behind their back, it is not even more impolite to do so when they are but a few feet away and in earshot."

"I was just asking," said Tom, "there is so much that's different, so much I need to know, so much I need to ask."

"The boy is right, there is much he has to learn, not just about trygalls, but about the whole land of Trymyll."

"Well, he could have asked me." Howel said in a slightly sniffy voice.

"Sorry," said Tom "now don't take this the wrong way, but it's difficult to have a discussion with a sixty-foot purple dragon, or even a Jack Russel dog, it just doesn't seem natural, if you know what I mean."

"No, I don't think I do," Howel said in a very snooty voice.

"Hey, go easy on the boy, this morning, he had never seen a dragon, let alone one which talked, it must be strange, give the lad a chance."

"He was happy to hear about dragons earlier."

"Now he has met a trygall and has learnt a little of them."

Tryg came over and signalled to Flintock that the dinner was prepared. Flintock waved his hand calmly towards the table, as he did the food appeared, plates high with hot steaming food. It all smelled delicious and Tom, Flintock and Tryg tucked in eagerly. There was a roasted hare, rabbit pie, stuffed and spiced pheasant, potatoes, greens, carrots, and even peas. Tom avoided the greens. He was not impressed with Tryg's table manners as he ate with his hands and threw the bones over his shoulder.

While they ate, Flintock drank a very frothy looking ale, Tryg was drinking what looked like herb tea, and Tom had fresh, homemade lemonade.

Tom soon realised that Howel was missing.

"Where's Howel?" he asked.

"He doesn't eat with us; he'll be back after he's eaten. He'll find a deer or two or maybe an ox. It's not pretty to watch, but he is a dragon after all."

Tom wasn't sure if he was joking or telling the truth but decided not to dwell on the thought.

"So, tell me young Tom, where are you from? Tell me a little about yourself." Flintock asked.

"Well, not much to tell really, I am Welsh, from a small mining town in the south of the country, I only have my mum at home, my dad left when I was a couple of weeks old and took my brother with him. I was doing okay, but my ma was ill, so I was looked after by this posh couple, Mr, and Mrs Hadley Smythe, who turned out to be Howell in disguise. Don't ask me how though. And it was Howell that brought me here, but you know that of course don't you."

"Well, I was the son of a tribal chief of the Yoruba peoples from Benin in West Africa. I travelled, or rather was bought here as a young boy because my natural and latent magic powers frightened my people. Had I not fled all those years ago with my great-uncle, who was a hidden wizard of great power, the tribe would have probably killed me."

"What's a hidden wizard?"

"A hidden wizard, well it's a wizard who lives an ordinary life, never showing their power or magic in any way. They also suppress their 'spark' for want of a better word, so other magical people cannot sense their power, so for all intents and purposes, they are just ordinary people."

"Why would they want to hide then?"

"Well, often they are there in secret to look after someone special and to protect them. For my great-uncle, it was me he had to protect, in secret and out of sight. Hidden."

"Wow, are there many hidden wizard then?"

"Who knows, if we knew, they wouldn't be hidden would they. Now, eat up," said Flintock, "Llewel the Elder will arrive in the morning. You must get a good night sleep as we have far to go tomorrow and in the days that follow."

Tom was shown a room to the side of the main hall. It was a bedroom, the bed in the centre of the room was probably bigger than his old bedroom, apart from the bed, there was a big leather sofa, a small desk with a lit candle and chair, and a bookcase full of old leather books all set out on a stone slab floor with a red patterned rug. The rug had a dragon pattern woven into the middle which looked the same as the one on his ring. There were drapes around the bed which heralded the same motifs as the carpet. In the fireplace, there was a roaring fire with a large leather padded Chesterfield chair next to it which looked both warm and cosy. The room was probably bigger than most houses back home! On the bed were his own pyjamas, on the floor his slippers, and hung beside the bed his old dressing gown. He could hardly believe his eyes, but that was a feeling he was becoming used to now.

He quickly got changed, went over to the washbasin, and was not surprised to find his toothbrush, flannel, and towel there. In fact, he didn't think anything much would surprise him now.

He washed, cleaned his teeth, and jumped into bed. He slept a fitful and dream-filled night with dreams of dragons, trygalls and wizards, castles, mountains caves, his father, his brother and the ring which he dreamt was glowing and emitting a bright light like a beacon in the dark signalling to the whole world that he had arrived.

Somewhere in the distance, he could hear his voice being called, repeatedly. But this was not the voice of Hadley-Smythe, Flintock or Howel, or anyone he could remember, but somehow it was a voice he recognised. But from where.............?

CHAPTER 4 - LLEWEL THE ELDER

Before he knew it, it was morning and he heard another voice calling his name, this time he recognised it, it was Flintock calling him for breakfast. As they tucked into sausage, bacon, eggs, and fried bread, he thought quietly about his dreams, and wondered whether to share them with Flintock but decided it was nothing, just the excitement of yesterday and so he said nothing.

As they ate, he also pondered all the events of the previous day, if his friends at school could see him now, he thought.

"SCHOOL!" he shouted involuntarily, "School! Mrs Glynn will kill me! It's Monday and we have a maths test today; she'll think I've bunked off on purpose! Boy am I in trouble."

As soon as he had finished saying it, he realised it was silly.

Flintock spoke reassuringly, "Don't worry, she won't miss you. She thinks you have moved to Cardiff to be with your father."

"Is that where he lives then, with Jon?"

"No Tom, not Cardiff."

He could sense awkwardness in the air but that was broken by a knock on the huge doors at the front of the hall. Tom had yet to work out why, the door on the outside looked small and flimsy, like a shed door, because that is what it was. But the door this side was a huge oak door, ten feet high with massive wrought iron hinges and lock.

The doors swung open and there stood a small wizard, a very

small wizard, barely four foot six inches of wizard, maybe a little more, Tom knew he was a wizard because he had all the normal wizardly things you would expect, a dark long flowing cloak of indeterminable colour, long pointy and slightly bent hat, long greying and unkempt beard, a staff with a globe affixed to the top and trainers on his feet. 'Trainers!' thought Tom, now that somehow ruined the image.

Llewel the Elder stood before them, a very unimpressive looking wizard, not that Tom had seen that many to compare him with, but against Flintock, not astounding at all. There he stood, not much to look at, but that's all there was.

"Don't let your thoughts run wild Tom," Howel whispered.

Tom took the hint, he knew that Howel had caught his thoughts and was warning him not to articulate them.

"Allow me to introduce you," began Flintock, but before he could finish.....

"I have not travelled halfway across this dangerous country for elaborate introductions," Llewel the Elder said impatiently, waving his hands dismissively, "I am Llewel the Elder, in fact, I am a Llewel, High Elder of the Council of Blaenoraid," he said with both arrogance and pride, "and you are Tom Jones. There, now we all know each other, there's much to be done! So, introductions over, breakfast nearly over. We need to get a move on with little time to waste. Any food left? I could murder a bacon sandwich."

Tom took an instant dislike to him.......

Howel caught his eye again and placed a paw against his lips as if to say, "Do not say what you are thinking."

Llewel the Elder spoke, "Do you know why you are here?"

"No," said Tom.

"You are here because something is draining the magic out of Trymyll and according to the mystics, you are the man...I mean boy, who is foretold to reverse it. The firstborn of Llewellyn the wizard."

"I'm not his firstborn, Jon is. So, you've got the wrong son."

"No, you are the one, best not ask questions now. You, dear boy, believe it or not, are here to save the day," Llewel said, this last part with sarcasm, scorn, and disbelief.

"And how am I supposed to do that?" asked Tom, again in his poshest Welsh accent.

"It is your destiny, and whereas we will help in any way we can, we actually have absolutely no idea as to why it is happening and no clues as to what to do. In fact, it is estimated that at the current rate of decline, all the magic will be gone in a decade, ten years at the most," said Llewel.

Tom wanted to point out that ten years and a decade are the same but thought better of it,

"But first, you need to be rid of those ridiculous clothes. Stick out a mile you will," Llewel flicked his wand and Tom's tee shirt and jeans disappeared and turned into a sort of wizard looking set of ill-fitting and rather grubby clothes with an almost green cloak to cover the worst. Tom did not like them at all. They itched, they smelt, and they were several sizes too big. He looked ridiculous.

"I'm not wearing these rags!" he shouted, "They're old, smelly and they don't fit. I want my own clothes back. Now!"

"Don't be petulant with me boy," Llewel the Elder said sharply.

"Then give me my clothes back! I'm bigger than you, so unless you want a black eye!" he exclaimed, clenching his fists.

"No, no, no," said Llewel, "you cannot talk to a High Elder of the Council of Blaenoraid like that. I am particularly important, and demand respect."

"No, no, no to you too, where I come from you earn the respect of others, you don't demand it."

"Now stop it, Tom, please," said Flintock, "your clothes are safe and, in your room, I'm sure I can sort you out something a little more suitable quite quickly."

The clothes he was wearing morphed into different shapes and fits as Flintock stood staring at him. Eventually, it settled into some leggings, a shirt, a tunic, and another green cloak. This time they were clean, didn't itch and smelt freshly laundered.

"There, that will have to do for now," Flintock said as he finished.

"What nonsense," exclaimed Llewel, "the clothes I gave him were perfectly adequate."

Flintock ignored him.

"Tell us what you know."

"You will not like this my boy, but our powers began to fade when your father came through the cave after the Dwarf Wars, unlike others, he keeps returning to the parallel world you call home, we cannot be sure, but the power does not seem to leave with him but weakens a little soon after he returns."

Flintock continued the story, "Your world used to be a magical world, but nearly all the power is gone now, mainly because no one now believes. Wales was the last place in Britain to retain any real magic power, but that is weak now and only just enough remains to keep the link between our worlds. Driven out be technology and disbelief. We know that the power is not leaking from here to there, it is just fading. Also, and of course, it is not that we are no longer believing, we all know the power of magic in its many forms, but some are losing it fast."

Then Llewel resumed, "We would like to believe that there were dark forces at work, that this was something orchestrated by Asmodeus the Dark, another High Elder, previously banished from the council. But his power, and the powers of his dreadful legions of dark wizards are just as affected. It's got so bad; we've started talking to him again after many years of ostracising him and his kind."

Tom was still reeling from the accusation against his father. He did not speak but held his tongue, his anger, and his dislike for Llewel the Elder increasing. He may not remember his father, know his father or even like his father, but he was still his dad and he didn't like anyone bad-mouthing him, especially not this midget of a wizard.

There was a short silence while they all absorbed the conversation followed by another pause while they all waited for someone to speak. Tom broke the hiatus by asking as calmly as he could...

"So why do you think my dad has anything to do with it?"

"We cannot be sure," answered Llewel, "but he goes from our world to yours frequently. He says he has business to attend to in the other world. Then when he returns a few days later, certain of us lose some of our magic powers. We don't know why, and while the power returns after a while, it is always weaker than before. Anyway, enough chatter. We must away to Castell y Blaenoraid. For the Council of the High Elders await. But first, we must hide your true name and give you a new one."

"What?" said Tom, "What's wrong with Tom, it's very Welsh and I like it."

"To protect you from incantations," answered Howel, "an incantation is a spoken spell, often against a person, but for it to work, the person saying the spell has to know your whole and real name, so we must never call you Thomas Jones again, but instead....."

Tom interrupted, "Tom," he said, no one ever calls me Thomas for a start and no one ever, ever, calls me Thomas Jones, not even at school. Anyway, that's not my name. I have another name, but no one ever uses it. So just call me Tom," he repeated with irritation.

"What do you mean you have another name? What's your name then boy?"

"It's private and no one, and I mean no one ever calls me by my real name."

"What?" said Llewel rather stupidly, "your name is Private? Private Jones, not Tom Jones at all?"

"Don't be stupid," Tom said sharply and with some malice.

"You can't talk to me like that, I am a High Elder of the Council of Blaenoraid."

"So you mentioned and like I said. You earn respect, you don't just get it."

"What about Daffyd?" said Llewel sheepishly, "that's quite Welsh."

"NO! Call me Tom or I'm going back, in fact, I am going back."

"You can't do that," said Howel with an air of concern, "you'll get lost in the forest and eaten by weird wolves."

"Don't you mean werewolves?" asked Tom.

"No, I know exactly what I mean, weird wolves, werewolves are a completely different thing. Weird wolves are much…….well, weirder."

"Meaning?"

"Well for a start, they don't bite you to drink your blood and turn you into one of them, they just eat you. They have the bodies of wolves and large bat-like wings. They're as big as a pony, completely silent in flight and on the forest floor. Like werewolves, they only come out at night, the rest of the day they look like big bunnies and eat grass. Like I said, weird. You only know of their presence if you can see them or smell them."

"Smell them?" repeated Tom.

"Oh yes. At night you'll smell them alright, from two or three hundred feet, they are disgusting! Absolutely no refinement, not at all like us dragons. We may eat people occasionally, but at least we have manners. And yet, during the day they frolic and play in the sunshine and are both friendly and delicious."

"Delicious?" said Tom.

"Oh yes," Flintock joined in, "and you only need one to make a rabbit pie big enough to feed fifty stout knights!"

"Enough! Enough!" cried Llewel the Elder, "we must be on our way, not talking recipes. It's several days of walking from here even in a straight line, which it never is. There are bound to be diversions. We could be walking for a week."

Tom did not like the sound of that!

CHAPTER 5 - TRYMYLL.

Trymyll is a land of seven cities. Each city has a castle, chateaux or large fortified house at its centre, and the city and surrounding lands are overseen by a High Elder, each High Elder has seven elders working for and reporting to them and each of the seven elders has seven senior wizards working for and with them.

At the centre of the land is Castell y Blaenoraid, the biggest castle, where the Elder of Elders holds domain. His name is, not only unpronounceable, but know one seems to know what it is, so he is just referred to as, the Elder. No one knows how old he is, they just assume he is an old and wise wizard, he wears a huge dark cloak which has a deep hood, so no one can see his face. He is surrounded in mystery and magic. His voice is exceptionally soft, and people must strain to hear him. But as he seldom speaks, this is not a great problem. His attitude is always one of 'don't speak unless what you have to say is of the utmost importance'. So, on the rare occasions he does speak, everyone listens. The High Elders of the six cities beneath him are usually the only wizards who ever hear him speak anyway. the Elder, plus the six High Elders form what is known as the High Council of Blaenoraid or the Council of Elders.

Each city has a name, each name has a meaning.

Castell y Blaenoraid is the capital of Trymyll, its name simply means 'The Capital.' It is set right in the centre of the land, high on a hill and overlooking all around. The countryside is lush, green, well-wooded and populated with deer and wild boar, both of which are good for eating. Being set high on the hill the view stretches to all the mountains which surrounded the Land of Trymyll, it is a most beautiful and magical city. There are rules and enchantments which control the city. You cannot apparate within the city walls. The council chamber, which is at the centre of the castle and inside the bailey, is encased in enchantments so that no magic can be performed inside of it. The council chamber is also the courtroom and deep beneath it are the dungeons of Blaenoraid. A place which would be feared in any other castle, but the dungeons of Blaenoraid, were quite comfortable, clean, and well lit.

Wrth y Môr, or castle on the sea. A bit of a misnomer as there is no sea in Trymyll. It stands in or rather on a vast saltwater lake. So big that you cannot see from shore to shore. When the wind is up, there are large waves and storm conditions, it looks like a sea because of its size, but it is, in fact, a lake. The castle setting is quite secure as it is built on an island about half a mile out into the lake. There is only one way in is along a long and narrow causeway which could be magically sunk if the castle is ever under attack and the drawbridge is raised. Around the castle swim sea monsters, multiple Kraken and a Manticore who also defend the castle if required, though in over four-hundred years, the drawbridge had never been raised and the causeway had never been sunk. Along the shoreline around the causeway entrance is the town of Wrth where the inhabitants live a happy life, eating drinking and fishing for the saltwater fish from the lake and freshwater fish from the may rivers that feed into the lake and run through the town. At this moment, it's High Elder is Llewel. His whole and unspoken name is Llewel Mathias Gaynor.

Goleuedigaeth was an interesting city. All the residents are female, all incredibly wise and all very magical. Although they have a High Elder, one High Elder Aneta Stepanek, from Eastern Europe, and the normal seven elders who oversee the forty-nine senior wizards, the city of Goleuedigaeth is run by consensus rather than by an authoritarian High Elder. Men are allowed in the city, but none live there. The city is beautiful in every way with fragrant flowers adorning each road, alley, balcony, windowsill, and doorway, in fact, every nook and cranny. At the centre there stands a most elegant seven towered castle, well when I say castle, it looks more like an eighteenth-century French Chateaux. The scent of the city can be picked up for miles around, so sweet, it seems to draw you in, once in the city, you were overcome with a sense of peace and tranquillity. It is the city of Enlightenment.

Fourth on the list is Gwir. High Elder Traveon Baughan is their leader. The castle itself looks very ordinary, the city that surrounded the castle is plain and grey. The opposite of Goleuedigaeth, Gwir looks harsh, severe, and serious. This is the Castle of the Truth. Set right in the north of the country and near to the Dragonlands this city and castle is a stronghold of battle wizards. All trained in the art of attack magic and defensive arts, but also fearsome knights with heavy armour, broadswords, mace, and shields. They ride destriers, large, fearless warhorses, bred for battle. This ferocious band of wizards are disciplined, it is ruled over by a strict and severe High Elder who thinks truthfulness, loyalty, honour, and bravery were the marks of a good wizard. Although a very grumpy sort of wizard High Elder Traveon Baughan is just the sort you need on your side if you ever go into a battle.

Next was Mynydd and the accompanying castle. Set high on a mountain to the very south of the land of Trymyll, Mynydd sits above the snow line, it is cold and snowy even in the hottest of summers, a particularly hardy breed of wizards live there, they are few, High Elder, Govannon Staley of the Elven community, seven Elven elders and forty-nine Elven wizards. Unlike most of the the other High Elders, Govannon Staley was not elected, his title was hereditary and passed from father to eldest son or daughter on death. Apart from a few bakers, cooks, and tradespeople, no one else lives in Mynydd, less than one hundred souls in all. The rest of the Elven Community live in the valleys below, bathed in the sun and lush with vegetation. They too are great soldiers, archers and horsemen and horsewomen, yes, men and women. They hold equal sway in the elven community and the women are the finest archers in the land and always fight alongside the men. No one wants to live in the actual castle, no one even wishes to visit. It was a terribly dark, cold, damp, wretched existence. Why anyone lived there anyway, no one could remember. They knew it was important to keep the castle occupied and active but could not remember why.

At the another extreme, Dolydd. The Castle in the meadows. A sun-drenched pleasant and well-populated city set in the vast pasture lands of Trymyll. Dolydd is the breadbasket of Trymyll, most of the grain, meat, vegetables, and fruit comes from the area surrounding Dolydd, where there are warm summers and mild winters. Who wouldn't want to live there? The High Elder, Brangwen Binning, or Bangers as most call her, is as much a farmer as a wizard and High Elder, she is a happy, congenial, and fun lady, enjoys her ale, wine, and song. She does not enjoy or respect the formalities of the council, so rarely attends, instead, she attends in person while at the same time being at home in her farmhouse castle. She is, as they say in Trymyll, in the neither here nor there.

One city was different from the others, called Castell yr Tywyll, it is there Asmodeus the Dark Elder is in charge, banned from the council, he has seven dark elders and forty-nine dark wizards running the show. Set apart from the other cities, from the distance it looks dark, there is always a black cloud shrouding the city, dense poisonous and even flesh-eating plants climb the walls all woven by the magic of the dark elders to keep snoopers out.

But there are problems in Trymyll, big problems, in fact, problems so big that even Asmodeus has been allowed back to attend some of the Council of Elders, to show unity to solve the problems.

The magic was leaching out of Trymyll and the Wizards were losing their powers. Sometimes bringing disaster, as a flying wizard might suddenly lose the power of flight whist high in the air and come crashing down to land. Someone might transform either themselves or someone else into an animal and not be able to change back, they could apparate, but instead of arriving where they envisaged, they would find half their body in a wall or buried up to their waist and be unable to escape. All sorts of terrible things were happening because the magic was disappearing.

Back in Tom's world, certain parts used to be very magical. Magic now is as rare as hen's teeth, even in Wales, previously one of the most magical places on earth and the birthplace of dragons. Modernity and technology drove it out, and slowly people stopped believing in magic, so it disappeared, almost. In the modern-day, most so-called witches and wizards are fakes and phonies, possessing little if any actual magic or power. But even now there are some powerful wizards living hidden amongst us. You never know who, you never know where. But they are here, it may be your neighbour, your mother or father, it may even be your best friend, or your worst enemy. Nobody knows, for they are hidden.

Not so in Trymyll, here magic rules, it is a way of life, everyone has magical powers of some sort to a greater or lesser degree. Some are very magical and become wizards, some less so, they are called phobls and are found living as farmers or carpenters or bakers as an example, but even they have some magic. A farmer can enchant a plough to make a straight furrow without the need of a horse, a carpenter can straighten warped wood or drive out woodworm and a baker sift his flour and knead his dough on a magic kneading table without even rising from his bed. They all seem fine, it is the higher wizards who were losing their powers, not the ordinary people, not the phobls.

Trymyll is an equal opportunity wizardly kingdom and both elders and wizards can be ethnically diverse, male, or female.

But as in our world, the males were usually in any positions of real power.

CHAPTER 6 - ASMODEUS THE DARK ELDER.

On the other side of the kingdom, Asmodeus the Dark High Elder was vexed, in fact, vexed was not the word, he was incandescent with rage. But whenever he was angry, light would emit from his body and little flashes of lightning shot out from him, Not a good trick, as it was ruining his image as Asmodeus the Dark, as when angry, he was, in fact, Asmodeus the really quite bright flashy High Elder. The fact that his darkness could not hide the light annoyed him even more and in a vicious circle of incandescent jiggery-pokery, he got lighter and brighter as he got angrier and angrier. Of all the powers and magic that had weakened, why not this one? The one which he could not control. It made some of the dark wizard's snigger, not that any of them would dare to even curl a lip in amusement, as diminished powers or not, Asmodeus was still more powerful, darker and more evil than any of his cohorts.

Unlike the other High Elders, Asmodeus was not High Elder by either election or consensus, Asmodeus bullied and fought his way to the position just as all the previous incumbents of the post at Castell yr Tywyll had done. One day, it would happen to him. He would be deposed by another power-hungry despot who wanted to rule the roost instead of Asmodeus.

"The boy is here! The boy is here! How did he get through the cave without me knowing?" he raged.

"Calm yourself my Lord High Elder," said Lodi, one of the dark wizards, "we do not believe that he is the so-called saviour of Trymyll, he is just a boy."

"Don't fool yourself, it is him," raged Asmodeus, "It is him!" he repeated, "find him, bring him to me."

"But why is the boy so important? He's just a boy, not a great wizard, not even an acolyte. He has no power, no magic, no spark, nothing that we can sense or detect."

He then calmed completely and in a very ordinary and non-scary voice said.

"He is wearing the ring of the elders. A ring of great power which can only be worn by one who is worthy to wear it. If he were not the chosen one, the ring would have left him as soon as it was placed on his finger. If an unworthy person removes it, then it will return to the true owner immediately."

"Then how do you propose we obtain this ring of the seven elders?"

Asmodeus ignored the question. He needed thinking time. Instead, he asked.

"Who is he with?"

"He is with Llewel the Elder, Flintock and a trygall."

"Llewel the Little" he mocked. "That fool is all politics and no magic. Flintlock is a sentimental, soft-hearted fool and the trygall will have no loyalty to any of them."

"What do you command oh Lord High Elder?"

"Just fetch him or the ring. If you can't get the boy, bring me his finger or hand, I care not which or how!"

Lodi was a little squeamish about blood and stuff like that. He neither favoured cutting off Tom's hand or even his finger. He thought that bringing the boy in one piece would be his best choice, after all, he didn't want to leave a trail of his own vomit for the others to follow.

One of the other elders spoke, in his most sycophantic tone of voice, "Most High Elder Asmodeus, why is the ring so important? If no one may wear it unless the ring chooses and accepts that person, what good is the ring to you?" He chose his words carefully as he dared not mention that Asmodeus may not be worthy enough to wear it.

"Because, you fool, when I am the Elder of Elders, I will be worthy to wear the ring and then the ring will protect me from all. I will be both invincible and indestructible. The mightiest, most powerful wizard ever to walk the land.

No one thought it wise to argue with him the fact that that having a high office, even the highest in the land, may not make him any more worthy to wear the ring.

Lodi bowed deeply and withdrew. At the city gate, out of the defensive enchantments which guard the city from outsiders entering and from unauthorised exit by anyone wishing to leave, he opened a small and very ordinary looking gate, walked through, and as he did he was transported to the other side of the kingdom to a large wood, close to a small hut he could not see, in a clearing he could not see, with smoke rising from the chimney he also could not see. This was as close as he would get as he could sense that the area was surrounded in enchantments and magic, a step closer he might set off a rolling sequence of spells which would end in his certain discovery and maybe his imminent demise. From a distance and shrouded in an obfuscation spell which prevented others from realising he was there, he watched and waited for the unlikely and unsuspecting group to appear.

His wait was short. Within a few minutes, they emerged from nowhere as if walking out of a mist that was not there. They were still preparing to leave but had only come out of the shack to have a look round for possible danger and to get their bearings for the day ahead.

Lodi could not see where they had stepped from and to be truthful, he didn't really care, but the tracking spell they had placed on Llewel's trainers had led him to this spot, and that was close enough.

He would use a stun and bind spell. He raised his wand, there was a large flash that shot towards the group followed by another flash and Lodi fell, stunned, and bound to the forest floor. In front of Tom was hovering a large gold shield, which as he looked, started to fade, and then seemed to withdraw back into the ring he was wearing.

No one really saw or understood what had happened except Llewel.

"Boy, show me your ring," Llewel examined the ring closely, "and how long have you had this ring?"

"Forever," said Tom.

"Don't be stupid, you're only thirteen. You could not, therefore, have had it forever or you'd be four and a half billion years old, so, let's try that simple question again, perhaps I'll reword it to make it simpler for you. How long have you been wearing this ring?"

"Well, as long as I can remember, I've always worn it I suppose. My dad put it on my finger when I was a baby before he left."

"Have you never wondered why, as you have grown, the ring continues to fit and has not, as your fingers got bigger, dug into your flesh, cut off the circulation and made your finger drop off?"

"No," said Tom.

"Then you are more stupid than I thought."

None of this was helping his ever-cooling feelings about Llewel the Elder.

Llewel continued..., "Have you ever taken the ring off?"

"Yes, once I took it off and put it in my pocket when we were making bread at school, Mrs Glyn told me it was not hygienic to wear a ring while cooking, but when my hand came out again, the ring was back on my finger. Another time a bully from school took it off me and ran off, but when I looked down, it was back on my finger, another time......," Llewel held up his hand to cut him off in mid-flow.

"Enough! Have you ever wondered why?"

"No," Tom said.

"I somehow thought not," Llewel's voice mellowed to almost a friendly tone, "Tom, you have an incredibly special and very magic ring on your finger. The ring is called the ring of the seven elders. At the moment this, this, an excuse for a wizard," he explained, pointing at Lodi, "came through a portal and cast the spell at you, it then bounced back leaving him both stunned and bound by his own spell, the ring reacted throwing up a golden shield which reflected the spell straight back onto himself."

"It was enchanted several millennia ago by the seven Elders of Trymyll. It then vanished. Legend and myth surrounded it......," Flintock was stopped in his tracks by Llewel.

"Enough, too much information will confuse the boy and inform the prisoner."

He waved his wand around Tom's head and muttered a few incantations.

"There, that's wiped what little brain he has of all we have just said about the ring."

Tom didn't wish to disavow him of his little trick, but he remembered everything he said, the ring had in fact reflected that spell back to Llewel so that Llewel had now forgotten what was said.

"Now, what was I saying? I seem to have forgotten what we were talking about. Oh well, never mind. Back to the problem in hand.

He flicked his staff and the bound and still stunned dark wizard disappeared back through the portal to face his fate with

Asmodeus the Dark Elder. Which would not be too harsh, his reputation was far worse than reality! Probably just get a good telling off.

"Anyway," said Llewel, "the ring's far too powerful for you, I will have to look after it for you, just until we get the Council of High Elders, then you can have it back so you can give it to them."

"This should be interesting," muttered Flintlock under his breath.

"Come on hand it over," said Llewel, now returned to grumpy, bad-tempered, and arrogant mode.

Tom handed over the ring, Llewel popped it into his leather purse and tied the leather lace. Llewel then looked at Tom with a slightly vindictive smile on his face, he looked down at Tom's hand and the smile vanished, the ring was back on his finger.

"I could have told you that would happen," said Tom.

"Give!" said an even more irritated Llewel. This time he took out his wand, placed the ring in his purse again, whirled his wand around the purse muttering something unintelligible, there was a flash of light.

"The purse is sealed, nothing can get out of there until released by me," he smirked again. The smirk disappeared as soon as he looked again at Tom. The ring was back on his finger again!

"Oh well, have it your way then, but the High Elders will want their ring back. Mark my words they will. Mark my words, mark my words," his voice trailed off at the end to more of a mutter as he repeated the last bit of his sentence several times as if he were trying to convince himself.

Excitement over it was time to hit the road to Castell y Blaenoraid. The small troupe returned to the 'shack,' collected some extra rations for the journey and exited it again, Howel the dragon, still in small Jack Russel terrier form, Llewel the Elder, Flintock, Tryg and Tom. Flintock released all the spells and incantations around the clearing and handed Tryg a small bejewelled gold and glass phial suspended on a long gold chain. A flame shot from nowhere and the hut disappeared in a cloud of smoke, the smoke then swirled round and round like a small whirlwind and shot into the phial ready for the next time they needed it.

CHAPTER 7 - THE WAND TREE.

Once they were out of the hut, Howel said his good-byes.

"It is not good that you walk with a dragon, I don't know why, but it seems the others think that I stand out a little and may draw attention to you. I will depart for now, but we will meet up again later."

Speech over, Howel unfurled his wings and launched sky wards. Within a minute, he was just a dot on the horizon and then seconds later he was gone altogether. Tom marvelled at his speed, he no longer seemed like a comedy cartoon character, but now a great, mythical, magical, and fearsome fire breathing dragon.

Tom walked with Flintock. He mused in his mind his new friends, he really liked Howel, he was so funny, he liked Flintock, he was kind, and despite his hideous looks, he had warmed towards Tryg. But he still didn't like Llewel the Elder.

They walked in silence for some time, after about an hour, Llewel spoke first and broke the silence. Much to the surprise of them both, he announced....

"The boy needs to learn some magic, to do that he needs a wand, so first, to the wand tree."

Tom thought for a moment, then said, "A wand tree, I never knew that magic wands grew on trees."

"They don't," said Llewel sharply, but without explanation, "it's about a day's walk from here to the Wand Wood, the wand tree is in the middle of the wood, you can't miss it, it's massive, ten times the height of any of the other trees."

Flintlock continued, "It will take us out of our way a little, but it is worth the detour, then we can start some lessons."

Tom was not impressed by the word 'lessons', sounded a bit too much like school.

"When we get there, it is just a small copse of trees, the wand tree is in the middle, you can't miss it," repeated Llewel as if only what he said mattered, "but a word of warning, once you're there, don't ask questions. The tree doesn't do questions. However, you need to find out as much as you can about your wand, but without asking questions!"

Tom was perplexed. What on earth is the little dwarfen wizard on about now? How can a tree not like questions, it's not like it can hear you or answer back, and anyway, how can you find out about anything without asking questions?

About mid-day on the morrow, they arrived at a large plain. Set in the middle was a small wooded area, he could see the wooded area, but all the trees looked the same height, as they got closer, he could see that there was every tree he could name, and quite a few he could not name, all huddled together in the wood. He could see Oak and Ash, Birches and Beeches of many types, Poplar, Elms, Pines of all sorts, many types of Eucalyptus, Irish Yew, English Yew, even fruit trees like Apples, Cherry, Mulberry and Pear. So many trees, all different, but all the same height. The trees which should tower above the rest like mighty Redwoods and the trees which should be tiny like Elderflower were all the same size. There did not appear to be a mightily tall tree in the middle at all.

"There," said Llewel, "right in the middle, can you see the tree that towers above the rest? Ten times higher than all around? That's the tree to go for."

But Tom couldn't see the tree in the middle. To him, they all looked the same height.

"But they all look the same height to me, I can't see a massive tree anywhere."

"Don't be a daft lad. Look, it's massive, humongous, right in the middle. Look!" Llewel said getting agitated and pointing at an empty space in the sky.

"The wood and the trees look different for different people," Flintock said to Tom quietly, "don't worry. When I came here it was just oak trees, hundreds and hundreds of oak trees all packed together so tightly that I couldn't get in."

Quite soon, they reached the edge of Wand Wood. They all stopped and looked at the wood. What was first described as a small copse, now looked like a massive forest of identically sized trees. Thick dense forest with, as Flintock had said, no apparent way in.

Llewel repeated the instructions on how to talk to the tree. Although Tom wasn't really listening.

"How are we going to get in there?" Tom asked nervously.

"We?" said Llewel, "Not we, but you, and only you. We can't go in, we already have our wands, only acolytes may enter."

"Unless you come for a repair or replacement," added Flintock, "but then you get the same wand as before."

"Well, what do I ask for then?"

Llewel snapped back, "Can't tell you that, it's between you and the tree, strictly confidential."

"But what do I know about wands? Come on, help me out a bit."

"No, no, no," said Llewel, "there are rules about these things, now in you go."

"Well how do I get in?" asked Tom a little nervously.

"Just walk boldly up and they will let you enter," Flintock said, "but don't forget, no questions."

Tom didn't quite hear the last bit as he was already walking excitedly to the wood. The trees seemed to part, and he found himself in the Wand Wood, with the path leading into the centre, the path opening up as he walked and closing again behind him. He looked around nervously, all the trees looked dark and menacing and all still the same height. Most looked as if they had faces and some were even talking to each other. Looking at him and then passing comments and snide remarks to each other. Giggling, even laughing at him. This place was creepy.

He was carefully looking around for a tall tree when he heard what sounded like a scream and a loud creaking noise, he looked up and saw the trees in front of him changing, growing, expanding, joining together to form one huge tree and a clearing appearing around it. The scream was not a scream at all, it was the sound the wood made as it grew and merged and grew and merged and grew and grew. Within a couple of minutes, he couldn't see the top of the new tree, it seemed to disappear into the sky itself.

Tom decided he had found the wand tree.

As it grew, a knurled face appeared on the trunk with woodpecker holes for eyes and an owl's nest for a mouth, a nose from a broken branch with just one leaf and branches sprouted out like arms, the roots then seemed to grow up from the ground as well and what looked like an old-fashioned stand-up desk appeared in front of the tree.

"Next!" said the tree, "Next one please, hurry along, I've not got all day. Next!"

"There's only me here," said Tom.

"Then you must be next," the tree said, "and how may I be of assistance?" Before Tom could answer, the tree asked, "name a wood."

Tom was confused, does he mean, name a wood like oak, elm or willow? Or does he mean to name a wood like the woods in the valleys back home? Elkin Wood, Fernley Forest, or Piney Copse?

Tom said, "Do you mean like oak, elm, willow? You really need to help me here......"

Before he could finish the sentence, the tree retorted, "oak, elm, willow and yew it is then."

"I never said yew!"

"Yes you did. Very strange choice, no one has ever asked for a wand of four different kinds of wood before, occasionally three, often two, but never four, and no one has ever, ever asked for yew. Oh well, never mind, oak, elm, willow and yew it is. But don't mention the yew wood to anyone or they'll all be back for one."

"But I was told you can't, you only get one chance at a wand."

"Interesting choice though," the tree said, casually ignoring Tom.

"Name a stone," said the tree, "precious or otherwise."

"What, you mean like a diamond, ruby, and emerald or like coal, flint or granite?"

"You can't have six, three's the maximum, and that's pushing it. Most times I only give one or very occasionally two. Diamond, ruby and emerald it is then."

"No! you misunderstand, I was just asking a question, not giving an answer."

As he said it, he remembered what Llewel had said, just as he thought it, the tree said, "He did tell you, didn't he, I don't do questions!"

'How did the tree know that'? Thought Tom.

"I know most things," said the tree.

"But I didn't say anything."

"You didn't have to," said the tree, irritatedly.

Tom suddenly realised he was holding a wooden staff, exactly his own height, with a jewel set in the top which shimmered in the light. It didn't seem to weigh anything; it was as light as the proverbial feather. He wanted to know more but knew he could not ask questions. How could he find out about what he had in his hand without asking questions?

"It's a bit big for a wand, it doesn't fit in my pocket," he stated out loud.

"It doesn't have to," the tree replied, "just say or think 'wand' and a wand will appear, 'staff' and the staff will appear, and 'wand be gone' and it disappears altogether."

Tom thought hard, how to ask the next question without it being a question.

"It's not very big. Well it is now, but I'm only thirteen, by the time I'm grown up, it'll be a tiny staff, more like a walking stick."

"No it won't, it will always be the same height as you. As you grow, the staff grows, as you shrink, the staff will shrink."

Tom didn't quite understand the last bit, but anyway, he was thinking about his next non-question.

"Doesn't seem very powerful," he said.

"Oh, but it is! And with your very surprisingly wise choice of materials, it will be a very great wand indeed. Oak is for strength and endurance powerful in war and battle. Elm is the tree of great wisdom, something you lack now, but the wand will guide you, and willow, second only to wych-hazel for its healing and restorative powers, and the yew will make it a very fine bow should you ever need one. But don't tell people about the yew, I've never granted four kinds of wood before. Ever. Never ever. Never," his voice trailing off towards the end.

"The yew, of course, is only good for one thing, and that's for making a longbow, I suppose it might come in handy if you come across a roundhead or some marauding feudal knight from the middle ages."

"Now," the tree suddenly started again at full volume, "the stone in the top. Diamond, the giver of light to fight against the darkness of evil, and again giving great power and strong pure magic when needed for defence or attack, diamond is the hardest material known to man and with it, you will be able to cut through many defensive shields. Ruby, the firestone, allowing you to control fire and emerald, the water stone and giver of life itself. Harness the power of that wand and you will be a great wizard young Tom."

"Next!" shouted the tree.

Tom looked around to see no one.

"But there's only me here," he said.

"Then my work here is done. Goodbye"

Tom was about to say thank you when he found himself outside the wood standing next to Flintock, Llewel and Tryg. They were all staring at him.......

Expectantly......

He stood there, empty-handed.

"Show us!" Llewel and Flintock said as one voice and with the excited tones of a kid at Christmas, "Show us!" they repeated slightly louder.

Tom thought for a moment and then said "Staff" he wasn't expecting anything to happen, but it did, there he was holding his new staff with a strange jewel set in the top made of diamond, ruby and emerald.

They both gasped when they saw it.

Flintock looked delighted at the new staff, Llewel looked jealous and slightly envious. Tryg didn't give a fig about the new wand, he was simply happy for Tom and even happier to see Llewel upset.

Tom then tried it out, "Wand," he said, and the staff instantly became a smaller version of his staff. Every detail was the same except it was the same length as his forearm.

"Wand be gone," and he stood empty-handed. He kept going

through the cycle, over and over, laughing as he did it.

"Stop, stop," said Flintock smiling, "you'll wear it out!"

"Yes," said Llewel, "there's a lot more to magic than making a wand appear and disappear. You have so much to learn and so little time to learn it. Quite ridiculous, quite impossible. Now stop playing with it and tell us what you learnt about it."

Tom explained everything that had happened in the Wand Wood and everything that was said, missing out the bit about the yew tree and having four different kinds of wood. Flintock was amazed that he found out so much, Llewel just made a "Humph" sound at the end of nearly every sentence.

"Why do we have both a staff and a wand? Why not just one or the other?"

"Well," started Llewel in an almost friendly tone, "the wand is really an everyday magical instrument for small but no less powerful spells, mainly using the power of the wood as the channel for the power. That is why it is held thus."

Llewel the Elder held his wand delicately in his hand, the jewelled end resting on the top of his purlicue, the fleshy bit between the thumb and forefinger, the tapered wooden part facing away. It can also be held between the thumb and forefinger with the jewelled end in the palm of the hand, this is often the stance for single combat or spells which need a bigger gesture. To demonstrate, he flicked his wand at a small shrub, and it burst into flames, he flicked again, and it extinguished itself.

"Now the staff is mainly for bigger spells, fighting battles, big and powerful magic using the power harnessed in the stone." he banged the staff on the ground and a mighty flash came from it and they were surrounded by a huge ring of fire.

"Very good defensive shield if under attack from all sides."

He then raised the staff and lunged forward, and fire sped away into the distance setting on fire everything in its path. He lifted the staff again and the fire stopped dead, waved his hand and all the flames disappeared. Llewel seemed to take some pleasure in its destructive force.

"Wow!" said Tom with a gulp.

"Not really, anyone can do it with the right mindset. As you can see, my stone is Ruby, so fire is a big part of my defensive and attacking magic. The trick with wand work is imagination and visualisation. Visualise what you want to do and send that visualisation down into the wand. With practice, you can do most things."

"Now, that bush I scorched just now, see what you can do with your wand. Don't forget, visualise and transmit."

"Wand," said Tom. The wand appeared. He gingerly pointed the wand at the bush. Llewel the Elder and Flintock watched eagerly. They expected little, maybe either a puff of smoke and a twig to catch fire, or he would blow the whole bush out of the ground. But instead, it was not what they expected at all. Tom didn't even try to make the bush burn. Instead, he gently waved his wand and restored the shrub to better than its former self, new growth, flowers, and a wonderful scent.

"Staff!"

He then raised his staff and held it aloft in his right hand and raised his left hand as well, a soft green light came from the jewel in his staff and radiated out, all around where the grass had been burned by Llewel the Elder's defensive ring of fire and all across the plain where he had sent his fire like a cavalry charge of burning destruction, grass grew, flowers bloomed, and all was restored. Tom wanted to be a healer, a repairer, a restorer, a renovator, not a destroyer.

Flintock smiled. There is more to the boy than he thought. Much more. Llewel the Elder just grunted.

"Enough for one day," said Flintock, "Tryg, do your stuff."

He handed Tryg the small phial, in which Tom could still see the thick grey smoke swirling and twisting as if alive, removed the stopper and released the smoke. The smoke curled, expanded, and thickened. When it cleared, there was the shack, the broken garden shed, the many-roomed mansion, the almost home from home he had stayed in the previous night.

Flintock walked around it staff in hand, muttering, "There, all in place. No one can see it now except us and Howel should he wish to join us here."

"Well, whoever it was earlier knew where we were this morning, so they might be back tomorrow with reinforcements," said Tom.

"Yes, I'd been thinking about that, how did they know where to find us?" said Llewel. Then in a low tone that he thought Tryg could not hear, "Can you trust your trygall? They have little loyalty you know."

"I would and have trusted my life to Tryg, and for the record, he's not my trygall," Flintock said pointedly, "he is free to live as and where he wishes, but he wishes to stay with me."

"Then think about how Asmodeus found us," he sneered, "think about it well."

That night was quite restless for Tom, he thought about the verbal disagreement between Llewel the Elder and Flintock. After he had gone to bed for the night, he heard them arguing about it again, and again after Tryg had left to forage food for breakfast. All night he seemed to be thinking about how they, whoever they are, had found them so quickly. As he slept, he heard the voice calling him again. By morning he was just as tired as when he went to bed. But up he got and put on a cheerful face and went out into the great hall for breakfast.

CHAPTER 8 - THE ROAD TO CASTELL Y BLAENORAID (AND MORE LESSONS) ...

Next day they set out early after a good breakfast. They walked for some time before Llewel started to talk, or should we say lecture. First, he talked about wands and staffs, the different woods, and the power of the stones, he then went through Tom's staff, itemising each attribute.

"Oak is for strength and endurance powerful in war and battle," he said. It was word for word what the Wand Tree had said which Tom had then related to Llewel. But then he added, "but what does that mean? Eh boy? What does that mean?"

He didn't wait for an answer, which was just as well, as Tom hadn't one anyway.

"Well, you can harness the power of the wood, oak is an extraordinarily strong and hard wood, used to build great structures, call upon it when you need strength, visualise it helping you. For example, if you are tired and flagging, you can use a staff to help you on your way, anyone can do that with any bit of wood. But with the magic of an oaken staff you can draw down strength and endurance from the very trees around you, you could walk or even run for days if required without getting tired. You could summon the trees of the forest to march with you as a great army. You could draw that strength into your body from the trees. Oh, such power you could have in your staff and wand," he tailed off at the end, almost whimsically, almost as if he coveted Tom's wand, "but that takes years of practice, and we have not years to practice, only days."

Tom didn't know what he meant by that but held the thought in his mind for later discernment.

"Elm is the tree of great wisdom, something you lack now, but the wand will guide you," He continued, again quoting the wand tree, "hold the wand's crystal and meditate on any problem, and you may receive the answer as a thought on the wind, blown in from the great elm forests of Trymyll where the mystics of the old order live, contemplating life's problems day and night, seeking wisdom from the forest itself. Of course, you may not get an answer, it all depends of course, it all depends," Llewel did not elaborate on what it depended on though.

"And willow, second only to wych-hazel for its healing and restorative powers. But you have not only seen that but remarkably somehow showed that power. Where that came from only the Maker knows. Not even a wizard yet, not even awarded a wizard's cloak, and yet somehow...."

He drifted off again in his thoughts. He never mentioned the yew wood Tom thought. Then he remembered that he hadn't told them. 'Just keep that to me then,' though he didn't know why.

"Now, the stone in the top. Diamonds, giver of light to fight against the darkness of evil and again giving great power and strong pure magic when needed for defence or attack, diamond is the hardest material known to man and with it, you will be able to cut through many defensive shields.

Ruby, the fire stone, allowing you to control fire. It won't make you a Firemaster, but you will be able to use fire for both attack and defence, and at the other extreme, you can even draw down a little warmth on a cold winters evening to relieve the chill of the night. And finally, Emerald, the water stone, and giver of life itself. Never have I seen a wand with three kinds of wood and 3 gemstones melded into one. Never.....," again, his voice drifted away slowly.

Tom thought about his so-called lesson and realised that Llewel had not taught him anything that the wand tree hadn't already told him.

As he finished speaking, over the horizon they could see smoke or dust or something.

"Now what?" said Llewel, mainly to himself, "probably only a dust storm," he continued answering his own question.

"No!" said Tom, "it's not."

"And how would you know?" Llewel sneered.

"I can feel it, it's moving this way, people on horses and a couple of dragons heading straight for us."

Llewel and Flintock looked at each other, Flintock with a slight look of worry, Llewel with a dismissive look on his face, rolled his eyes.

Tom slammed his staff into the ground. Around them a thicket began to grow, gorse, brambles, nettles, ivy, and small trees, all intertwined in such a way as to look and feel impenetrable, it grew around them and then arched over them like a dome.

Several minutes later, the hoard galloped past and the mighty dragons flew above them, scouring the ground for their prey.

Then, as quickly as they arrived, they were gone.

"I was just about to do that," lied Llewel, "you should not have done that, you don't have the experience, the control, or the knowledge, you could have smothered us all with that trick, we could all be dead!"

"No," said Tom, "I envisioned exactly what happened as it happened, developing the thought as I went along, not only enclosing all around us but the top canopy as well so the dragons could not see us and imagined the cavity in which we stood so we would all be safe"

"I don't know how you did it," said Flintock, "but it was powerful and well executed. Tell me again, no tell us again, so Llewel can hear how you formed the thicket" he emphasised the 'you' with a hint of sarcasm for Llewel.

"Well, like I said, I didn't just bang down my staff and form a small thicket, I envisioned what was happening as it happened, so I started with the bushes, trees, thorns, gorse, weaving and developing the thought spells one on another to form first the thick impenetrable outer defence, while also visualising the canopy above and continuing to imagine the clear area where we stand, so it wasn't a spell like you would normally expect, but a continuously developing interweaving and interwoven envisioning spell of what I was trying to develop. Having said all that, I haven't a clue what I was saying then and don't even understand what I just said, or even where that little speech came from!"

"Enough of this nonsense," said Llewel "it was just luck, now we must progress."

Llewel raised his wand to clear a path out of the thicket.

"Stop," said Tom, "I haven't finished...."

Llewel held up his hand to stop him, "I doubt if it is worth hearing, we have no time to stop, we must press on."

He raised his wand and flicked at the thicket, but nothing happened. He tried again, again nothing, "Staff!" he said, his staff appeared, and he struck it on the ground....... Nothing!

"No," said Tom, "you stop talking for a while and listen for a change. I also envisioned that only I could break the spell as a precaution against hasty action from either side."

Again, he had no idea where his words were coming from.

Flintock raised an eyebrow and a small smile. 'This should be interesting he thought'

"You cannot talk to me, a High Elder, like that, how dare you question my authority."

"I don't know what this wand has done to me, but I feel very different now, I feel as if I have all the power the world could offer, so, close it and listen!"

Tom raised his voice and continued, "As far as I'm concerned, you have no authority. Not over me anyway. I didn't want to be here; and I still don't want to be here. As far as I'm concerned, I've been kidnapped by a small obnoxious and bad-tempered wizard with no manners."

This time it was different, Tom looked at Llewel straight in the eyes and Llewel had something happen to him for the very first time. He had no answer. But recovered quickly and after some seconds, Llewel started again.

"You need to learn respect young man."

"Wrong, I've told you before, you need to earn respect, it doesn't just happen because you're a grumpy old wizard or have a grand title!"

Flintock's small smile increased to a small grin. Though still out of sight of Llewel of course.

"That is twice they have nearly found us, so before we go anywhere, we must find out who or what is betraying us," Tom said, now a little calmer, but still quite angry.

"It is obvious to me, it's the trygall, they have no loyalty to anyone or anything, he must have alerted them when he went out hunting last night."

"How dare you," said Flintock, "Tryg is my friend and he would not betray us, so apologise to Tryg."

"Perhaps you two are in it together? You and your hideous little friend, both traitors to the cause."

Flintock flinched as if to go for his wand, but decided better, maiming a high Elder would not go down well with the Council of Elders, he knew he could out magic Llewel at any time, but the council tended to stick together.

"Why don't you accuse Howel while you're at it," said Tom, "after all, he's not here to defend himself."

"Well, good point boy, at last you may have said something sensible, yes, it could well be him, I for one have never really trusted dragons," Llewel said with a certain satisfaction, "I don't quite know why I have one or even how I come to have one, now I mention it!"

"Stop being stupid," Tom snorted.

"You've gone too far this time," barked Llewel, "you do not talk to a high Elder like that!"

"Yes, I know, you're a High Elder of the Council of Band-Aid, you've mentioned it before. I said stop it and I meant stop it! Staff!" said Tom.

Tom's staff appeared in his hand, he placed his left hand around the huge gemstone set in the top, closed his eyes, and began to concentrate. Under his hand you could see light of every colour swirling in the stone with occasional beams of pure white light darting through the gaps in his fingers.

"Stop it," said Llewel, "you cannot harness its power like that, it could kill you."

"Shush," said Flintock, "be quiet and watch, it is amazing, something neither you nor I have seen before."

Tom relaxed and the light show stopped.

"It's you!" Tom suddenly exclaimed, "you're the one who's been leading them to us."

"Rubbish!" Exclaimed a very vexed Llewel, "how dare you even suggest such a thing. Why would I? I am a High Elder! How dare you! How very dare you!"

"No. Not you personally, those ridiculous looking trainers you wear are what's leading them to us."

"How?"

"I don't know how or even care how, just take them off."

Llewel gingerly took off his trainers with a very hang-dog expression, he picked them up off the ground as if they were somehow now disgusting. His socks were almost beyond description, the heels so worn that they looked like potatoes in a netting sack, both his big toes poked out at the front. His feet were appalling, with black dirt under the toenails and a strong smell of something horrid. Llewel started to wave his wand about them and exclaimed.

"A tracking spell, someone has placed a tracking spell on them, I will get rid of it immediately."

"No," said Tom, "we can use it to our advantage. Can we get Howel here to help us?"

"And how do you think the dragon can help?" said Llewel regaining his sneer and air of assumed authority.

"Then he can take the trainers, tracking smell and all, sorry, tracking spell and all, and drop them on the far side of Trymyll. Then we'll see how quickly they sus that one out," Tom said with almost a smile, "hopefully, by the time they work out our little ruse, we will be in Castle Band-Aid."

"Agreed," they both said at once, "but it's Castell y Blaenoraid, not Band-Aid." continued Flintock. Llewel had agreed with some reluctance, he had quite an attachment to his trainers. He then dug out a more wizardly looking pair of pointy shoes from his bag and put them on. Tom thought that they looked much better than trainers on a wizard.

"We will be very safe to stop here tonight," said Flintock, "here Tryg, do your stuff, we have enough food in store until tomorrow, so if Llewel would be so kind as to summon Howel, his dragon whom he doesn't really trust, and then we'll make a plan for tomorrow."

It appeared even Flintock was getting bolder and jibing Llewel now.

Llewel flicked his wand around, and a small bird appeared in the thicket, he whispered in the bird's ear, Jon made a small exit gap in the defences and off it went as quick as a flash. Half an hour later they heard wings beating above them as Howel landed. There was an audible pop. Tom envisioned a tunnel into the thicket and in trotted a small mongrel of an indeterminable breed. But to Tom it was a Jack Russell called Howl.

CHAPTER 9 - A NIGHT TO REMEMBER....

That night they all slept soundly, all except for Tom. Again, he awoke in the night to the sound of someone calling his name. As always, he knew the voice but didn't know who it was. Suddenly, he was very awake, or so he thought. He seemed to be flying at incredibly high speed across the countryside, just about mattress height, he sped across fields, through woods and forests, down narrow paths, through towns and villages, down narrow alleyways, up and over hills, never touching anything and always at a constant height. He was beginning to feel quite sick when he stopped abruptly, very abruptly. Well, he stopped, but his dinner continued its journey a few extra feet and onto the floor in front of a tall hooded person, a wizard he presumed, but did not know, he also did not know whether a friend or foe.

'Wand!' he thought, almost instinctively.

"Tom, Tom, no need for wands," the wizard said in a quiet and calming voice, "I am your friend, not your enemy. I will not harm you because you are very dear to me. I have watched these past days at how you have developed since receiving your wand."

The stranger's wand peaked from under his cloak and the sick was all cleared up.

Tom recognised the voice at once, it was the voice that had called him each night since he arrived in Trymyll. Why hadn't he told the others about his dream voice, he might not be here if he had. Tom was, for the first time, frightened. Very frightened.

Tom felt he could do nothing anyway, he felt most strange, he was there, he knew he was there, in the room, possibly halfway across Trymyll standing before a strange wizard, but at the same time, he knew he wasn't there and that he was still asleep in his bed. He also knew this was not a dream but a reality and he knew that he was wide awake and fast asleep all at the same time, if fact, he realised, he understood nothing of what was happening at all.

"I need my ring back," he said.

"Well you can't, it's my ring, not yours, my dad gave it to me when I was a baby."

Even as the words left his mouth, he knew.

And yet he felt no emotion, no love, no anger, nothing.

"Tom, you no longer need the ring, I gave it to you for your protection, both at home on the other side and as you started your journey here in Trymyll. But now you have your wand, possibly, in the right hands, one of the finest and most powerful wands ever made, you do not need the ring. It must be returned to the High Elders for safekeeping."

"What do you know about my wand?"

"More than that fool Llewel the Elder knows, that's for sure. Come sit and I will explain. You will not understand some, most or all of what I am going to say, but I will try to keep it simple."

There was a pause while Tom sat, the hooded figure sat next to him began his story but did not reveal his face.

"You have worked out who I am, and you are probably wondering where I have been all these years and why I left you and your mum behind."

"You can say that again!" emotion had returned, "because you're a complete loser if you want my opinion."

"No, I had no choice. Did your mum ever speak ill of me or of

Jonathan? I'll answer that for you, no she didn't, because she knew why I had to go and why Jon had to come with me. What she didn't know for sure, but probably suspected was that you would have to follow me as well."

"Why? Why did you leave and take my big brother as well?"

Anger flaring hot again.

"It is difficult to explain. I thought I had a life in Wales, I was the last wizard left in the country. I was the guardian of the mines."

"No, you weren't you were just a stupid miner like the rest," Tom said heatedly.

"No," he said calmly and quietly, "I was a miner, that is true, though actually I was safety manager for the mine. But my 'other' job was to protect the miners in Wales from things they would not understand or even want to believe. I kept the dwarfs away. Dwarfs have very deep and dark magic, they live way down, deep in the earth, and mostly shun contact with mortal humans. Any they met usually disappeared. As the mines were sunk and new shafts and seams opened, I had to make sure that the new seams went nowhere near where the dwarfs lived. There were many a rich seam of coal, so rich we would still be digging them out today if I hadn't made them appear as solid impenetrable granite rock."

"Where'd they go then?"

"Who?"

"The miners who bumped into the dwarfs?"

"That does not matter now. When the last deep mine closed, my task finished. I was summoned back to Trymyll for a greater mission. Magic was slipping away on this side as well. It was not that anyone here stopped believing, everyone believed in magic as I am sure you know. No one knew why it was happening. I was the last of my kind and legend held that my firstborn son would herald a new time of magic and all our lost powers would be restored."

"So, what went wrong?" Tom interrupted.

Well, Jon came through with me, but nothing, nothing happened, nothing changed, Jon had not the power or skill to do any meaningful magic beyond a few cantrips, minor spells of the sort even some humans could do."

"Why?" Toms anger evaporated, and inquisitiveness took over.

"At first I thought that he cannot be my son."

A hint of bitterness and sadness hung in his voice.

"What? Never. Mum wouldn't do nothing like that!" Tom's anger was up again.

"No, you're right, she wouldn't, and she didn't."

"Where is Jon now?"

"He's still with me, he is learning some magic, but he'll never be a great wizard. But he is my eldest son, and I love him dearly. I discovered sometime later that the mystics had misinterpreted the prophecy. It didn't have to be my firstborn, it just had to be my son. Which of course is where you come in."

Tom was silent for a while, "But what can I do? I'm not a wizard or anything, I can't do magic. It must be a mistake."

"No, it's no mistake and you've already done magic. I tell you, one day you may be the greatest wizard who ever lived."

"Tell me about the wand. You said you knew more than even Llewel the whiny Elder did."

"Ah, the wand. I have studied wands for many years. They tell you that you only get one chance, one wand, one choice. No one ever explains to you before you go and see the Wand Tree, just how important it is. No one ever suggests what you should ask for. It's an unwritten and rather stupid rule, when you meet the wand tree, you're on your own. No one knows where the rule came from or even if it's a real or made-up rule. I now know it's a made-up rule. The tree knows best and if you don't ask for a specific wand, the tree will decide for you. It's all a lie, there are no rules, just stupid folk law. It's all humbug. Some wizards, not knowing any different have gotten themselves the stupidest wands going and the magical power to match. I know one who has apple wood and a piece of coal. Loved his stomach too much and thought it would be good for making apple pie. Can't even do that properly, because he can't control the temperature, they always come out burnt! No, yours is special, because I made it so."

"How? When I was in the wood I was as confused as anything and stupid lists came out of my mouth that sounded more like a recipe instead of a simple wand request."

"Well I know that because I broke all their stupid made-up rules and told you what to say."

"Don't be daft, I was talking gibberish, it was hardly coherent, even took the Wand Tree by surprise."

"Exactly, the Wand Tree has rarely given a wand like it, three wood types and three precious stones melded as one. Exactly what was needed, exactly what you asked for and exactly what I suggested."

"What do you mean?"

"Well, I, with the help of Howel and his mind-bending and highly confusing powers, and by the way, he is actually my dragon, not Llewel's, we wove the thoughts into your head quite a long time ago and when faced with the Wand Tree, it all came tumbling out."

"Not his dragon? Why does Llewel the stupid Elder say that Howel is his then?"

"Again, a clever dragon that one, he has some quite amazing and magical powers, after he suggested to Llewel's little brain that he was, in fact, his dragon, he took him on as his own."

"What about his actual dragon?"

"He doesn't have one, he doesn't like dragons, always scared they'll eat him for his magic powers. Terrified of them he is, doesn't trust them and never owned one! Although, dragons are very much like cats. Do you own the cat? Or are you owned by the cat and enslaved to it? Do I really own a dragon? Or is it just toying with me?"

They both chuckled at the thought.

"I don't believe any wizard owns a dragon, it is a partnership of mutual respect and camaraderie, love almost. Yes, it's almost like love."

"What about your wand? What's it made of?"

"My wand is incredibly special also. Despite what you were told, after I had studied wands for some time, I returned to the wand tree and asked it for a new wand. Mine is also oak for strength, wych-hazel for healing and elm for wisdom, so slightly different to yours. My stone is made of diamond, emerald and ruby, exactly as yours is."

"Do the elders know you have a new wand?"

"No, they didn't know what my first wand was made of, so they also don't know what this one is either made of or capable of."

The was a short hiatus, then Tom said, "I should be getting back; they might look in on me to make sure I'm okay."

"And if they do, they will see you're sound asleep in your bed because that is where you are."

"So, I'm not here like at all, this is all like a dream?" Tom asked questioningly.

"No, no, you are here as well, or more exactly, you're in what is called the neither here nor there, confusing I know, one day you will understand, now, the ring please."

"But it won't come off."

"Yes it will, now give."

Tom gave up the pretence that the ring was stuck and slid it off his finger and placed it on the table between them, he didn't want to have direct contact with whoever was in the cloak. He watched and the ring disappeared. He looked down expecting it to be back on his finger, to his surprise, it wasn't. A feeling of peace overcame him, it was as if he knew the ring was now back where it belonged, with his father, wherever he was. He had a feeling that his father was, but also wasn't there. He was really confused and just did not understand.

"Don't tell the others about this, they may not understand either."

Before he could question that last remark or even say goodbye, he felt a jolt as what seemed like an invisible rope attached to his belly button pulled him back along the exact same path he had come by, but in reverse and seconds later he found himself back in his bed, fast asleep just as he always had been.

Next morning, he woke. He looked at his hand, there was no ring. So, he hadn't dreamt the whole thing after all. He felt sick in his stomach, what would Llewel say when he found out the ring was gone. What would he say, what could he say? He was frightened again.

Tom got up, washed, and dressed and went gingerly out to the main hall where breakfast was being prepared.

They turned to greet him but instead with one voice exclaimed; "What on earth has happened to you? You look dreadful."

Tom didn't know quite what to say, he could hardly tell them the truth, he panicked slightly, then said.

"Oh, I was sick in the night, sorry, but it's all cleared up now."

Not exactly a lie, but not exactly the truth either. He went and sat down and tried to eat his breakfast, it was difficult because he was also trying to hide his hand so that no one would notice the missing ring. Llewel the Elder was looking at him suspiciously. He knew something was up, and he just stared at Tom with his normal malicious look on his face.

Tom suddenly started, "Oh, forgot something, excuse me," and disappeared back in his room. What could he do? How was he going to get out of this problem? He sat on his bed and started to cry with fear. That ring was obviously something very special, if they thought he had lost it there would be big trouble, if he told them his dad had taken it back, they wouldn't believe him as no one could get into the shack without setting off all the alarms. What can I do? What can I do? What can I do? He rocked back and forth, as the phrase just went over and over in his head. Someone said his name, this time he knew it was his dad. It felt and heard as if he were in the room. He looked up and saw the cloaked figure he had met last night standing by his bed.

 "How.... How did you get in here?" he said slightly timidly.

"I didn't," he said, "I'm neither here nor there, just as you weren't last night. Just listen, don't talk or they", he paused and nodded at the door, "may hear you. Take out your wand, take down one of the brass curtain rings and re-imagine it into a facsimile of the ring."

Tom jumped up, stood on a chair and took one of the rings, put it on his finger, pointed his wand at it and thought hard, picturing the ring of the elders on his finger, slowly at first and then more quickly the curtain ring re-formed, reshaped and morphed into the ring. He looked up to acknowledge his father's help, but he was gone. Again...

He then put a few more brass curtain rings in his pocket, just in case. In case of what, he had no idea, it just seemed like a good idea.

Tom jumped up and exited into the main hall, they were all still eating breakfast, he resumed his place at the table and carried on as though nothing had happened, the others also carried on as if he had never left the room. He had a strange feeling inside; he must have been gone for fifteen or twenty minutes and yet all were behaving as if nothing had happened. Very strange that Llewel had not asked in his normal condescending tone where he had been for so long. Very strange indeed.

CHAPTER 10 - A DETOUR AND A TRAP.

After breakfast, Tryg dispatched the shack back into the phial and handed it to Flintock, Tom opened the thicket and allowed them all out to continue the journey. He closed the exit and left the small wooded area intact, but spell free so that if the others, whoever they are, returned that way, they would not suspect their hiding place.

Howel had left at daybreak, trainers in his claw to dispatch them somewhere, far away to lead whoever was following them on a nice little detour.

Howel flew high in the sky heading for the Dragonlands.

About noon, Howel returned, "Where did you drop them then my scaly friend?" asked Flintock.

"In a dragon's cave on the very edge of our land, amongst a pile of bones so they will now think you have all been eaten by a dragon and be very scared of the magic and years the dragon has inherited."

For once, even Llewel laughed with them, well smiled anyway.

"Lessons, lessons," exclaimed Llewel, "you must have more lessons, we have to teach you so much, and yet you and we have so little time, so little time. You must have more lessons, so little time."

Tom had noticed that sometimes if Llewel had no one else's words to repeat, he would say everything several times over himself.

They had walked for a couple of hours now across farmland full of crops and livestock and were approaching a wooded area when they noticed there was smoke curling up from within. They entered the woods cautiously, not knowing what to expect. Birds were singing, leaves were falling, all seemed peaceful and in order. They came upon a clearing and a farmhouse; the thatch roof was ablaze and there were a couple of gravely injured men lying outside the house.

"Stop! This might be a trap," Llewel said, stating the obvious, "tread carefully and silently. Wands out and ready."

As they approached the burning house, they could hear a woman weeping inside. They moved quickly to investigate, there was indeed an unbelievably beautiful young lady inside, tied hands and feet, sobbing. Trig started dealing with the fire, drawing it away from the house and into himself. Flintock went into the house to tend to the girl, Tom rushed to the injured men to see if he could help them, Llewel just stood there looking as if he were doing nothing, which he was. His eyes darting left and right looking for danger.

Tom started to heal the men as quickly as his young and inexperienced power could cope.

"Who did this to you," he asked.

"She did," they replied, nodding towards the girl in the house.

Flintock started to untie the girl, "Who did this to you?" he asked.

"They did," she answered, nodding towards the two injured men.

"Very interesting," said Llewel, "two badly injured men tied up a girl and left her in a burning house and at the same time a young woman bound hand and foot kicked the what-sits out of two fit and strong young men in their prime? Very interesting indeed!"

Tom suddenly found fear, dread, and despair creeping into him again.

"This must be a trap of some kind," said Tom "we need time to think this through."

As he spoke there was a rush of wind, then silence. Tom looked around, everything was still, nothing moved, the leaves that had been gently fluttering down from the trees, stopped in mid-air as if frozen, suspended and still, a sparrow flying from tree to tree stopped in a wing beat, unmoving. His companions stood like waxworks in a museum, unblinking, stony-faced. Flintock was kneeling tending the bound girl, Llewel was just standing there keeping his distance, his head twisted and his eyes peering into the distance as if he were looking for an escape route and Tryg motionless sorting out the last of the fire, licks of flame suspended mid-air, unmoving.

Rubbish, Tom thought, now what have I done? He sat down sharply,

"Wand away," he said and hoped for some inspiration.

Tom was alone and yet surrounded by people. He needed to do something, but he didn't know what, he needed some help and advice but didn't know who to trust. He knew his dad would know what to do but he wasn't there. But that had been his life up to now. Flintock was his best bet, he was sure he could trust him and equally sure he would not trust Llewel.

"Wand," he said. He went over to where Flintock was kneeling and motionless, pointed his wand and envisioned him moving again. Tom nearly jumped out of his skin when Flintock stood up again as if nothing had happened and looked around.

"How did you get here? You were outside a second ago."

Then he saw the others, all frozen in time, saw the leaves suspended in mid-air, saw the look of fear on Tom's face, looking at Tom he stuttered.

"How? How did that happen?"

"I don't know, it just did," Tom replied.

"Has it happened before?"

"I don't know, it might have done, I don't know."

"Don't tell the others," they said in unison.

"We need to work out what and how this happened, keep it to ourselves, Llewel is already both jealous and suspicious about you and your power," continued Flintock.

"Why would he be jealous?"

"Because you are already doing things that some elders could not do. I think you have an amazing and inherent gift, you are your father's son, your father is a very great and powerful wizard who has chosen a different path to many, he could and should be a High Elder, if not the Elder, but has chosen not to be. Llewel thinks, and it's important you don't let on I've told you this, he thinks you are not who you claim but another powerful wizard appearing as a boy, also, he neither likes nor trusts your father."

Tom didn't know now what to say, he really didn't understand, so he just said nothing. He didn't know his father, but the last bit did not help his ongoing relationship with Llewel the stupid Elder!

"But I assure you, you can trust me, I have in these few days been both amazed by you and grown fond of you, I have always counted your father as a true friend, I will make sure that we get through this without anyone, especially you, coming to any harm, we will deliver the ring and then we'll find your father."

Tom nodded in appreciation at his candidness. He was still scared though, even more scared as he knew that he no longer had the ring to protect him.

"But what about this, it looks like a trap to me, what do we do now?"

Not very reassuringly, Flintock said, "Actually, I haven't a clue."

Flintock didn't need long to consider the next move. Out of the air stepped Asmodeus wand pointed directly at Flintock and Tom.

"One move Flintock and your dead," Asmodeus snarled.

"Well, greetings to you Dark Elder Asmodeus."

"My title is High Elder Asmodeus you pathetic excuse for a wizard."

"I suppose this little charade is your doing?" said Flintock.

"Yes, clever little ruse just to slow you down long enough that I could pinpoint where you were and arrive before you left. Of course," he moved his head slightly in the direction of the two men, "they didn't tie the girl up and she didn't beat them up, stupid peasants are so easy to manipulate into believing what you want them to believe. I'm keeping you at the end of my wand because I know I can't hurt the boy while he has the ring. You boy give me the ring."

Tom stepped forward gingerly, took the ring off and gave it to Asmodeus.

"Well, that was much easier than I thought, it seems that I am in pathetic company, the boy is no better than his father."

A spark of light emitted from his wand which knocked Flintock off his feet and about 10 feet backwards landing heavily on the ground with a violent crack.

"That was for your insolence. Oh, forgetting my manners, thank you Thomas son of Llewellyn."

Asmodeus did a mock bow and then stepped backwards and disappeared to wherever he had come from.

Tom rushed to where Flintock had landed. He had landed badly and had a compound fracture of a bone in his forearm. Flintock moaned, so Tom and his wand started to work. He envisioned the bone back under the skin, then slowly imagined the bones knitting together and the skin healing. Flintock was mended within about ten minutes and sat up.

"Well thank, your healing powers are amazing. But why did you give over the ring so quickly without even an argument, you know he couldn't hurt you all the time you had the ring. I take it the ring is back on your finger as usual?"

"No," said Tom, "it's not. He has the ring."

"NO! This is a disaster, quick, release the others from your time freeze, we must tell Llewel all that has happened and warn them at the Castell y Blaenoraid."

"No," said Tom, it's alright the ring is in safe hands. Just don't tell Llewel."

"What? What do you mean?"

"Just don't worry, it'll be okay, I promise, just keep this as a secret between us."

"Don't worry!" he said, voice rising to a falsetto, "Asmodeus has the ring and you say it will be okay!"

"He hasn't, he just thinks he has the ring. The ring is safe, believe me, please trust me on this, the ring is safe, it's just that I don't have it now and neither does whoever you said that was have it either."

"What do you mean you haven't got it and he hasn't got it? Where is it?"

"I can't tell you, it's just safe. Believe me."

Tom then took one of his spare curtain rings out of his pocket and again, re-imagined it to look exactly like the ring of the elders.

"There, no one need ever know."

"You're smarter than you look," he said smiling at Tom, "now, what do we do about this lot?"

"I'm not sure, if this is what happened last time, then it just sorts itself out."

"What do you mean, last time?"

"Another secret for you to keep, I think. This morning at breakfast I went to my room and then came back to breakfast, how long was I gone?"

"Only about a minute, why?"

"I was gone twenty minutes at least."

"What? How? What were you doing in there?"

"Can't tell you, I promised I wouldn't tell anyone."

"You've got to trust me."

"And you've got to trust me," said Tom, "I can't tell you yet...... but I will when I can."

The leaves began to flutter down, the sparrow continued in its travels, first the girl, then the two lads and finally, but only a split second later, Llewel and Tryg re-animated again.

"Right," Llewel said as if nothing had happened "where are we, what are we doing, what's going on?" He seemed a little confused, but once the girl and the two lads started shouting at each other, Llewel tried to take command again.

"Stop! Stop!" he shouted, "stop at once, all of you," he paused, he continued, "right, what's been going on?"

The three started shouting and pointing at each other, each accusing the others of doing something.

Flintock intervened.

"Quieten down, all of you and listen. Whatever you think happened probably didn't happen, someone may have, and we don't know who, but probably a mischievous imp," he fibbed, "has befuddled you and left the scene. It's a good job we came along when we did, as we probably scared him off, or you all might have died or at least been robbed. So, stop shouting and let's sort this all out,"

"Staff," said Tom.

He held his staff aloft, a blue hazy light emitting from his gemstone and the house began to put itself in order. The thatch was restored, the broken furniture rebuilt, all the spilt and knocked over broken pots and crocks came together again, the plates and cooking utensils returned to where they should be, and an aura of peace descended over the whole place.

"There," he said, "sorted."

"I was just about to do that," lied Llewel, "I do wish you would stop interfering, and stop doing magic you don't understand. You could be putting yourself and all those around you in danger. I neither know nor understand how you know so much, it is most unnatural, so you should stop now and don't do any more until you have been taught how to properly control it."

"Anyway", he said loudly, trying to take control again, pretending to all that he had both sorted out everything and that it was all under his control, "everything seems to be in order now, so we had best be getting on our way. Good day to you all, good day."

"But," Tom started, "the two lads are still not healed, and we haven't eaten since breakfast."

"Well, we really haven't the time to linger here, healing peasants and eating the few scraps of food they may have. No, we must move on, now!" his voice raised at the end to make the point.

"You go if you want to," said Tom, "I'm staying until these people are properly sorted out and well enough to fend for themselves again."

"You will do as you are told, young man. I am in charge here, not you; I say when we move on, and that is right now!"

"Well," retorted Tom, again in his best Welsh accent again, "you are not the boss of me, I don't belong in this world anyway, so I don't have to do anything you say anyway."

....and with that, Tom disappeared!

CHAPTER 11 - TEACHING TOM.

Tom had not realised he had disappeared even after he reappeared in the room he had met his father in the other night. He thought it was another 'neither here nor there' experience. His father spoke.

"Tom, sorry about that, Llewel was getting me very frustrated so I intervened and brought you here to be with me."

"But I'm not actually here am I? I'm there as well."

"No, this time, you really are here, physically and in the flesh."

"How did you do that?" Tom stuttered.

Tom felt an overwhelming urge to hug his father, but fought it off, as he still had not come to terms with his father's disappearance all those years ago. He desperately needed a hug but now was not the right time or the right person.

"Come look...."

In the centre of the room was a fire pit, he waved his wand over it and as they looked into the flames they could see Llewel the Elder jumping up and down in rage, Flintock standing quite still with a slightly bemused look on his face while Llewel spent his rage. Tryg was nowhere to be seen, he probably thought it was wise to stay out of the way for a few minutes.

"Can't you magic Flintock and Tryg here too?" asked Tom.

"Sorry son, this is between you and me now. I'll let Flintock know you are safe, but I can't bring him here or even let him know where we are, if you, Flintock and Tryg all disappeared, the High Elders might not understand and accuse him of treachery."

"Shame, I quite like Flintock. So, why now? Why bring me here now and not earlier?"

"Well, that's twice and almost three times that Asmodeus has found you, so who's letting him know where you are? And whose letting him know where you might be next? That is the question I need answering."

"Well it must be Llewel the stupid Elder, mustn't it?" said Tom.

Llewellyn smiled at Llewel's new title.

"You shouldn't call him that, I know he hasn't earned it, but a High Elder still deserves a little respect."

"Sorry," Tom said unconvincingly.

"Trouble is, once you told Flintock that you no longer had the ring, then you put yourself in danger."

"How? Flintock would not betray us, he said that you and him were besties."

"Yes, we are 'besties' as you call us, but, small as it might be, it was a risk I was not willing to take."

"But how did it put me in danger?"

"I'm afraid it's all about the ring. All the time they thought you had the ring; you were a valuable commodity. Put simply, once you no longer had the ring, you were, in many ways, and to some people, surplus to requirements. It's not you anyone is interested in, it's the ring. They think the ring is the answer to the disappearing magic in Trymyll, which incidentally, it's not."

"But what about you, has your magic been getting less powerful?"

"No, and neither has yours. In fact, although I have now brought you here so that you can fully realise your magic, I can sense that you already have more power than many wizards I know, and your power is growing exponentially. But now you need to learn how to control both your power and the urge to use it."

"Meaning?"

"What do you mean by 'meaning'?"

"What does," Tom's speech slowed to single syllables, "what does expo tent shelly mean?"

His dad laughed.

"It means that your power is growing faster and faster as each day passes. With that wand, you could, and probably will, become one of the greatest wizards ever known. Even greater than the Elder of Elders, whose name is and shall remain a mystery to all."

"Who's he then?"

"Well, the Elder of Elders, he is the highest wizard in the land, He is always referred to as the Elder. The other elders believe that this is because his real name is unpronounceable, but in fact, they have never been told his name at all. They cannot recognise him, because they have never seen his face, and they do not recognise his voice because he speaks so little and so softly."

"Wow, how do you know all these things and the High Elders do not?"

"Oh my goodness, the wisdom of the wand is working its magic on you already!"

"And how did he become the boss elder anyway?"

"Too many questions for now, when you are ready, everything, and I mean everything, will be revealed to you. Now, I believe you said you were hungry back there. Come let's eat and meet your brother Jon."

Tom and his dad moved into the next room, there was a table piled high with food, but Tom had no eyes for the food, he just stopped and looked over at his brother. He was a few inches taller than Tom, but apart from that Jon looked exactly like him. Same long and curly ginger hair, blue eyes, freckles over his nose and skinny as a rake. For what seemed an eternity, they both just stood there staring at each other.

Jon spoke first, "Hi Tom," he said quietly.

"Hi," Tom replied sheepishly.

There then followed another staring competition while they both stood eyeing each other.

Their father spoke first, "Come on, let's eat, Tom must be starving."

It was very strange for them both, seeing the brother they had never seen before. Well, Jon had seen Tom, but he was so young he couldn't remember him, and Tom had seen Jon, but only through baby eyes. So, neither knew the other.

They tucked into the food and soon the conversation was flowing, they talked of rugby, how Wales was doing in the Six Nations Cup, whether they should replace the prop forward or not. Was their fly-half up to the job? They talked about football and how Cardiff City was placed in the F.A. Cup. Then Jon remembered to ask after their mother, the mood then went sombre.

Tom then spoke quietly and with reverence, "She's fine in herself, happy and that, but not well at all. She's in a wheelchair now and must carry oxygen around wherever she goes. Da, if I could go back, I could help her, couldn't I? Make her well like?"

Llewellyn almost welled up to hear Tom call him da for the first time. Tom also noticed what he had said, and for the first time realised he felt affection for his father. He rushed to him and hugged him and, also for the first time in his life, tears rolled down his face. Tears rolled down both their faces. They just stood there, hugging each other, and loving each other for what seemed like an age.

Jon coughed, "Don't mind me like," he said.

Llewellyn beckoned him over, they all hugged, they all cried tears of emotion. They were family.

"Yes Tom, we can all go back and visit, but only once the job here is done. But don't worry about your ma, she's fine. A miraculous cure came over her soon after you left. I'm afraid that was all part of the illusion created by me and Howel, so you would have to go and live with those terrible Hadley Smythes. Really sorry about that, but you know how Howel is, likes to think he's a very posh dragon indeed."

"Why did the Hadley-Smiffs say they were Welsh then? They didn't sound Welsh at all. And why did I have to go live with them then?"

Well, the first bit is easy. Howell is very Welsh, he is a Welsh Dragon, born and bred in Wales. Just like the one on the Welsh flag."

"But that's Red!"

"Red? Don't tell me they've got it wrong," Llewellyn laughed, "anyway, Hadley Smythe or Howel to give him his real name, had to work quite hard to 'bend' your mind and get you ready to come over to this side of the veil. Your mind is very firm and quite closed to probing by mind-benders, that is why he was calling you to the cave for a couple of months, but could not get you to go in. It's also why, when I called you in your dreams, instead of your 'self' coming over to where I was in the 'neither here nor there,' you wouldn't budge. Just lay there snoring. Llewel the Elder tried several times to probe into your mind because he thought you were someone else, the fact that he failed only made his paranoia worse. With some people, mind-bending is just so easy that even a non-magical human can do it, like on the hypnosis shows you see on the television where they get members of the audience to dance like chickens, but others, like you, are a very hard nut to crack, but we had to get into your mind before you came over."

"Why?"

"Because Trymyll can a dangerous place, so Howel and I had to be able to read your thoughts and give you thoughts as well, it's not mind-reading or control, it's just thoughts and suggestions. For example, had you gone into the Wand Wood without some subliminal suggestions, you also might have come out with a wand that couldn't even make a good apple pie!"

"What is your wand made of Jon?"

"It's similar to yours and da's, but unlike you and da, I just can't connect to it." Jon said in a dejected sort of voice.

"Yet," said Tom.

"No, I don't think I'll ever connect to it properly," said Jon.

"Yes you will. You're my big brother, so you can do anything I can do and more. That's what big brothers do."

Llewellyn felt quite proud of Tom, he was an encourager as well as a healer and restorer. And who knows, perhaps he is right. They just needed to find a way to unlock the power of Jon's wand, to get him and his wand connected.

"But first, I have a confession, sort of, well, maybe more good news and some bad news," Llewellyn said almost sheepishly, "good news is, you really do have the potential to become a great wizard, the bad news is, as I sort of said before, most of the magic you have done up to now wasn't actually you, but me acting through your wand. But the next news is either good or bad depending on your point of view. For the next while, I will be teaching you how to do it all by yourself."

"Lessons," Tom said, "I did think it was all a bit too easy. But much as I hate lessons, this one will be worth it, so let's start soon before I go off the idea!"

"Come, let's go into the next room, it's my little schoolroom. I think you'll like it."

They went through a door and stepped out into a vast desert plain which went on, completely flat until the sky met the earth. The sky was azure blue, the sand as white as snow. It was incredibly hot, and a bright sun hung in the sky.

"Oh," said Tom, "I thought you said the next room, but we're outside."

"No, we're not actually, watch."

Llewellyn flicked his wand, the sky darkened, the moon appeared, stars twinkled and there was suddenly quite a chill in the air. Another flick and they were in a vast mountain range, snowy peaks disappearing into the distance an icy blast penetrating to their very bones. Then in a dark damp cave deep in a mountain with the grunts of animals and unknown horrors all around. Then at sea in a small boat bobbing up and down on the waves land nowhere to be seen and dark clouds gathering on the horizon. In a cell deep in a castle, rats and mice scurrying around with bones on the floor and a stench of death in the air. Then in a vast forest thick with trees and the sound of birds and animals. Then atop a castle wall looking down on a vast army and finally in a small room with a single table and some chairs. All these different scenes flashed before him in a matter of seconds, no time to take too much in and no time to be frightened.

"Welcome to the training room, we are deep in the castle, below the kitchens, below the deepest dungeons, below the deepest part accessible from anywhere in or out of the castle. You can only enter through a hidden door in the castle unknown to all but me and guarded by spells and incantations, impassable by anyone or any thing."

Tom wished people wouldn't keep using the phrase 'any thing', he found it rather frightening.

"Here, we will begin your training. It is all illusionary so you can't come to any real harm, but you will feel and experience it all as if you are really there, you can see, feel, hear, taste and sense everything as a reality, but of course, it is just an illusion. Fear and emotion will be real. Very real. But nothing beyond what you can endure."

"What do you mean by that?" stuttered Tom.

"Training is tough, but you have to be equipped both physically and mentally for every eventuality. You will not like some or even most of the training. You may not like me at the end of your training, but you will thank me at the end for the experience and for the fact you will be prepared for most of things that Trymyll can throw your way."

Tom did not like the sound of that at all, but not wanting to disappoint his father, he knew he had to go through it. So, with gritted teeth he said.

"Okay da, let's do it!"

"Now, when you faced danger over the last few days, you coped very well. When the hordes of Asmodeus came trouncing across the plane, you created the impenetrable thicket and copse which you then enchanted so no one could get in or out. How did you do that?"

"Well, envisioned what was happening as it happened, so I started with the bushes, tree, thorns, gorse, weaving and developing the thought spells one on another to form first the thick impenetrable outer defence, while also visualising the canopy above and continuing to imagine the clear area where we stand, so it wasn't a spell like you would normally expect, but a continuously developing interweaving and interwoven envisioning spell of what I was trying to develop. Having said all that, I hadn't a clue what I was saying then and didn't even understand what I said, or even where that little speech came from!"

"Precisely," said Llewellyn, "now have a think about what we have discussed previously and answer my last question, which was, how did you do that?"

Tom's mind was in a whirl and he had to think quite hard even to remember the last question. Suddenly it dawned on him what his dad had said. He then repeated what he had said almost word for word.

"I hadn't a clue what I was saying and didn't even know what I said, or even where that it came from!"

"Exactly," his dad said, "now answer your own question."

"It was you. I couldn't do any of that really, but you were watching and formed the spell and the speech in my mind."

"Well done," his dad said, "but now you're on your own, you will have to form your own spells, something you can do, and will do with a little training. But you will have to rely on your own wit and wisdom, and wisdom can and will flow through your wand. One remarkably interesting trick, which I have never seen before though. You can stop time. I have obviously been watching over you since you arrived here in Trymyll and could not help but notice how when you returned to your room during breakfast the others didn't notice you missing for more than a minute despite you being gone for nearly twenty. Just before Asmodeus popped out of nowhere you sensed a trap and again time stood still. It only happens locally, the whole world doesn't stop, just what is in the immediate area, hence Asmodeus was able to pop into your time bubble and not be frozen as well. It's awesome and it didn't come from me, so it must be to do with your connection to the wand. The wand wants to protect you so locally freezes time when the right triggers are in place."

"Oh," said Tom, "I thought that was you as well."

"No, not me, you and your wand. So, make sure you don't lose that wand. Ever!"

"Can I lose it then?" asked Tom?

"Well yes, it is possible to have it taken from you in the right circumstances, however, a wand always returns to its owner."

"Meaning what?"

"Well, a senior Elder can confiscate your wand if you are misusing it, but if the taking is unjust, it will just return to you as soon as you say 'wand'. If an adversary took it, in battle, you only need call it and it will return. But if the wand is enclosed in a cold iron case, then the wand will not and cannot return until released. But let's hope that never happens. Well, that's enough for one day, let's have some supper and get some shut-eye, because tomorrow....

JOSEPH R. MASON

"Let the training commence!"

CHAPTER 10½ - MEANWHILE, BACK AT THE COTTAGE...

"What in the Makers name happened there? Where did he go?" said Flintock.

"What do you mean? Where did he go! What have you done with him, you idiot wizard?" Llewel shouted.

"Me? What do you mean what have I done? More like what have you done."

"I have done nothing. It must have been you and your dreadful trygall. I have done nothing."

"Well that's true, you've done nothing since you arrived apart from upset people and rub them up the wrong way. And don't bring Tryg into this, he's not My trygall, he is a free, a free, a, a..," Flintock didn't know quite what to say, he couldn't say 'a free man' because he wasn't. But he didn't lake to say animal or beast, because Tryg was much, much more than that. Flintock suddenly got his voice back, "he's free to come and go as he wishes, and he wishes to stay with me. Your only job was to get the boy safely to Castell y Blaenoraid and you haven't even managed that. My job was just to tag along with Tryg to provide company and a friendly face for Tom because the council knew he wouldn't get that from you."

They had completely forgotten about the two young men and the girl. They stood there open-mouthed in amazement at what was going on.

"Excuse me," the girl said sharply.

Llewel jumped slightly.

"Yes," he retorted rudely, "what do you want? Don't just stand there gawping woman. Say what you want to say!"

"Don't worry, I will!" she said pointing a finger at Llewel the Elder and jabbing him in the chest, "You are the rudest and most irritating little man, little wizard or whatever you are, I have ever met. I'm not surprised the wee skinny boy cleared off. With you for company, so would I!"

Llewel went to speak, but before he could, she was off again.

"The boy, he wanted to help, he wanted to make sure we were all alright, he was nice. But you, you shrivelled up little excuse for a wizard wanted to just leave me there in a burning house bound hand and foot. I could have died! But did you care?" her voice was now at a pitch that could shatter glass. Llewel the Elder was now more like Llewel the paler or Llewel the very scaredier! Llewel tried to interject again.

"I haven't finished yet. So, don't interrupt me," she continued, "because that is also very rude. Your mate here was willing to help, the boy was willing to help, but you, you, you… Oh. Words just fail me I'm so angry!" She then stopped jabbing him in the chest and took a step back.

"Well?"

"Well?" stuttered Llewel the Elder.

Before he could get a word out, she was off again.

"And what do you mean by 'we really haven't the time to heal poor peasants and eat the few scraps of food they have'? We are not poor as you so rudely put it, we are farming folk. We have plenty, we are not peasants, we are landowners and farm several thousand acres of our own land. We have livestock, sheep, cattle, pigs, goats, and hens, we have corn, wheat, fruit, and vegetables in abundance. Our barns are full to overflowing SO WE

ARE NOT POOR!!!" she finished the sentence at a crescendo and with a voice loud enough to burst eardrums.

"Well, well, well," he continued, still trying to think what to say, "well, I'm s, s, sorry?" he said lifting his voice at the end turning it into a question to see if it was the correct answer, "well, yes, I'm sorry. It was all a bit of a shock coming across you and your friends here."

She stopped him short.

"They are not my friends," she shouted, "they're my blooming brothers!"

"Well, yes," said Llewel, missing the point, "but I wouldn't describe them as blooming, more blooded when we found them, but they both seem a bit better now."

"Aaaargh!" she screamed, "You stupid little excuse for a man, that is not what I meant, and you know it!"

With that, she delivered an exquisite left hook that sent Llewel the Elder high into the air and onto his back.

She then turned to Flintock and said, in a completely normal voice as if nothing had happened.

"Excuse my manners," and turning to her brothers barked, "boys, we have guests, get some lunch on."

Well, she may have been beautiful, but she had a tongue on her like a bad-tempered blemonpuss and a vicious left hook which would stop most men but was especially suited to a small and diminutive wizard.

Sometime later, when tempers had settled the six of them, Llewel, Flintock, Tryg, Terrwyn Merrick and her brothers Rhioganedd and Menw sat down to a hearty meal prepared by Tryg and the brothers. Roast Pork with apple sauce, roast potatoes and several different vegetables, Rhubarb, and ginger crumble with custard to follow, and all washed down with some rather favourable homemade sloe wine. Terrwyn ruled the roost here, she dominated both her brothers and the conversation.

Llewel said nothing, he ate in silence. After they had eaten their fill, Flintock made sure that they were all healed to the best of his abilities. Rhioganedd and Menw offered to help them look for the boy as they knew the woods around like the backs of their hands. But Flintock politely turned down their offer of help as he knew that wherever Tom was, it was a long, long way from here. So, the two wizards and the trygall went on their way. It was not long until evening, so after walking for an hour or two, they set camp in the woods in the usual manner.

The evening was spent in silence, Flintock had little desire to speak to Llewel and Llewel, for a change, had nothing to say. They had eaten a good lunch earlier with the family Merrick, so they had a light supper of wild mushrooms with polenta and pan seared kale and then all turned in for the night.

Next morning, there was a silent breakfast, they broke camp in the normal manner and continued on their weary way.

Llewel still had not spoken. Even after half a day of walking, not a word. Flintock was quite enjoying the peace but decided that eventually, they had to talk about Tom and where they think he might be. So, he broke the silence.

"What do you think happened back there then?"

"Oh, I agree with you, probably some passing imp started it all."

"That is not what I was talking about."

Flintock really had lost all respect for Llewel the Elder or he wouldn't address him this way, "I was talking about Tom, and you know it."

"Well, I have been giving the situation some thought, which is why I have been so quiet."

Flintock knew that wasn't true, he was quiet because of what Terrwyn Merrick had both done and said. It was, after all, a most magnificent left hook. Flintock smiled to himself as he replayed the moment in his mind.

"And what have you concluded from your long meditation?" he

asked with a hint of sarcasm.

"Well, that's just the thing, absolutely nothing."

"Okay, I have to admit I have come to the same conclusion. But what do we do and say when we get to Castell y Blaenoraid?"

"Again, I have been giving that some thought as well but have concluded that again, I haven't a clue. Any suggestions Flintock old friend?"

'Flintock old friend?' Flintock could not believe his ears, he knew that Llewel the Elder despised him, in fact, he knew that Llewel despised everyone. Llewel had no friends, and no one wanted to call him friend either.

"Well, we could always tell the truth and say that he just disappeared before our eyes. We could tell of the great and powerful magic he had been doing without any training or foreknowledge so he probably could have been able to apparate using his own power?"

"Then where would he go? To apparate you have to visualise your arrival point and apart from the cave and the thicket he produced or the wand tree he won't be able to visualise anywhere else in the whole of Trymyll."

"You could send Howel Back to the cave to check there, but it would be sealed, so Tom could not enter. But at least Howel could check. I doubt if he would return to the thicket or the wand tree."

"But! Ah-ha, an idea, the shack! What if he visualised the inside of the shack?"

"No," Flintock rolled his eyes in disbelief, "the shack is not a real place, just an illusion, so he would not be able to even leave where he was unless the target actually existed. So, it's back to plan A, tell the truth."

"Well, I don't like that idea at all. We still have three days of travel, let's see what else we can come up with."

That night, while they were both sitting by the fire warming and just about talking to each other. Llewel was plotting, Flintock could see it in his eyes, in the way he was behaving, in the way he was being friendly. Too friendly.

"How about we come up with a story about Asmodeus? We could say that he suddenly appeared, snatched the boy and disappeared before you could do anything to stop him."

Flintock thought that was too close to the truth in some ways.

"Before I could do anything? How about before YOU could do anything." Flintock replied, emphasising the word you.

"Oh no, quite out of the question, the council would never believe that I, a great and powerful wizard could not deal with Asmodeus, whereas you, a very ordinary wizard, could not possibly win against his power and magic."

"Well, these are the error points in that statement. First. May I remind you that you are the one supposed to be protecting Tom, you are the one tasked with getting the boy to Blaenoraid. And might I ask, where were you supposed to be when Asmodeus popped in to say hello, in the privy? Secondly. I am not an ordinary wizard, I too am an Elder, I am far more powerful than you, and more powerful than you will ever be. But I chose not to seek high office because I know that most of the so-called High Elders are a load of backstabbing sycophants who love power and glory more than anything else! If I were the Elder of Elders and may the Maker forbid, I'd have banished most of you decades ago."

"Now, now, my dear old friend, it will look far better and be far more believable if you bore the brunt of the blame. I will, of course, speak up for you to make sure they don't meet out too harsher punishment for losing the boy and the ring!"

"And thirdly," Flintock bellowed, "I am not your dear old friend, I am not even your friend at all. You have no friends because you want no friends and have always gone out of your way to be as obnoxious as possible to every person you meet! Now, if you would like to step outside for a dual with wands, please be my guest. I will flatten you before you even draw your wand."

"Now, now," Llewel said meekly, "that it should come to this, I am shocked and hurt by what you say, of course I have friends, many close and dear friends," he lied, "but I will not demean myself by brawling in the street to settle a small difference of opinion."

Flintock could not believe his ears.

"Then how about we say that I was out the back in the privy when Asmodeus popped by and you lost the boy and the ring."

"No, no, that will not do at all. For a start, it isn't true. My version is better by far," Llewel stammered.

"What do you mean 'it isn't true'? It has as much truth as your version of events. I'll tell you again. We tell the truth. The boy just disappeared, vanished, apparated, gone, vamoosed!"

"Oh, have it your way then, but they won't like it. Mark my words, they won't like it all."

"They won't like it if you lie to them either, and remember this, Llewel the Elder, neither will I," Flintock paused to allow that to sink in, then continued.

"Why don't wait for High Elder Aneta Stepanek, she can then determine which of us is telling the truth."

"Oh no, no, no, I'm sure it won't come to that old friend."

Flintock raised his voice to answer.

"It will if you breath one word of a lie, and you'll have both me and the boy's father to deal with. And while I'm shouting, stop calling me old, and stop calling me friend. Because I am not now, and never will be your old friend!"

CHAPTER 11½ - LET THE TRAINING COMMENCE...

Next morning, after a good breakfast they left Jon and entered the little schoolroom. Llewellyn took his wand and said.

"Scene 1. Out on the plain."

Tom found himself outside, white sand stretching to the horizon where it met a pure blue and cloudless sky, just as he had momentarily seen the day before. There was no wind and no movement. Tom looked round; nothing between him and the horizon in any direction.

His father spoke, Tom looked round to see where he was, but he was still completely alone.

"Tom, you have a special power which we discussed yesterday that did not come from me. Twice yesterday, time stood still for you. I have no real idea of how you did it, how it works or why. I do have a theory about what triggers it, but it's only that, a theory, an idea. We need to develop and control it, see how it works, understand it. It is something I have never seen before. First, I'll send by something small, a butterfly, try and freeze it in time and space."

Tom sensed movement in his peripheral vision. It was a butterfly, flying in its normal erratic fashion, darting up and down and from side to side in the random fashion typical of the species.

Tom looked at the butterfly, pointed his wand at it, screwed up his face and willed the butterfly to stop. Nothing happened, the butterfly continued in its own way. Another came, Tom went red with concentration the veins on his neck stood out, but nothing happened, the butterfly continued fluttering across in front, up, down, to the left, to the right and into the distance.

"Well that didn't work," his dad said, "let's try again."

Another butterfly wafted by. Tom concentrated. Stared at it, glared at it, screwed up his face again in concentration, his eyes felt like they would pop out of his head. He strained so hard that an involuntary botty burp popped out. That completely ruined his concentration and he nearly fell over laughing.

"No Tom, no time for laughing, this is serious. You have to learn how you did it; in fact, we have to learn, so you can repeat it whenever you need to."

Again, a butterfly came by, and as before did flutter by.

The next butterfly was different, as it came close, it turned and looked at Tom. From nowhere it opened a huge unreal and exaggerated mouth and rushed at him. It terrified him to his very core. The mutant butterfly stopped. Hanging in the air as if dead. Then disappeared as Tom's dad ended the 'show.'

"Well that was my theory, and you may have just proved it. The power is fear-based. When you are frightened, very frightened, somehow your wand stops time. Let's try again."

Another butterfly came bobbing along. Tom tried to stop it but again failed. In the corner of his eye, he sensed movement, he turned to see a huge Blue Dragon descending on him from nowhere. Again, before it could strike, it froze, hanging in the air as if he had just hit the pause button on a DVD. Again, his dad made it disappear.

"I know it sounds silly but try to remember that fear and save it for whatever happens next."

This time a small bird flew by. Tom tried to feel scared, but he couldn't. The bird just carried on.

This went on for hours, butterflies, birds, dragons, rabbits, hell hounds, more birds, more butterflies, more dragons, more hell hounds. Nothing worked. The scary ones, he froze in time, the everyday birds, animals, and insects, just carried on as if he were not there.

The room reappeared. Tom stood there exhausted, wet with sweat and exertion, his dad sat in a comfortable chair smiling at him.

"Don't be despondent Tom, we'll get there, don't worry. That'll do for today, let's rest up, eat, talk, sleep and try again tomorrow."

They went through to the main living area. Jon was there looking and feeling slightly left out and with a hint on jealousy asked.

"So, how'd it go today?"

They both spoke at once.

"I was rubbish."

"He's making good progress."

"Come on, it can't be both, which is it? Rubbish or good?" Jon smirked. He liked the idea of boy wonder wizard not doing as well as expected.

"Both," said his dad, "we were working on a bit of magic which Tom can do, but just doesn't know how he does it."

"That doesn't make sense." said Jon.

I know it doesn't," his dad replied, "and don't ask about what bit of magic as Tom's training is strictly between Tom and me. You know the rules Jon."

"What rules?" asked Tom.

"Because every wizard's magic is different, a teacher and pupil never discuss their lessons outside of the classroom, even with family."

"Why?"

"It's difficult to explain the rule, but for a change, there is a good reason behind it, it's not one of their made up rules. Because every wizard's magic is individual, if they start talking about what they can and can't do and how they can and can't do it, another acolyte may, by using the same method, get it completely wrong and endanger both himself and those around them. It's a bit like acting. A good actor can be very convincing about an emotion like sadness, but they all use different methodology and visualisation to give the appearance of sadness. Some do it by thinking of a close relative or friend that has died and that still both makes them not just look sad but be sad. They can shed tears very convincing. Another might remember a childhood event which hurt them so much they are still upset by the very thought of it. While another just think they are peeling onions and just the thought makes them cry. Alright, maybe not the last one," Llewellyn laughed.

Tom listened intently, trying to think of what made him scared, he could think of nothing. Then he remembered Mrs Glynn, his teacher. She scared the pants off him, just her name brought him out in a cold sweat. Yes, he thought, tomorrow I'll just think of Mrs Glynn!

Over supper, there were many animated discussions about all the normal topics. Tom already knew that you don't have to say "wand" or "staff" to make them appear, you only had to will it in your mind. Tom thought he would just test the waters with the thought of Mrs Glynn. He willed his wand out and hid it below the table out of sight, He thought about missing a homework deadline and Mrs Glynn and then wove that thought with the vision of stillness. The talking stopped, Jon froze, a potato on his fork halfway between plate and mouth, his father, mouth open, mid-sentence, stopped. Tom moved out from his chair and touched his dad with his wand, envisioning him moving, and he reanimated, carrying on his ramble about Cardiff City FC. A few words later he stopped, looked around, Jon was still, very still, the flames in the fire no longer flickering and the curl of smoke perfectly stationary. He smiled at Tom.

"How did you do it then?"

"Just thought of Mrs Glynn, she scares the poop out of me. She's worse than Miss Trunchbull!"

They both smiled, Tom touched Jon with his wand under the table, re-imagining him moving and everything returned to normal. His brother hadn't noticed a thing.

Next day, after breakfast, it was straight into the training room.

"First, back to scene one."

Tom was back in the desert again, under the scorching sun. A butterfly came into view, as it approached, Tom saw Mrs Glyn in his mind and a missed maths test. The butterfly froze, his dad then send a few more butterflies, birds, and other harmless creatures just to check it was not a fluke. Then the desert dissolved back int the classroom.

"Well done Tom, but keep practising until you can do it without thinking, but also, don't make it your get out for every situation. There are many more magical ways to get out of trouble. So be both imaginative and inventive. Know what you want to achieve, then weave that thought down into your wand and make some magic."

"Scene two," his father announced, "Back to the plain, but now it's night, so keep your wits about you."

He was right, whereas yesterday it had been scorching hot sunshine, now the temperature had plummeted and was almost freezing. With no light pollution, Tom could see a myriad of stars and planets. He remembered something Hadley-Smythe had told him one night when they were looking up at the night sky.

"If it's a star, it twinkles, if it's a planet, it's a steady light, and if it flashes on and off, it's either a plane or a UFO."

He remembered them both laughing at that, probably the only funny line Hadley-Smythe had ever said.

Tom wasn't scared, just slightly apprehensive about this situation, there was no moon, so apart from the stars, no light at all, "Staff" he muttered in a shivering mumble. His staff appeared. Now what? he thought. Can't see a thing. Then he remembered his stones. Diamonds, the giver of light to fight against the darkness. Ruby, the firestone. Tom said and thought "Light!" and the top of his staff burst into a brilliant light that pierced through the darkness for what seemed miles. Tom held his staff high, and the light spread out all around him.

"Well," said his dad inside his head, "you have now achieved two things. You have a light which allows you to see everything around you in any direction for many miles, but you also have a light which enemies, animals and other frightening things can see and be attracted to. So put that light out. You need a torch, not a lighthouse beacon."

Tom hadn't thought that one through. 'Wand', he thought. He then did two things, made the stone light up again, but not so brightly and he imagined the light to emit in one direction only, so now it acted more like a torch and not a lighthouse. Better, he thought. Then he thought about the Ruby and about how a little warmth might not go amiss, he felt a trickle of warm energy race through his body. So now he could see, and was not quite so cold.

"What next da?"

He didn't wait long, a long snake slithered along the ground towards him. The snake was a good twenty feet long and well over a foot in diameter. Toms immediate thought was to freeze time, but he knew he couldn't use that trick every time he had a problem.

He weaved a thought of a jet of fire coming from his wand, and a flame shot out like a small flame thrower. He directed it towards the snake and the snake slithered off in the other direction, unharmed.

Then he was back in the small schoolroom, his father, as usual, sitting in the armchair.

"What's the matter? Why am I back so soon?"

"Nothing's wrong. Just a change of scene. Scene three, a snow-capped mountain."

Llewellyn had no sooner spoken, and Tom was on top of a mountain. It was freezing, many degrees below freezing. 'Ooh!' thought Tom, 'I need some warmth.' He radiated some heat around him from his ruby stone just like he did in the night scene a few minutes ago. As he did, the snow he was standing on started to melt at an alarming rate, within a few seconds he was down to his waist and then, moments later the hole he was melting was higher than him. He looked down, the hole was filling with water as the snow melted and he was already up to his waist in freezing water. He began to panic; he had stopped radiating heat but the latent heat he had produced was still melting the snow and he was still sinking. It reached his chin before....

He was back in the room again. Completely dry as if nothing had happened, but still shivering with the cold.

"You didn't think that one through either, did you?" his dad said, "Before you do anything, unless you are in mortal danger, think. Do a risk assessment. What will happen if I do this, what will the consequences be if I do that? Think, think, think. As it was, you were in no danger, but if you suddenly found yourself in the mountains of Mynydd, you might be in serious trouble."

Tom had no idea where Mynydd was and didn't bother asking.

There was a pause while his dad thought a little.

"Tom, what exactly did Llewel teach you about magic in the few days you were with him?"

"Well nothing really, just went on about how dangerous it was and how I shouldn't meddle with it until I had lessons. But although he kept on about it, he didn't teach me or show me anything. The only thing he could do was light fires."

"That bloke is absolutely useless. He should have been called

Ron the Elder, Ron being short for moron! Did he talk about flying or levitation at all?"

"Only to say it was too dangerous to fly because wizards had fallen from the sky when their magic failed."

"Mmmm. He would say that, that guy fears his own shadow. If he thought about it too much, his brain would probably fry. Flying and levitation are good tools both for travel and for avoiding ground-based predators, if you could have levitated you would not have sunk ten feet into the snow just then. You don't have to be a hundred feet in the air to get out of trouble. For a snake, for instance, just a few feet could put you out of harm's way, and if you must fly, although it's not my favourite form of transport, again, you won't die if you only fall a few feet. Flying has its place though and it's something you should learn. So, let's do it."

CHAPTER 12 - FLYING LESSONS.

The training room turned into what looked like a huge gym hall, in fact, huge doesn't describe it, it was about six hundred feet from wall to wall in each direction and a good hundred foot high. Big enough for several football pitches and still room for a burger bar in each corner. The floor was very strange, it moved, it was like a massive bouncy castle.

This time his dad joined him.

"Right," he said as his staff appeared, "flying and levitation are one and the same. But we start with levitation as it is easier not to fall when you're not moving."

"Don't we need broomsticks?"

"No, you don't, you watch too many wizard films. All you use is your staff. You don't have to, but when flying it is good for directional control. Some female wizards ride a rather awkward side-saddle position, but most don't, all us men sit astride with the stone to the front. Two reasons for that, at night you can use it to illuminate your way and in battle, you can unleash some mighty magic when flying. Observe."

Llewellyn sat astride his staff and gently pushed up with his legs and rose a few feet in the air.

He landed. Stowed his wand and said, "Now watch."

This time he just stood there and just floated up into the air.

"See, you can also easily levitate without a staff as well."

Llewellyn landed again.

"Just think up and imagine yourself floating when you push off with your legs, as I said, you don't need your staff, you can just float, but most people are more comfortable using their staff."

Tom sat across his staff. Up, he thought, and up he went. Right up to the ceiling! He then thought down, and down he plummeted. Llewellyn caught him before he hit the ground.

"Don't worry, the floor would have caught you if I didn't. Think up but think about a couple of feet this time."

Tom tried again, this time more successfully, but his balance on the staff was very unsteady and he wobbled and then plonk. He fell off...

"Don't worry about the wobbles, it's just like when you learnt to ride your bike, a bit shaky at first, but you soon get used to it and then you never lose it."

"How would you know?" Tom said, bitterness returning, "You weren't there. Father Seamus O'Reilly taught me to ride."

"Oh, did he now?" his dad said, in a thick Irish accent, "Did he really now."

Tom fell off his broom.

"What, you sounded just like him there," realisation dawned, "it was you; you came disguised as Father Seamus O'Reilly every week to see me and mum, it was you wasn't it?"

"That it was," he said, keeping up the accent and at the same time morphing into Father Seamus O'Reilly.

Tom welled up, he had thought his father had deserted them, when in fact he came every week to check on the two of them. He picked himself up and fell into his dad's arms for a long hug.

"Now try that again and keep trying until there's not a wobble in sight," he said still in his Irish accent.

"You can drop the Father Seamus act now."

Llewellyn morphed back to his normal self.

Tom soon had the lift-off and hold position, but not until he had hit the ceiling a few more times, hung upside down several times and fell off the staff altogether many times more. But after a couple of hours, he was there, he could sit astride his staff and only a slight and occasional wobble.

"Right," said Lewellyn, "almost there, now we will try some actual flying. Keep it low and slow. Have you ever ridden a Segway?"

He knew the answer but still asked anyway.

"Of course not."

"Well, you know the principle of it. You lean slightly forward to go forward, slightly back to stop and go backwards, lean left or lean right for directional, control, but on a staff, you also must envision forward, back, left, right. Okay?"

"No, not really, but I'll give it a try."

Tom leaned forward slightly and thought about moving forward. But instead of moving slowly off he shot forward like a greyhound out of a trap and he was heading straight for the wall, he panicked and couldn't think how to stop. He hit the wall, but as he did, everything slowed down, and he sank deep into the wall and bounced back out again. The wall had looked solid enough, but, like the floor, was soft and sponge-like, absorbing his impact and returning him to the hall.

"Let's try that again, but maybe not quite as fast."

Tom tried again, and again, and again, and again. He was really having trouble controlling speed. He was either shooting forward like a bolt from a crossbow or slower than a slug in a salt marsh. The concentration was immense, beads of sweat appeared on his forehead. He was not going to give up easily, and eventually he started to have some control. He could finally keep a good height, hold a good pace, and turn from left to right.

"Enough!" said Llewellyn, "we'll call that a day, actually, slightly more than a day, we started after breakfast and it's now way past supper time. We'll return tomorrow."

"What! We didn't even stop for lunch!"

"How time flies when you're having fun."

The vast hall faded, and they were back in the classroom again. Llewellyn opened the door and they stepped out into the living quarters. Jon had prepared supper and eaten his, so he sat with them while Tom and his dad recounted the stories of the day. Jon was full of admiration for his little brother, but also just a little jealous, so he especially liked the parts when Tom hit the wall, fell off or was left dangling by one arm a hundred feet up in the air. Jon always liked to hear about Tom's little failures. Brotherly love and all that!

Eventually, they started talking of home.

Jon started, "So what was going to school like? From what I've heard it must be great. All that learning, and friends, and rugby, what's it like?"

"Oh, it's not that great. After a while it gets a bit boring. The teachers are bossy, and it doesn't end with school, then there's homework as well."

"Sounds fun to me," said Jon

"Don't you have school then? Can you read and write and stuff?

"Of course I can. It's simply different here. I have what's best described as home school, but it's not anything like what you did, dad does some of it, Flintock does quite a lot, even Howel does some. But a lot of stuff just arrives in your head. One day you know nothing about a subject, the next day you wake up with it all swimming about in your brain. Weird. Oh, and I also get to visit other people my age in Flintock's town for what they call 'social interaction'," they both sniggered but didn't know why.

"Where's Flintock live then?"

"He lives in a place called Wrth y Môr, it means 'place by the sea.' It's great there, you can go boating, fishing and of course swimming. No rugby though. I tried to show them, but they weren't interested."

"Perhaps we can go together and teach them!" they both laughed at that idea.

They talked for a couple of hours together about life in Wales and life in Trymyll, comparing, exaggerating, boasting, and arguing about which was best, right up until bedtime.

That night Tom had a fitful sleep full of dreams about flying, crashing, falling off and awkward landings, so was not exactly fresh and ready to go when called for breakfast the next morning.

Next day was better than the last, Tom didn't fall off very much, he didn't crash into the ceiling, he didn't crash into the floor, he didn't crash into the walls. By the end of the day he was able to control his flight quite well, swooping, turning, climbing turns, diving turns, stall turns and even a loop the loop as a finishing flurry. Tom was quite pleased with himself. His dad was incredibly pleased. Jon was indifferent.

Day three of flying lessons was a disaster. This time the training room morphed into a green forest with hills, caves, and rocky outcrops, with birds, deer, wild pigs, toads, and rabbits roaming about. Tom had to fly at staff height avoiding all these obstacles. Tom hit trees, he hit a deer, the deer then chased him until he hit another tree. He argued with his dad, he shouted at his dad and his dad shouted back.... He bumped into just about every obstacle he could find.

"Why can't I fly above the trees? I won't keep hitting things then," he said.

"Three reasons, one, it's dangerous, if you come off you have a long way to fall. Two, it's dangerous because you are too visible above the tree line, someone watching out on a hill or a lookout platform would see you and could bring you down with a spell or an arrow. And three, because I said so!"

Tom's shoulders ached from collisions with trees, his arms were bruised, his legs were scratched and chaffed, and he had twigs and pine needles in his hair, his knuckles were split, and bleeding, and his pride was hurt. He had done so well the day before, even finishing with a victory loop the loop, today, he was rubbish.

Tonight, over supper, Tom was disappointed and angry, his dad wasn't feeling sorry for him at all, and Jon was loving it.

Next day Tom was on his own. His dad had business elsewhere. Tom was let loose in the forest to learn to fly all on his own.

Tom found that with his father watching, he tended to get flustered. He couldn't see him watching, but he knew that he was still there, and he was so afraid of his dad seeing him fail, that he failed. But without his father, he thought he could get on far better.

He mounted his staff and kicked off. Moving forward through the forest he moved off, not too fast, swinging left and right around the trees. He kept his level, one staff height in the undulating landscape.

It was not long before he picked up speed, his confidence was growing, he was beginning to enjoy what he was doing, when crunch! Headfirst over the end of his staff, laying on his back looking at the sky. He had hit a tree stump. He as concentrating on the trees around but had not seen the stump of a tree left from when it had been felled. That's not fair he thought. This isn't a real forest, just a magicked up one, so there should not be a felled tree here anyway. He heard the crack of a twig. 'Wand', he thought, his staff disappeared, and the wand was in his hand. He rolled slowly over onto his front and then raised himself up being careful not to make any noise. He peeked over the top of the bracken and saw a man walking and whistling with a woodsman's axe slung over one shoulder. The man stopped. Looked directly at Tom and said.

"Well hello young Tom, your dad said I might see you here today."

"How do you know who I am?" said Tom, then thinking it was a silly question, the woodsman had already answered it by referring to his dad.

"What are you doing here?" Tom asked.

"Well," he said, "I look after the woods, I cut out the dead and diseased trees, keep the undergrowth tidy and generally look after the place."

"But it's not real, it's not a real forest, just one my dad magicked up."

"Oh no, it's real alright. It's not part of the training room, when your dad wants to come here, he apparates you in from the training room, so it's a very real forest. I live here in a cottage over yonder with my dear wife and we both look after the forest. I was just on my way home for a brew, care for a cup?"

"Yes, I'd love to, but dad said I have to learn to fly and learn to fly well."

"I know that, but you've got to rest up a bit or you'll exhaust yourself. Come on, I expect Mrs Cadwalader's made some cakes too. Oh 'n by the way, my name is Traveon, Traveon Cadwalader, keeper of the Forest of Llewellyn the Brave. But you can call me Traveon, cos that be my name, and you can put your wand away, you'll come to no harm in these parts."

Tom stowed his wand.

The walked a short way down a valley and Tom could see a small cottage, smoke coming from its chimney, set in a clearing, and surrounded by a pretty garden, roses over the door and a white picket fence. They soon arrived. Inside, Mrs Cadwalader was just taking cakes from the range and had already brewed a large pot of tea.

"Ooh, young Tom," she said almost excitedly, "been expecting you, so I made some cakes and a big brew."

Tom was both thirsty and hungry, and he hadn't had a cup of tea since arriving in Trymyll. Let's face it, when is a thirteen-year-old boy not hungry when there is cake involved?

"Milk and sugar?"

"Yes please, two sugars please."

Mrs Cadwalader gave over a mug of hot tea and a warm rock cake.

"Well young Tom, what brings you to the forest? Learning to fly I expect, that's the normal reason people come to these parts."

"How do you mean? What people?"

"Oh, your dad's a very generous wizard and possibly the best in the land."

"Not possibly Lynessa, he is the greatest wizard in all of Trymyll," interjected Traveon.

"Well, as I was saying, your dad is very generous with his time for such a busy man. He's trained several acolytes here in Trymyll and they all pass through these woods at some time or other while they tries to learn how to fly. But none of them can fly, not well anyway, not very well at all some of them," she said as if trying to emphasise the point, "they hits trees, hits boulders, gets stuck in caves, they scratches 'emselves, bruises 'emselves even breaks the odd bone here and there. But no matter, I patches them up and then I shows them how it's done."

Tom looked quite shocked at that suggestion. Mrs Cadwalader was short and plump with rose red cheeks and thick, thick spectacles. She just looked altogether the last person you would imagine on a staff flying through the forest.

"Oh, I knows what you're thinking. She don't look like a first aider," she laughed, "no, my little joke, you're thinking, she don't look like a flyer, aren't you?"

Tom didn't answer, he didn't have to...

"Come outside when you've had your cake and brew and I'll

shows you."

A few minutes later, the three of them stood outside.

"Staff," she said, and a most elegant staff appeared, no more than a pencil in width and with a large pearl stone set into the end.

"And before you ask, yes it will take my weight."

She then burst out laughing with such a joy that Tom couldn't help but laugh too. She pushed off and went into a vertical climb at such speed she became just a dot in the sky. Then followed the most magnificent aerobatic display, complete with vapour trails and coloured smoke and even stars. Multifarious loops and barrel rolls. She wrote letters in the sky then dived down at what looked like the speed of sound into the trees, then away, weaving, ducking, diving corkscrewing around trees rocks and boulders and all at a speed which made her just a blur, then she headed straight for Tom but before he could duck, she stopped dead in front of him not an inch from his nose and stepped down from her staff.

"That was unbelievable," said Tom, "may I see your staff?"

"Of course, my dear, here."

Tom took the staff in his hands, gently as if it were fragile and he was afraid he would break it, it weighed, well, it weighed nothing. It was as light as the air that surrounded it.

"What's it made of Mrs Cadwalader?"

"Well, it's not wood, it didn't come from the wand tree, it came from an old wizard who lived over two millennia ago. He was completely blind and yet could see better than anyone else of his day, where his blind eyes were there were two large pearls. One of those blind eyes is held at the end of my wand. The wand itself is fashioned from the fourth finger bone of a Golden Dragons wing, so it has incredible strength but exceptionally light in weight. This was the wand and staff of his son who was the greatest flier ever to grace the skies. He was my ancestor, and the wand has been passed down through the generations to the oldest child be they male or female. Now it is mine. Alas, we are without children, so when I pass on to the other side, the wand will choose a new owner. But it will be owned at a price, whoever next this wand claims as its own will also be blinded in both eyes from that moment, and yet they too will be able to see more than they ever saw before."

Tom didn't understand what she meant and nearly dropped the wand when he heard it. He instantly thought that he hoped it didn't pick him. But then he thought, why would it? There are many, many wizards in Trymyll the wand could pick. Anyway, Mrs Cadwalader was still relatively young, she still had years before she would die. He hoped.

"Will you teach me to fly like you can Mrs Cadwalader please?"

"That's the thing young Tom, you already can, you just have to conquer your fears."

"How?" he stumbled over just that one word.

"Believe," she said, "just believe. Believe you can do it, and you will do it," she paused, then surprising said, "here, mount up on my wand and fly."

Tom sat astride the thin and delicate looking staff and kicked off. He too shot up into the sky at breakneck speed until he was just a dot, then down to the forest floor, he sped on, he skimmed around the trees, around boulders, down caves and out the other side, he had never flown so fast in his life yet he had no fear of falling off and he didn't even touch, let alone hit any of the obstacles he was coming across. Then he shot up into the sky and did exactly what Mrs Cadwalader had done, giving an impressive aerobatics display, zooming down again and along the forest floor right up to Mrs. Cadwalader and stop. She didn't move, she didn't even blink. She just stood there holding her staff. Tom looked down.

"What? But I had your staff, how come I'm sitting on mine?"

"Oh, deary me young Tom, I don't lend my wand to no one, I just makes them think I does."

"But I was holding your wand, I sat astride your wand, I rode your wand."

"No, no dear, you may have thought you did, but my wand is very magic indeed, so, even though you have a really closed mind for suggestions and that, it ain't no match for my wand. It is, after all, the fourth finger of a Golden Dragon, and you knows how magic they are," she said laughing, "that my dear is all your own work on your own stick. And a fine one it is too. Never saw a wand before with four kinds of wood for a starter. Very handy having yew in your wand."

Tom started, "how do you know about the yew? It wasn't meant to be yew, after I stuttered out the oak, elm and willow, which wasn't an answer, but part of a question, I started to say 'You got to help me here', and the wand tree mistook the word you for yew."

"Oh no deary, the wand tree never makes mistakes. It were yew for a reason."

"But why, what good is yew anyway, the wand tree said it was only good for making bow and arrows."

"I suppose if no one knows then no one will tell you."

"Tell me what?"

"Bet they told you three commands, wand, staff and wand away, either spoken or thought."

"Well yes, there aren't any more."

"Try bow," she said.

"Bow?" said Tom as a question. His staff disappeared and he was holding an Old-English Longbow, and he had a quiver at his side with three arrows in.

"Now deary, see yonder on that apple tree. There be three apples left on it. See?"

"Yes"

"Take one arrow and take 'em down," she chortled.

"How can I hit three apples with one arrow?"

"Like I said earlier. Believe."

Tom took an arrow from his quiver and noticed that as he did that it was at once replaced with another. He pulled the bow back and lifted the knock to his eye to get a straight aim.

"Don't aim at one apple, concentrate on the three of them, imagine them all being hit."

Tom loosed his arrow. As it sped towards the apple, the arrow seemed to split into three and all three apples exploded into fragments.

"No need to look for your arrows dear boy, you'll always have three in your quiver."

"How do you know these things? Who are you really?"

"Who me? Oh, I'm me, without a doubt. But don't be fooled by appearances. I may look like a woodman's wife, 'cause that what I am. But you can be a Woodman's wife and a wizard all at the same time you know. You see, me and Traveon, just want a simple life out here in the woods. You'll learn soon enough, those wizards in the outside ain't all they seem. High Elders are worse. They all be conniving, backstabbing social and political climbers. We been there and done that. Now we want none of it. So, your old man, the gent that he is, set us up here to look after the forest."

"Traveon, are you a wizard as well?"

"Oh yes, course I am. Used to be an Elder an all, we both were. People wanted Lynessa here to be a High Elder, and she was for a while, but we soon realised, they wanted her to move up just so she'd look out for them, do them favours and like. So, we just decided one day to quit. Oh, the commotion that caused, no one ever quit before. Up till then, elders stayed elders or moved up a notch. No one ever went down on their own, unheard of. You can be stripped of your position, they said to us, but you can't quit, 'specially not a High Elder. So, we asked them to show where it says that in the rules. Well they couldn't, 'cause they makes up the rules as they goes along. So, me and Lynessa here, just disappeared, help of young Llewellyn of course, and here we are."

They heard someone approaching and Tom turned to see his dad walking down the valley.

"Business all done then?" asked Mrs Cadwalader.

"For today, but more tomorrow. How did young Tom do at his flying today?"

"He flew like a good 'un. Not seen a flier like him for thirty odd years. Can't think who it was now, but I'm sure you'll remember him," she said laughing.

They all knew exactly who she meant. Llewellyn blushed, just a little bit.

CHAPTER 14 - ARRIVAL AT CASTELL Y BLAENORAID.

Two days passed relatively slowly but without incident and without much communication between the two wizards. Flintock was still brooding about the things Llewel had said and done. Llewel was still trying to think of a plan to get him off the hook and implicate Flintock in Tom's disappearance. As they rounded the top of the last of the hills, there in the distance they could see the central city and rising above it, the daunting view of Castell y Blaenoraid. The castle of the Elder of Elders, meeting place of the Council of the High Elders, the Council of Blaenoraid.

They stopped to take breath and view the castle. They both wondered what fate awaited them as they returned empty handed, no boy, no ring. But still hardly a word was uttered between them.

Llewel the Elder had hatched his little plan and was just about to play what he thought was his trump card.

"This whole journey has taken too long. We should fly in the rest of the way, if we stay at low level we should be safe if our flying fails us."

Llewel didn't apparate, he was too scared he would end up inside the castle wall rather than next to it.

"What do you mean by we?" Flintock replied, "Tryg cannot fly, do you expect me to just leave him here while we fly off into the distance?"

"He could easily make his own way at twice the speed he is doing now walking with us. He will only be a couple of hours behind us."

"And what sort of welcome would an unaccompanied trygall get at the city gates? They would not only not let him in, but they would also drive him away."

"Well, I'll go on ahead and let them know we are all safe and on our way."

"We are not all safe and on our way. We do not have Tom or the ring."

"No, you misunderstand, by we, I mean me, you and Tryg."

That was the first time Llewel had ever refereed to Tryg by his name. Flintlocks gut told him that Llewel had hatched a plan which was not going to end well for him or Tryg. But before he could say another word, Flintock was astride his staff and moving away fast.

"Stop!" shouted Flintock, "Stop! Come back here or I'll break every bone in your body," but before the sentence was finished, Llewel had vanished into the distance.

"Right Tryg, now for our own little trick. Come here and hold on."

Tryg and Flintock joined arms, and with that, they both vanished from where they were and reappeared just outside the city walls.

Once out of sight, Llewel flew cautiously, just in case he did fall off, and so, two hours later he arrived at the city and stepped down from his staff. The guards did not challenge him, you don't challenge a High Elder when he enters the city. Neither did they acknowledge him, normally a High Elder would be greeted and welcomed by the guards at the city gates, the guards always made an exception for Llewel the Elder. He never even noticed the insult despite being repeated often.

He made his way to the castle, again the guards stepped aside, but did not acknowledge him with even a polite nod of the head. He entered and went straight to the council chamber and requested the clerk to convene a meeting of the High Elders immediately. Only four of the High Elders, including Llewel, plus the Elder of Elders where physically present in the castle at that time. The other two, Govannon Staley of the Elven community and Brangwen Binning of Dolydd appeared, but not in solid format. They were in the neither here nor there.

The council chamber was round, a double door for entry. In the chamber there were six seats set in a circle. Opposite the main door was the chair of the Elder of Elders. Much larger than the other chairs. More throne than chair, ornately decorated with gilt; behind the chair a single door which led to the vestry of the Elder. The acoustics of the chamber were perfect, so all could hear when the Elder spoke, he spoke little, but the chamber was almost designed for that rare occasion. In the centre of the circle was a round table. At this table sat the clerk to the Elders, the clerk to the Elder of Elders, the minute taker, who curiously didn't write anything down, but was able to recall every word spoken in every meeting going back for as far as anyone could remember. The fourth chair at the round table was empty. There was also a small gallery where other invited guests sat and a sort of dock for when the chamber was used as a courtroom. The whole room was only about forty feet in diameter.

the Elder of Elders entered and took his seat, the High Elders who all stood awaiting his entry, all sat down. As was his custom, he did not speak but instead the Clerk to the Elder of Elders opened the meeting and then asked the question they had all gathered to have answered.

"High Elder Llewel, High Elder of Môr, Castle by the Sea. What is your news of the acolyte Thomas Jones, son of Llewellyn the Brave, the ring of the seven elders, Elder Flintock and the trygall?" the clerk always spoke in this very grand way, always titling every person correctly and precisely.

Llewel worded his answer carefully to not actually tell a lie.

"All are well and in safe hands. Flintock is only few hours walk from here and will be with us shortly."

The Clerk repeated, "the acolyte, Thomas Jones, son of Llewellyn the Brave, the ring of the seven elders. They too are safe and in good hands?"

"Oh yes," he said, "the very safest of hands."

He didn't lie then either, but he didn't know that he was telling the truth.

We will await their arrival and reconvene at that time. Adjourned!"

With that, the High Elders all stood and awaited the Elder of Elders to vacate his throne and leave the chamber. As soon as he had gone, the other High Elders also dispersed, leaving as a group, all chatting happily together about the expected turn of events. All except Llewel, who they ignored to a man and woman, neither nodding to him nor acknowledging him in any way. This act of ostracism was in his mind a mark of respect, because in his little mind, he believed that they all felt a little inferior to himself, meaning he must be superior to them.

Meanwhile, unbeknown to Llewel, Flintock and Tryg had arrived at the city some time before them having apparated to just outside the city limits to await his arrival. They entered, not through the main gate where Llewel had entered, but through a small side gate where Flintock knew there was only a single guard. As he approached, he muttered a small obfuscating spell causing the guard not to challenge him, and then pulled his hood right up to hide his face. He went straight to a tavern he knew which was frequented by Llewellyn. He cautiously looked around. In a dark corner away from the main lounge area he saw who he wanted and he and Tryg moved over to the small alcove to greet his friend.

"Llewellyn the Brave," he said.

"Flintock the Elder, Tryg," he replied, "Flinty, I have been expecting you as I am sure you were expecting me. Sit quickly, I have much to tell you but little time as I should be elsewhere at this moment."

Flintock went to speak, he needed to tell him that his boy had disappeared, "Hush and listen," Llewellyn continued, "I have both the boy and the ring, so fear nothing."

Flintock looked shocked but half expectant.

"Llewel the stupid Elder is up to no good, he purposely tried to get here before me to speak to the council. I am sure he will try to blame me or Tryg for Tom's disappearance."

Llewellyn smiled.

"What's so amusing about that?"

"Llewel the stupid Elder, that's what, it's exactly what Tom called him when I apparated him in," they both smiled.

Llewellyn ordered some ale and roasted meat for them and an herb tea and meat for Tryg, Flintock pulled his hood close as it arrived.

"Don't fear the council, they all despise Llewel as much as he despises them. They will know soon enough that both Tom and the ring is safe. You have my word on that."

"Llewellyn my friend, you have a very gifted boy, he was doing magic and spells beyond what most experienced wizards could do and doing them well. Llewel was livid, he kept telling him to stop before he hurt himself or someone else, but he was so in control. He was amazing and Llewel was so jealous. Whenever Tom did something amazing, Llewel would either say that he was just about to do that, or that Tom was lucky to get away with it. But Tom's magic was way above anything Llewel could do."

Llewellyn smiled broadly at his friend Flintock. Then it suddenly dawned on Flintock.

"It was you wasn't it? It was you working your magic through the boy and his wand. Brilliant!" he exclaimed as he clapped his hands in joy.

"Yes, I'm afraid it was, with Howel's help of course, he was never far away, but well out of sight, when he first received his wand from the wand tree and Llewel did his little scorched earth demonstration, I picked up the signal from Tom that he wanted to be a healer and restorer not a destroyer, so that is why I then changed from what would have been a most fantastic firework display ever seen, to restoring the plain to better than it was before. I was a little disappointed, I had such a magnificent display already in my head, spell-woven down to the last flicker and pop, but Tom didn't want it that way. It was me that built the thicket around you on the plain when the hordes of Asmodeus came calling, and it was me also who healed the poor Merrick brothers and your broken arm."

"Thanks for that, painful that was."

"But keep this all to yourself. The council will want to question you about this later, tell them all exactly what you saw, but make out it was my boy who did everything on his own. But I'll tell you what I didn't do, it wasn't me that stopped time, that was all Tom. First job when he came to me was to work with him on controlling and mastering that little trick. It took a whole day, but we cracked it in the end, so now he can hold time at his will. I'm so proud of him and still only thirteen years old. But I must go, I need to get back, so we'll catch up later."

"How'd he do it then? Get back where?"

Llewellyn just tapped the side of his nose and then disappeared. 'What!' thought Flintock. You can't apparate in the city bounds. How did he do that?

The council reconvened. This time, for the first time anyone could remember, the fourth chair in the centre was occupied. In it sat a man dressed from head to foot in black, his hood pulled over his face so no one could see him.

The Clerk to the Elder of Elders spoke, "Elder of Elders, High Elders, Clerk to the High Elders and any others present," he nodded towards the stranger in black, "we have reconvened as foretold at the arrival of Flintock the Elder into the city. He has arrived at a side gate a some while ago with his trygall, but the fact was not reported for some hours, he then proceeded at once to find refreshment at a local hostelry where he met with Llewellyn the Brave. There was no sign of the boy Thomas, the son of Llewellyn, or of the ring of the seven elders. The boy Thomas and the ring of the elders were in your keeping. You, Llewel the Elder of Môr, Castle by the Sea, are requested to explain to the council, your declaration at the previous meeting that they were safe and in good hands?"

"Well," sneered Llewel the Elder, "Flintock, the incompetent fool must have lost him and the ring. They were fine last time I saw them. He should be stripped of the title of Elder if you ask me."

A tall and elegant woman with long black hair that partly obscured her face before flowing down to her waist raised her hand.

"High Elder Aneta Stepanek of Goleuedigaeth has the floor," announced the Clerk.

"Tell us High Elder Llewel," she spoke in a firm Eastern European accent, "remembering who I am, High Elder Aneta Stepanek of Goleuedigaeth, from the city of Enlightenment, who already knows the truth. But for the benefit of others here present, where and when did you last see the acolyte Thomas, son of Llewellyn and the ring of the elders?"

She fixed her eyes hard against his, now he could not lie even if he tried, he tried to look away, but he could not. High Elder Aneta Stepanek knew the truth and would tell it anyway.

"Three days ago, by a farmhouse on the Great Plain. We had walked into what I thought was an ambush and during the argument about what to do afterwards, he just vanished."

"So, are you telling us that a thirteen-year-old acolyte with no discernible magic apparated away from you, a High Elder and Flintock the Elder, one of the finest wizards in the land," and she added for good measure, whispering as if to herself, "a wizard superior to you in every way."

But because of the perfect acoustics, everyone heard anyway.

"Well yes he must have done, there is no other explanation, and although you call him an acolyte of no magic, his magic was powerful and growing. He could do things that many Elders could not do," a mumble of disapproval sounded round the room, "Yes, you may scoff, but he did. Once he had his wand, he was away. I taught him well, everything he knows, I taught him. I showed him how to hold his wand and demonstrated how to make a small bush burst into flames, I told him to try another bush to see what he could do, expecting either nothing at all, or for him to blow the whole bush out of the ground, but instead, he turned to my smouldering bush and restored it to be more beautiful than before."

He then told them of his restoration of the plain after he had torched that, the building of the impenetrable thicket when Asmodeus and his hordes came across the plain. Asmodeus, who had returned to the council because of the current crisis, blushed a little, but did not defend or deny his actions. He told of the tracking spell Tom had discovered on his trainers. Embarrassing both him and Asmodeus. He told of the healing of the Merrick brothers as well. He told them everything he could just to make them see that Tom was indeed already a powerful wizard who could easily apparate away if he wanted to. He even confessed that he was too hard on the boy and that was probably the reason he left anyway. He told them everything he could so they would not blame him.

"This is all very interesting," said High Elder Traveon Baughan of Gwir, addressing the council and not waiting to be introduced, but who can collaborate this amazing story? Why do we not see if Flintock the Elder tells a similarly unbelievable tale?"

"Warder!" cried the Clerk, "take Llewel, strip him of his wand and place him in a cage of cold iron and take him to the dungeon."

The council chamber itself was en-caged in cold iron, and enchanted so no magic could be done there, no pulling of wands to settle a dispute, no drawing of staffs to try an escape. The man in black stood, and although you could not see his form, you could feel the strength which seemed to emanate from his body. Llewel only came up as far as the heavy black leather belt around his waist. He was more Nephilim than man. Llewel gave over his wand sheepishly, which was placed in a wooden box, banded with cold iron, and locked with an iron lock. The round table split and then folded to the sides and an iron cage rose into the room, Llewel was led into the cage which then disappeared below, and the table unfolded and moved together, looking like the solid table most had assumed it was before. Llewel noticed that the very formal clerk to the Elder of Elders had failed to use his title of High Elder, that could only mean one thing, he was no longer a High Elder.

"Adjourned for one hour! Summon Flintock the Elder." The council stood, awaited the departure of the Elder of Elders, then they too dispersed out of the chamber.

An hour later, the council reassembled. Flintock the Elder was invited in and questioned in a similar manner. The difference was, Flintock gave clear concise answers. The boy disappeared three days ago after an argument with Llewel the Elder in which

Thomas's final and angry words to Llewel were "You're not the boss of me!" and then he disappeared. Several of the High Elders sniggered at this new turn of phrase. Flintock then also told of all the magic which Tom had performed, about how amazed they both were, about Tom's natural abilities and how High Elder Llewel wanted to stop him doing magic and criticised his every move. But Flintock continued to enthuse about the boy's abilities.

During his story, the Clerk intervened only once to tell Flintock that Llewel the High Elder was now just Llewel and to refrain from using his former title as it was no longer valid.

At the end of his long tale, there was a short discussion among the High Elders. Those who had scoffed before now seemed to not only believe but also seemed excited about the powers of the new young wizard. Perhaps he was 'the one', they thought.

Flintock knew that he had not told the whole story, he also knew that Aneta Stepanek would know that he had held something back, she was the Enlightened one who always knew the truth before it was even spoken.

When she rose to speak again. His blood ran cold, she knew he was holding something back and now she was going to expose him.

CHAPTER 15 - CASTELL Y BLAENORAID, THE TALE CONTINUES....

Flintock was worried, he knew that Aneta Stepanek of Goleuedigaeth knew more than she was letting on and Aneta Stepanek knew that Flintock, although he had been truthful, he had not told the whole story. Surely, she would continue her questioning until she exposed everything. He waited for the next question.

"Tell me Elder Flintock, do you know where the boy acolyte Thomas is now?"

"No, I have no idea at all," he said truthfully.

"And do you know where the ring of the elders is now?"

"No. I don't know that either."

High Elder Aneta Stepanek sat down again.

The Clerk to the Elder of Elders then asked a question.

"High Elder Aneta Stepanek of Goleuedigaeth," he spoke in his normal high and haughty manner, "you are the enlightened one and know better than anyone here. Does Elder Flintock speak truthfully and honestly?"

"My dear Clerk, every word he has spoken is true."

"Then you may step down Elder Flintock. You are free to go as you please."

Flintock didn't believe his luck. She must have known that he was hiding something. Llewellyn had spoken to him only hours before and told him that Thomas was only an acolyte and had little magic of his own, so why had High Elder Aneta Stepanek not caught him out when he spoke of all the amazing magic which he had witnessed Tom perform knowing it was not his own but by his father's.

The council all rose as the Elder of Elders left through his personal door and then they all filtered out through the double doors opposite the Elder's 'throne'.

As Flintock left, Aneta caught his eye and they walked out together turning away from the rest of the High Elders and going down to the next level.

"Don't worry my pet," she said in her thick Eastern European accent, "of course, I know it was not the boy, but his father who performed the real magic. But for now, that will be just our little secret!"

Before Flintock could question her, she turned again and was gone. Flintock went to follow her, but she was nowhere to be seen. What was she up to? He thought this is just the sort of politics and intrigue that kept him from seeking high office. He must find Llewellyn again and tell him what happened and ask his advice as well.

Flintock must first find Tryg as it was not good to leave a trygall alone and unaccompanied, and then he must find Llewellyn; but he had no real idea where to look. He headed back to the inn where he had met Llewellyn and where he had left Tryg. As he entered, he looked warily around and over in the small alcove they had met earlier he saw Tryg sitting with someone, but he could not make out who in the shadows. He went over, the hooded stranger looked up, it was Llewellyn.

"How did you know I needed to see you?" Flintock asked after exchanging greetings.

"You should know by now my friend. I know most things, even the things people prefer me not to know!" he said with a laugh. They sat in the corner alcove and ordered some ale and herb tea while they discussed the day's events.

"So, Llewel the High Elder is now just Llewel!" Llewellyn laughed as he spoke.

"Yes, and they are holding him in the dungeons for some reason. They have no crime or accusation against him, so why are they still holding him?"

"Oh, I expect it's just to let him cool off for a while and to remind him of his place, after all, he was not exactly truthful when questioned by the council."

"He doesn't have a place anymore, he's just plain old Llewel the Wizard." Flintock quipped.

"I know, but I somehow find it hard to be sad for him."

They both smirked at each other.

Tryg had a look about him which told them he was not happy.

"If only he could talk," said Flintock, "I wonder what the problem is with him, that is a look of disapproval if ever I saw one."

I'll tell you what, I have an idea, meet me in the Paddock Wood in one hour, we may be able to find out."

An hour later, Flintock and Tryg arrived at the Paddock Wood to find Llewellyn and a familiar looking Jack Russel standing there.

"Hello Howel," said Flintock.

"Oh, this is so undignified, I am a Purple Dragon, the finest in my class, and yet I am reduced to this life of a dog. It's really not natural, so unseemly, so undignified."

"I've had a check around, there's no one about, so you may change back if you...," Llewellyn hadn't even finished the sentence when pop! There he stood, all sixty foot of iridescent purple dragon. He shimmered in the evening sun, ever-changing hues of purple tinged with the red of the dying sun, huge scales like armour plate, a deep red glow in his throat and wings like a huge bat with vicious spikes at the end of each finger which could pierce through armour and bone alike. Howel flexed and shook every muscle in his body, making the ground shudder a little. He could look ferocious, he could be ferocious, but somehow, it was difficult to take him too seriously when he spoke. The full-on Oxford accent he had adopted, just didn't sound right.

"Right, that is better," he said having had his little shake to make the point, "now, how may I be of service?"

Llewellyn spoke, "It's Tryg really, he seems worried or upset about something and we hoped you might be able to tell us what is wrong."

"Well," he said, nuancing each syllable, "well, let me see. He is worried about Llewel, he thinks he may be trouble, although he knows that the ridiculous little imp of a wizard, my interpretation of his thoughts you understand, has and had no friends, he could still raise up a rabble to turn against the council."

"But why would he want to do such a thing. His punishment was just for his failure to deliver Tom and the ring," said Flintock, "surely now he would be wanting to ingratiate himself with the council to get back up the ladder again?"

"Well no, according to Tryg, who of course has the hearing qualities of a well-tuned owl, during the last couple of days of your journey, Llewel was muttering to himself, unaware that Tryg could hear every word, it seems that he is convinced that Tom is a fraud and he was going to make sure that no one believes in Tom or in his power or that he could save the magic in Trymyll. He believes that if he can turn the whole populace against both Tom and Llewellyn, then the boy will become so dispirited that he will believe it himself and then Tom's own magic will fail."

"Well that's not going to happen," said Llewellyn, "I'll make sure of it. I'll look after Tom and keep him away from any such thoughts."

"But then you have Jon."

"What do you mean by that?" he said slightly riled.

"Well," continued Howel, "on a personal note, from my own observations, unless some changes are made, Jon may also decide to undermine Tom in any way he can also. He is jealous and quite put out by the recent turn of events and may likewise do all he can to make Tom fail. The poor boy feels quite rejected. Up to now he has, for all intents and purposes been your only son, now Tom is here, he feels he has not just moved down the pecking order, he's not on it at all."

"That's ridiculous, he knows I love him. He knows I would never let him down."

"It is hardly my place to say, I am after all only a dragon, albeit a very fine dragon, but how much time have you spent with Jon since Tom arrived?"

That hurt, but Llewellyn knew it was true. He had neglected his older boy; he had spent all his time with Tom and left Jon to do all the household chores. He must put that right and soon. But how? He had to involve him with Tom's training. He wasn't sure how, Tom was learning magic, real magic. Poor Jon could hardly light a match without striking it.

CHAPTER 16 - JON & TOM PARTNER UP.

Tom continued his training for many weeks, but now it was different. Jon now accompanied him into the training room each day. Jon was not much good at the magic bit, but now he had an added enthusiasm which helped the little magic he had become better each day. Jon was also, for a fifteen-year-old, a good strategist. So, for the different situations that their dad placed them in, Jon worked out what needed to be done and then they both executed the plan. Working as a team was great, and it helped Llewellyn's problem which he had inadvertently caused by excluding Jon from his life, making him resent him, and his little brother Tom.

Tom was becoming more accomplished as a wizard and Jon was becoming quite the strategist. Llewellyn set out the various scenarios for them to practice. One of their first joint adventures was on the battlements of a castle, surrounded by a marauding horde of bandits.

Tom's first approach was to feed positive and calming energy across the attackers and then have a talk with their leader about a peaceful outcome. Jon thought it was not the best plan, but if he wanted to try it, they could not come to any harm, so give it a go.

Tom stood upon the battlements, staff in hand. He calmed the mob and stopped all the jostling and jibbing, he then called down.

"I want to talk about a truce with your leader."

Much to Jon's surprise, the leader stepped forward and agreed to talk. They went down to open the gate for a chat. Two minutes later they were hanging by their ankles in the castle dungeon.

"Not such a good idea after all," said Jon.

Their dad reset the scene. They were back on the battlements. This time Jon took control, briefed some of the men of arms who were in their crow's nests and lookout towers and called Tom to try again. Tom didn't quite understand, but he again held his staff aloft and radiated peaceful and calming waves down onto the mob. Again, they all quietened down. This time their leader stepped out to the front and called up to Tom to ask if he wanted to discuss the terms of his surrender. But this time as he stepped forward, there was the swoosh of an arrow, and their leader was dead. The mob then fled. Tom was mortified, how could Jon have done such a thing. Tom wanted to talk peace and Jon had arranged for the leader to be assassinated in cold blood.

The scene dissolved into the classroom. Llewellyn was there waiting.

"Dad, how could he do that, he shot him in cold blood just as we were about to talk!"

"Well first, you must remember that in these scenarios, no one dies, no one gets hurt because they are not really there at all. Secondly, if Jon had not arranged for that little show of strength, you and he would have been back in the dungeon hanging up by your ankles again. Had the horde taken the castle, many would have died, but by taking out one man, all survived," he turned to address his other son, "Jon, although what you did may have saved many lives, there are other strategies which you both could have used to frighten off the attackers. Now, they are just men, not wizards, they have no magic and do not understand magic. Go again and go back with a better and different strategy in which no one gets hurt, or I may just leave you hanging by your ankles until breakfast tomorrow!"

With that, he disappeared, and the boys were back on the battlements.

"Now what?" said Tom, "what can we do that will frighten them off?"

"I dunno," was Jon's reply, "what frightens people most apart from Mrs Glyn?" they both laughed at that suggestion. Although Jon had not met Mrs Glyn, he knew all about her from Tom, "Ghosts? The walking dead?" he continued.

"Well ghosts don't exist, and we can't empty the graveyard of corpses because that takes some very dark magic which no one is allowed to do."

"Why not?"

"I dunno, I suppose, because raising the dead means there would be a lot of dead people walking around who would be hard to kill because they're already dead, and because they wouldn't know who's side they were on they might come after us."

"Is that true?" Jon asked.

"No idea, just made it up, but it sounds reasonable to me."

"Okay, no walking dead, so what do we do Tom?"

"I'm thinking, what about you? Any thoughts?"

Jon was thinking out loud, "If only we had a Dragon, that would scare the what-sits out of them."

"Mmmm," said Tom, "we could always get one."

"Where from?"

"The fires in the castle!" said Tom clutching the stone of his staff, he concentrated on the ruby element. He envisioned a dragon made of fire, breathing fire. Through the power the ruby in his staff, all the fires in the castle suddenly flared up and he drew up the flames from all the fires to form the dragon, weaving the flames to form a body about forty feet long, golden in colour like burnished bronze with fire spraying from his mouth with every breath. The dragon launched off the battlements and flew around the castle, flames whooshing out of its mouth over the heads of the marauding horde. They turned on their heels and fled to a man. The dragon circling around and dived among them until they were over the hill and out of sight. Then the dragon vanished as quickly as it had appeared. Jon and Tom looked at each other, smiled and high fived. The scene dissolved and they were back in the room.

"Well done you two, another successful quest, even if it did take three attempts. Right, Tom, you're on supper duty, Jon is going for flying lessons in the gym. Tom exited the classroom just as it was transforming into the massive padded flying hall.

To start with Jon was no better than Tom. It took him a full first evening just to get off the ground, his flying training was taking place late afternoons and early evenings after a day's training with Tom, so he was tired already. He was bouncing off the ceiling, walls, and floor. Eventually, he managed to fly without crashing, stopping when required, turning, climbing, diving and general manoeuvres, but all at a slower rate than his thirteen-year-old brother. He was just too tired to concentrate fully on his flying.

Several days later, it was into the woods, he had a full day in the woods on his own while Tom had lessons with his dad on incantations and dweomers. Just like his brother, it hurt. Jon bounced off trees, stumps, rocks and just about anything and everything else in his path. By the end of the day, he was blooded and sore.

He tried again the next day but was not much better, but after four days he was getting the hang of it.

Day five he met with the Cadwaladers, Lynessa and Traveon, Traveon took him to the cottage for tea and rock cakes and the normal pattern unfolded. Well nearly.

Mrs Cadwalader again produced her amazing wand, fashioned from the pencil thin fourth finger bone of a Golden Dragons wing with the pearlescent stone of the blind wizard's false eye. Up she roared, looping, diving, whooping out loud, as she dodged around the trees at breakneck speed. Jon was transfixed, he was in awe of the fat old lady wizards flying skills.

"Wow Mrs Cadwalader, I wish I could fly like that, that was awesome!"

"Oh, I'm sure you could if you tried. Here take my staff and have a go."

"But how?"

"Just believe that you can do it and the staff will do the rest."

Jon mounted the staff, well stick really, he was afraid he might break it even though he weighed less than a quarter of what Mrs Cadwalader must weigh.

Up he shot at what to him was an unbelievable speed, as soon as he cleared the treetops, he lost his nerve, stalled, and plummeted to the ground.

Traveon whipped out his wand, pointed at the ground where Jon would hit and it instantly turned to a sponge-like texture, but without any change in appearance. So, when Jon hit it, he was expecting to die or something, but instead, he sunk into what felt like a huge soft, comfortable bed of feathers.

Mrs Cadwalader pretended to snatch her staff out of the air as it returned to her, in fact, of course, it had never left her.

"There, there my deary, that wasn't quite what we were wanting, but at least you're not hurt. So, let's try again deary. Don't forget, the staff is not what makes you fly, it's you what does it. You don't need a staff to fly, it just feels better and gives better directional control. So next time you falls off, don't plummet. Float."

Again, without Jon knowing she called out his staff transforming it, so it looked like hers, "Off you go again sweetheart. Don't worry, that happens all the time. Nearly everyone falls off the first try."

As soon as Jon was up and flying, she turned to her husband and said, "Well, that's never happened before!"

Jon was better this time, not so fast, but he was steady, he weaved in and out of the trees, around stumps, through the brick arches of the orchard wall and away into the distance, all without hitting a thing. A few minutes later, he arrived back at the Cadwaladers.

"There my dear that wasn't too bad was it?"

"But next time I won't have the magic of your staff."

"You didn't that time, here's my staff, look, you're sitting on your own stick!" She laughed. Jon looked down, there was his staff, he had been tricked.

"But!" he exclaimed, but before he could say more, Mrs Cadwalader said.

"I don't lend my wand to no one," and laughed again.

"Go on. Off you go, you can do it, you just needs to practice till you gets a bit faster. Go on, off with you."

"Thanks to both of you. I promise I'll practice, and thanks for the tea and cake!" and off he shot, well, maybe not exactly shot, but off he went anyway. He flew around all the trees and other obstacles for about half an hour. As soon as he landed and his feet touched the ground, he was back in the training room. His dad was waiting.

"Well. How'd it go then?" his dad asked.

"It was alright I suppose. I met this weird old wizard lady and her husband, Mr and Mrs Cadwalader."

Llewellyn interrupted, "They're not weird, just different."

"Well, she showed me a few tricks and then I could fly around all the time without hitting things or anything!" Jon exclaimed with excitement, "it's just," he hesitated, "I'm not very fast, but she said that would come with practice."

"Excellent news, then we must make sure you practice two or three times a week in the woods until you are like greased lightning!"

"It was fun, so I will, don't worry."

"I won't," his dad said with a wink.

The scene changed; It was raining hard and drops of water ran off their heads and down over their faces. 'Thanks dad,' they both thought. They found himself hiding in a cold damp camp full of hostile dark wizards. In the distance Tom could see Asmodeus the Dark Elder, ranting, as usual, tiny flashes of lightning emitting from him as he became angrier and angrier. First thought, how had he known that that was Asmodeus? He was distant and dressed very differently to the Asmodeus he had met briefly earlier. The wand he decided, was feeding him wisdom.

He looked at Jon, "That's Asmodeus over there, the flashy one."

They both giggled quietly.

"Find the boy!" he shouted, "he is here, I can feel it. The boy has tricked me once with his false ring, but he won't fool me again or he won't live long enough to regret it!"

Fear struck at his heart. Tom was sweating despite the cold. Sweating so much he wondered if they could smell him. No, daft thought, he couldn't even smell himself, so they couldn't either.

They needed to make a break for it, they needed to run away, but there was too much light with all the fires and burning torches. Even if they ran, which way was safe? He could use magic to put all the torches and fires out, but then they would not be able to see either so they might run straight towards the enemy.

Another thought, he could use his power to send soothing waves of magic and then negotiate their way out. No, last time he tried that, they both ended up in a dungeon, hanging by their ankles.

What about his bow? He could take out Asmodeus with a single arrow and escape in the confusion which would follow. Although he knew that Asmodeus was not a reality, it still went against his principles. He didn't want to kill anyone, even if they weren't truly there. Had he thought it through, he could, by concentrating on all the wizards, taken them all out with a single arrow which would split to match the number of targets.

What about a fight to the death? Break cover, face them, fight them, and defeat them? No worst idea ever. There were too many of them and they hadn't even had a proper 'magic' fight yet, so didn't even know how to do battle. He couldn't use the fire dragon trick again; they would know it was magic and counter it, or even turn it against them. He could use the old freeze time trick, but his dad will not be impressed with that. He couldn't use that every time he was in trouble. He wished he were invisible, then he could just walk out of here.

Tom and Jon both knew that these were not real events, they knew they could come to no harm, but it was not just magic and imagery which formed these illusions, their father had woven into it real emotions, real fear, palpable consternation and foreboding. In fact, terror and despair featured highly on their emotional scale.

Tom focused on his dad and they dropped out of the enemy camp and back into the training room.

"What are you two doing back here? You can't just pop home for a chat every time you're stuck. You must go figure things out for yourselves. So, what's wrong?"

"Da, can we make ourselves invisible?" Tom asked.

"Yes, of course you can, but that's for another lesson, it's difficult to perform and even more difficult to hold it. So back!"

With that, they were indeed back. Asmodeus was still doing his flashy bit as he got angry and they were still stuck in the enemy camp.

"Find the boy!" he shouted, "He is here, I can feel it. The boy has tricked me once with his false ring, but he won't fool me again or he won't live long enough to regret it!"

Oh, Tom thought, we're right back at the beginning again. Groundhog Day!

"Well Jonathan Jones, now what do we do?" Tom asked. He now had a theory that his fifteen-year-old brother, being older and therefore wiser would instantly have some strategic advice.

"Not a clue, but I'm working on it. We are on slightly higher ground here and there's a stream that runs through the camp. Using your emerald, you could stop the water further upstream and then release it suddenly, washing them all away."

"How long would that take? It's only a little stream we'd be here for hours before we had enough water to do anything. Anyway, they would notice if the stream suddenly stopped running by. I know I would," replied Tom.

They really didn't know the power of their stones. They could have, if they wished, conjure up an Olympic sized swimming pool of water or two and just dumped it on the camp. But they were acolytes, they were still learning.

"Right Tom, plan 'B,' we mount our staffs and skedaddle at high speed in different directions and outrun them?" his voice raising at the end to make it a question knowing that he wasn't even convincing himself.

"No, they might have better flying skills, let's face it, we only learnt ourselves within the last few days, they would have been flying for years."

"Alright, Plan B revision 1," Jon said with a little more conviction, "they will be looking behind things, in things and concentrating at ground level. If we fly straight up vertically into the sky until we are out of sight, then we just fly away. It's dark, there's no moonlight because of the rain, so we won't need to go too high. What do you think?"

"Sounds like a plan bro," said Tom, "let's give it a go. But before we do, we need camouflage, I'll change our clothing and cloaks to black, pull your hood up and cover your shiny white face and don't smile, your teeth will give us both away."

Tom quickly envisioned and wove a spell making and remodelling their clothes and boots to a light-absorbing black. He pulled up his own hood right over his head so that it hid his face. Neither could see each other. Time to go. They stepped over their staffs and pushed off, but as they did, they were back in the training room.

"What!" exclaimed Jon, "what have we done wrong now?"

"Nothing, perfectly sound strategy, more than a ninety-five per cent chance of success, maybe even as high as ninety-nine."

"Then why bring us back?"

"Simple, it's supper time. You solved the problem, so why let supper spoil? And we need to talk about tomorrow."

They sat down for supper, both the boys were hungry, they had worked hard today, they worked hard every day.

"So," said Tom, "what's happening tomorrow then?"

"You're going to meet some real dragons tomorrow, and they might or might not be friendly. Tomorrow, as you walk through into the training room, you will actually apparate away and step straight into the Dragonlands of Trymyll."

"What on our own? Up to now, it's been sort of virtual reality, you mean this time we'll actually be there?" Jon questioned warily.

"Oh yes, this time it's for real, but don't worry, I will be there with you, well, virtually anyway."

"What do you mean by virtually da?" asked Jon.

"I will be able to see everything that is happening from here and can be with you in the instant it takes me to apparate from here to there."

"Well," said Tom, now was his chance to ask a question which had been bothering him since his arrival, "well now we know where there is, but where is here?"

"You my son, are deep, deep, underneath Blaenoraid, the capital of Trymyll."

Tom had suspected as such, but now he knew.

"We are in a set of rooms which no one knows of which are inaccessible to all except us. There are only two ways in, there is a small door which is hidden by spells and enchantments deep in the bowels of the castle, or we apparate in, which is how I brought you here in the first place."

"So, where's the entrance then, the one we can't see?" asked Tom.

"That, at the moment is privileged information."

Tom dropped the subject and they carried on eating and talking.

The two boys chatted long into the evening, they decided to keep their dark black light-absorbing clothes and hoodies, they quite liked the look, a bit of a uniform. Unknown to their dad, they then started to recolour all their clothing to this shade. Llewellyn hadn't noticed or said anything when they reappeared back in the training room before supper, so to them, that was his approval. While they worked, they chatted.

"So, Tom, what's life like in Wales then? What do you miss most?"

"I miss my mates from school and rugby and all that, and of course I miss mum, but there's not much else I miss."

"Come on, there must be something you miss."

"Chips," was Tom's reply, "I miss chips, burgers, and chocolate."

"What are they then? Your mate's names?"

"What!" exclaimed Tom, "Oh, I don't suppose you've ever had any of them. No, they're foods. I'll try to explain, you won't understand, but I'll try."

"I'm listening," said Jon expectantly.

"Well, chips are potatoes which are cut into strips about as big as your finger and fried in hot fat until brown and crispy, you then put salt and vinegar on them and dip them in tomato sauce as you eat them."

"Oh, so what's so good about that then? Don't sound that special to me," Jon said.

"I said you wouldn't understand. It's not just food, it's an experience. You buy them down the chippy and then walk to the park with your mates eating chips on a Saturday evening."

"So?" Jon replied.

"What do you mean by 'so.' It's great, it's an event, a ritual, it's life itself. It was our Saturday evening thing!"

"Well, it doesn't sound that exciting to me. So, what's chocolate?"

"Now chocolate cannot be explained. It's an experience and taste like no other. If chips are life itself, chocolate is better than life."

"Don't be daft, how can chocolate be better than life?"

"It can't be explained. You must try it. If we ever get back home, no, when we get home, I'll take you to the chippy, buy you a burger and chips, and then we'll eat chocolate together. Only then will you know."

Jon didn't bother to enquire about a burger, if that was the best about home, he was better off here.

By the time they had finished their talking, they had a pile of black, light-absorbing clothes each. With a satisfied grin on their faces, they vowed to each other, in the way that kids of their age did, that they would, from this day forth, be known as the Boys in Black, or Boys of the Black, or The Wizards Black. They laughed as they came up with more and more ridiculous names, the final one being Mighty Wizards of the Black Cloak. In the end, they decided to be Boys of the Black Hood. They thought it had street cred. Important when you're thirteen and

JOSEPH R. MASON

fifteen.

CHAPTER 17 - TO THE DRAGONLANDS.

Next morning, there was a little tension over breakfast.

"I don't feel well, can't go for training today," Jon exclaimed.

His dad was having none of it.

"You look perfectly alright to me, now come on, eat your breakfast, you'll need all your strength today."

"Maybe, but I'm still not going."

"What do you mean? You're not going."

"Just what I said, little boy wonder wizard can go if he wants, but I'm stopping here."

"No need for that attitude, apologise to your brother," Llewellyn said sternly.

"No."

"Apologise!" he said even more firmly.

"Sorry Jon, I didn't mean it. But I'm still not going and that's final."

"It's all right da, I'll go on my own."

"I'm not sure about that, with two of you it would be a better and safer experience. I shouldn't really say safer because I will make sure neither of you come into any real danger, but Jon needs the experience as we much as you do."

"No, it's fine, I'll go on my own," Tom insisted.

"Okay, if you're sure. But Jon, listen up, you will need to go there sometime, so why not go with your brother, you're the eldest, you should be looking out for him."

"I know, but dragons just aren't my thing," Jon added more calmly.

"What on earth do you mean by 'not your thing'?"

"Exactly what I say, I don't particularly like dragons, to be honest, they scare the whatsits out of me."

"But you like Howel, he's a fine dragon, and he likes you."

"Yeah, for supper," he said sarcastically.

"Don't be daft, Howel wouldn't eat you, or anyone else for that matter, unless he had to that is."

"That's the problem, what if he decided he had to eat me. What if he got all paranoid one day and decided you, me, Jon, and everyone else was out to get him? He'd eat us all."

"No, he wouldn't, and you know it, Howel is a very gentle dragon, he hardly ever eats anyone," Llewellyn said with a grin.

"Anyway, why are we going there? Not to fight dragons I hope?" Jon questioned.

"No, don't be daft, that way you would get eaten! It's something all acolytes do; they go to seek out dragons and learn from them. Most dragons are incredibly wise, many have great magic which they sometimes share with acolytes if they take to them. Blue Dragons being the exception, a species to be avoided at all costs. Some dragons, especially purple ones, as you know already, can be a little stuck up, but don't worry, learn what you can from those that you meet of any colour except blue. You also go to see if you can find a dragon to partner up with. Very few do, most don't. Don't worry if you don't, only a handful acolytes ever pair up with a dragon, fully fledged wizards don't do any better. Most wizards are dragonless. Of the seven High Elders, only two have dragons, of the other forty-nine Elders, about five have them, even Flinty doesn't have a dragon to call his own. So, no worries if you don't get one to fall in love with you. You can always get another pet," Llewellyn smiled at the boys, "and don't forget, no one ever owns a dragon, it's a partnership of trust and respect."

"Alright, I'll go, but I'm not happy about this. You had better be keeping a close eye on us. And if I don't like what I see, get me back here quick."

"Okay, I will."

"Promise?"

"Alright, I promise. Enough already! Now, quickly through the door, half the morning's gone arguing."

The boys stepped through the door. They felt what seemed like a tug on their bodies and then a spinning sensation, a sudden stop, opened their eyes and there they were, on the far side of Trymyll in the Dragonlands. They had 'landed' atop a very tall mountain, the whole area was mountainous, lots of steep valleys, caves, densely forested areas and what looked like quarries in some of the valleys. They were above the snow line, so it was cold, very cold. They wrapped their black cloaks around them and drew a little energy from their wands to warm up but being careful not to melt the snow and sink. The boys knew that their dad could both see and hear them, so Jon asked.

"What's with the quarries da?"

They would hear any reply in their heads, not as actual spoken word.

"This is where the stone for the castles came from several thousand years ago, they quarried the area when the castles and surrounding towns were originally built. They don't quarry anymore; they use bricks just like at home; and just like at home, the quarried granite buildings outlast the brick-built ones by millennia."

"What do we do now?" Tom asked.

"I suggest you both mount your staffs and have a recce."

The boys did as suggested. They both sped down the mountain

at breath-taking speed and into the valley. Jon seemed to have gained a lot of confidence and had only slight problems keeping up with his younger sibling. They swooped across the bottom of the valley, into quarries and out again, up vertical faces and across plateaus and down the other side. Eventually, they came to a stop on top of a quarry as they could see smoke in the distance.

"What do you reckon that is?" asked Jon.

"Well it is the Dragonlands, so I'm guessing it might be dragons."

They continued cautiously, over the next crest and there in the next quarry were a dozen or so chickens, both hens and cocks and a large cockerel.

"Why are there chickens down there?" asked Jon.

"They're not, they're a family of Red Dragons. Watch."

He had remembered what Howel had told him, 'Red dragons are to be sought; they are very magical, faithful, trustworthy and have longer lives than any other dragons. Their metamorphic other is a hen or cockerel according to their gender. He just wished he knew what metamorphic meant, but he thought it was like when Howel turned into Howl the Jack Russel. He floated slowly down to the group of chickens. Dismounted, bowed, and said.

"Good morning Red Dragon family."

There was a dozen 'pops' as the dragons, of all different shapes and sizes 'recovered their dignity' as Howel would have put it. The largest male was a good sixty-foot-long, there were a couple of mature females about fifty-foot-long and a variety of small to medium-sized dragons which Tom assumed were their offspring.

The male spoke in a strong, deep, resonating voice which seemed to bounce off every wall in the quarry.

"Good morning to you young acolyte. May we know your name?"

"I am Acolyte Thomas Jones, a son of Llewellyn the Brave, and watching from the top of the quarry wall is Acolyte Jonathan Jones, eldest son of Llewellyn the Brave"

"Llewellyn the Brave, I know him, I suppose you have come to learn of dragons and to perhaps win a favour?"

"Yes please," Tom replied somewhat nervously.

"Well bring your sibling down and I will introduce my family to you both and teach you what I wish you to know."

Tom bowed again and flew up to where Jon was standing.

"You coming down? He wants to introduce himself and teach us stuff about dragons and things."

"Not blooming likely, we'll both be eaten alive!"

"No, we won't, Red Dragons are very nice and very trustworthy, and he knows our dad."

"Help me da, I'm too scared to go down there. He'll eat us both!" Jon said.

Their dads voice came through, "Don't be scared, I know this particular Red Dragon and his family. He is Odgar Caddell and his ladies are Rhedyn and Awel. Be polite and respectful and they will respond with the same."

Tom lightly gripped his stone and sent out an aura of peace and tranquillity surrounding his brother. Jon calmed down, mounted his staff and they floated down together.

"Jonathan, son of Llewellyn the Brave. You too are welcome. I am Odgar, and these are my females Awel and Rhedyn. We have between us nine immature dragons or whelps as you would call them; I won't bore you with all their names as I know you will forget them anyway."

That's true thought Tom.

"You have come to learn of dragons and perhaps to win favour or fellowship with one. I can and will teach you what I wish to teach you out of respect for your father, but all my offspring are here to stay and neither I nor my ladies wish to have a long-term fellowship with a wizard at the moment."

'Oh no', thought Tom, 'another few days of lessons'.

"Not at all," said Odgar, "the knowledge I give will be passed over very quickly indeed. Oh, and don't forget, I can get your thoughts, surely the Purple Dragon, Howel has taught you that much?"

"Yes, I know, but forgot," Tom said apologetically.

"Well then, keep your negativity to yourself," Odgar said sharply, his voice again bouncing all around the quarry, "hold your staffs upright and just below the stone. Move the stone and hold it against your forehead."

As they did there was a flash, and then what seemed like a movie playing at very high-speed flashing through their heads. It was so fast they did not even have time to see a single frame. In a couple of seconds, it was over. Finished.

"Wow!" said Tom, "that was fast. So fast I'm not sure I caught any of it."

"Oh, but you did, every single bit of it, and I also learnt every thought you have ever had as well. Let me prove what I say. You asked your father the other day if you could become invisible?"

"Yes, but how...."

"Think invisible."

Tom didn't quite know how to think 'invisible' but tried to imagine no one could see him. As he did, he began to fade and eventually disappeared.

"That is just one many skills which I have passed to you both.

"Jonathan, the first day that you and your sibling were reunited you said, that you could not connect to your wand. Well, now it is time to connect."

Jon had no idea what he meant but took his staff and held it aloft. He could feel the power surge from his staff and down through him, around him and back into the staff. He pointed the staff at a huge boulder, the power shot out and the granite vaporised. He pointed it at a piece of rock the size of a small car and willed it to rise. It rose effortlessly into the air. He was connected, oh boy was he connected.

"Whoooheee!" he yelped with joy!

"Apart from those two little tricks, I have invested you both with a many more, but you will realise them later as you go on with your quest. You may not realise now, but you know everything a human acolyte needs to know about dragons, again, you may not grasp it now, but when you need to know something, you will find that you already do. Now, off you go Jonathan, son of Llewellyn and Thomas son of Llewellyn. I, Odgar and the ladies Awel and Rhedyn wish you good fortune, sound magic and long life; good day to you both, and please give my kindest regards to your father," Odgar said with a deep bow.

"Good day to you Odgar Caddell, good day to you Awel and Rhedyn," Tom spoke first, and then Jon repeated. They both bowed courteously, mounted their staffs, and flew off again at great speed. Jon realised that he now felt completely confident in his flying and was now able to keep up with Tom quite easily. He now had no fear of dragons either, Odgar had taught him all he would ever need to know about dragons in a few seconds. He now knew for certain that the only dragons to fear and avoid were the Blue Dragons.

They continued their journey, up mountains and down into valleys, in and out of quarries, always keeping low to the ground to avoid being spotted by anything hostile. After about thirty more minutes, they came to an abrupt halt. They could sense trouble ahead.

They could hear a commotion of some sort up ahead and so, they pushed on slowly to the top of the next quarry, they stopped near the edge and peeked over. What they saw was both alarming and frightening. Down below they could see a Golden

Dragon and her whelp. Caught by their claws in iron traps, cold iron traps, or they would have escaped by now. There were three Blue Dragons down there too, these were baiting the Golden Dragon and trying to capture her baby Golden Dragon. The three Blue Dragons were being egged on by a dark wizard dressed head to toe in black.

"We've got to do something, that Golden Dragon is getting terribly upset and tiring. Once her strength is gone, they will easily capture the whelp. We have to stop them," said Tom.

"How are we going to do that, we don't have much chance against three Blue Dragons and a Dark Wizard."

"We have surprise on our side, we are also dressed in black, so he may not see us as the rescue party, I have a trick up my sleeve beyond the normal wand and staff, and I now know how to kill a dragon. Odgar must have taught me in his 'lesson' as he knows I would never use it against another dragon except in self-defence. We'll fly around the valley and then straight in over the top of the Dark Wizard and his Blue Dragons and position ourselves next to the mum, then, I'll deal with the dragons while you hopefully engage with the wizard."

"How do I do that?"

"Engage with your wand and staff, the wisdom of the wand will guide you and give you the power required."

"I hope you're right. Let's do it before I think too much and get scared!"

They swooped around and down at lightning speed and stopped dead next to the Golden Dragon facing the three Blue Dragons and the dark wizard.

Tom summoned all his courage and spoke, at least it sounded like him, but his voice was magnified many times and he could be heard quite clearly above all the commotion.

"Let these dragons go and be on your way or face the consequences of your actions!"

The dark wizard let out a sardonic laugh, "And how can two small boy acolytes of little consequence make me, and my dragons face any consequence?"

He laughed again, he thought to himself how amusing he was to use the word consequence twice in one sentence.

"We warn you. There are two of us and only one of you, release these chains and set the dragons free."

"There may be only one of me, but have you noticed my pets?" he carried on in his jovial mood and gestured towards the Blue Dragons, "there my pets, a little light lunch for you. Get them!" he said.

Blue Dragons are easy to confuse because they are not very bright, so instead of attacking straight away, all three of them just looked at the two boys.

Tom shouted at them, "Three of you and two of us, one of you's not getting fed today."

This confused them even more, they looked around at the Dark Wizard, as if to say, don't you mean, it's three of us and three of you!

While they looked round, Tom struck.

"Bow!" he said.

Instantly he stood there with his Yew longbow and a quiver of arrows. He quickly knocked, aimed, and loosed a single arrow which he knew would have a cold iron tip, he concentrated his thought on the scale just below the fire chamber at the base of necks. The arrow split into three and all three arrows sunk deep into the chests of the three dragons and deep into their hearts. They fell with a crash to the ground. Dead! The dark wizard lost his smile and pointed his staff at the boys letting out a massive energy burst. Jon banged his staff to the ground, and they were surrounded by what seemed like a hemisphere of solid energy. The spell ricocheted off and into the quarry wall, vaporising a few tonnes of granite rock. Jon dropped the shield and sent out his own burst of energy, every bit as powerful as the dark wizard's, Jon didn't have the qualms that Tom had about hurting or killing people. The wizard avoided the blast by apparating to another part of the quarry and letting off another burst. Jon volleyed this one with his staff, almost like a cricket bat sending it straight back to the Dark Wizard. This joust went on for several minutes before it came to a very sudden halt. The Dark Wizard just froze in time and space. Tom had taken control, frozen everything, and stepped out of the fray. He touched his brother with his wand, and he was at once re-animated. He was just about to launch another burst when Tom stopped him.

"Stop, it's over, he can't move."

At that moment, their father appeared beside them.

"Well done boys, you make me proud."

Llewellyn released the Golden Dragon from her shackles and then shackled up the Dark Wizard in the cold iron chains. He then released the whelp and used his chains to make extra sure the Dark Wizard was going nowhere. Tom then released his freezing spell on them all.

"Thomas, son of Llewellyn, Jonathon son of Llewellyn and Llewellyn the Brave, we are indebted to you. We thank you all for your help in this most difficult situation."

"How do you know us?" Tom asked, but then he realised he already knew. A Golden Dragon is the wisest of all dragons, why wouldn't she know?

"Exactly," said the dragon, even though Tom had not spoken. Being female, she was only about forty foot long. But magnificent, Tom had never seen anything so beautiful in all his life. She was exactly what he had expected and more, much more. Brilliant Golden scales covering her body, each one looking as if it was made from 24-carat gold and burnished to a brilliant shine. She smelled of saffron and incense. In relation to her body, her wings were quite small, not enough to fly with at all, but Golden Dragons do not need wings, they could fly because they are Golden Dragons. She hovered above the ground effortlessly, her wings just caressing the air, her young whelp next to her.

She was a Golden Dragon of ancient China, for Golden Dragons originated from the Taihang Mountains, a vast mountain range of northern China, stretching some two-hundred and fifty miles from north to south and forming the boundary between the Shanxi and Hebei provinces. They are found deep within the deepest caverns below the mountains of the north, shrouded with magic and unknown to man even to this day.

"Thomas, son of Llewellyn, we owe you a great debt for slaying the three Blue Dragons, as do we to you also Jonathan son of Llewellyn for your bravery in engaging with the dark wizard when so inexperienced in battle. That debt will be paid in full when the time is ready. Until then we return to our weyr."

With that, they morphed into sparrow hawks and flew away swiftly into the distance.

"What shall we do with him?" said Jon.

"We will take him back to Blaenoraid and throw him in the dungeons. The council will want to question him about his motives."

CHAPTER 18 - THE COUNCIL OF BLAENORAID.

Llewellyn, the boys, and the dark wizard arrived back in Blaenoraid a moment later, deep below the castle in the hideout they called home. Before the dark wizard could orientate himself, Llewellyn departed with him and deposited him in the castle dungeons, still bound in his cold iron chains. The dungeons themselves were lined with cold iron, so there was no means of a magical escape. He also confiscated his wand and incinerated it before his eyes. Llewellyn could see that he had made an enemy by the look in the dark wizards eyes, but that was just another in a long list of enemies. He then returned to the boys who were preparing supper.

Over supper, they discussed the events of the day.

"What did the Golden Dragon mean when she said that the debt will be paid in full when the time is ready?" Tom asked.

"No idea really," his father replied, "but a Golden Dragon will always do what it promises, so when she said the debt will be paid, she meant it. She owes you two and she won't forget it."

"So, what's on the agenda tomorrow?" asked Tom, "more training I suppose," he said in a world-weary way.

"No, not tomorrow Tom, tomorrow you will appear in the city and consequently have to go before the council to both explain your disappearance and give them the ring."

"But I don't have the ring."

"No, but I do, if you remember, you gave it to me weeks ago when we were first reunited."

"Yes, I do remember, of course I remember, but sometimes I can't separate reality, dreams and the 'neither here nor there'."

"Well a lot has happened in these last few weeks, it's not surprising."

"But what do I say about my disappearance, where do I tell them I've been?"

"Tell them the truth, tell them that when you came through the mountain, you knew nothing of the magic of the Land of Trymyll. You didn't even believe in magic at that point. As you progressed along the road to Blaenoraid you lost faith in the so called protector they had sent called Llewel the Elder, so a true and powerful wizard rescued you. Because he believed that you were in mortal danger. It was prudent not to reappear again outside of your hiding place until you had some level of proficiency at magic so you could protect yourself and those around you. Some of the elders may try to probe your mind to see if you are lying but don't worry about that, the only one who might get through is High Elder Aneta Stepanek, again, don't worry about Aneta, she is an old friend and very much on our side. However, I doubt if even she could read your thoughts and make any sense of it," he laughed.

Although said as a joke, Tom's mind was so naturally tightly closed that Llewellyn really did believe that Aneta would not be able to break into Tom's mind.

"What if they start asking awkward questions or questions about you?"

"Don't worry about that, the clerk to the Elder of Elders asks the questions on behalf of the Elder. He only asks these questions for the benefit of the High Elders. The Elder knows what is going on anyway and will not ask any questions you cannot answer. If any of the other High Elders start asking the wrong questions, they will be silenced by the clerk, reminding them of your age and that you are too young for vigorous interrogation."

"How do you know all these things da?"

"I just do, I know more about what goes on in council than most of the High Elders. Don't ask me why, just accept it as true."

Tom could see his father didn't want to continue this conversation, so stopped asking more questions despite having loads more.

The next morning, Tom wandered into town and pretended to look around the market just as anyone would do. He made sure that he became noticed by the castle guard, and word soon reached the members of the council. This was his first proper visit out into the world since his arrival in Trymyll. He had walked for a few days in the countryside but never seen a city before. It was very strange. It looked medieval and yet modern at the same time. They clearly had no planning laws here. You would see an obviously very ancient house, centuries-old and built of granite block next to a row of terraced brick cottages with slate roofs which looked as you might find in any town back home. There were lights hanging everywhere but all strung together with string. No sign of any wires to power them, but all as bright as any electric bulb. The streets were smooth and hard, not cobbled as he imagined, but not tarmac either, they were just solid and smooth, almost like they were a continuous slab of solid stone.

The market bustled with all sorts of people. There were what he called in his mind, normal people, human wizards and phobls, there were people with long pointed ears and sharp noses, he assumed they were elves, he had heard his father talk of elves. There were others with small pointy ears and wings on their backs who didn't seem to walk, but flitted here and there like dragonflies, Tom thought these must either be pixies or fairies.

He would ask later if he remembered. There were also dwarfs, short, thick set and powerful looking, an appearance of permanent bad temper on their faces. Most people gave them a wide birth. No one made eye contact with them.

The market itself seemed sort of ordinary. The fruit and vegetables all looked familiar, the meat stalls also looked much the same as a butcher at home, although some meats were different. One was selling leg of weirdwolf. Tom didn't think he fancied that. They seemed to have a lot of game, pheasant, partridge, hare, rabbits, and wild animals, even boar, squirrel, and hedgehog! The food stalls were all very cold, no sign of refrigeration, but they hung with a magical frost to keep the produce fresh in the summer sun, and the stallholders rubbed their hands together and blew into them for warmth, clouds of condensation hanging in the air. Yet a few feet from each stall, it was a warm and sunny day. Tom was amazed and amused by what he saw. He would have many questions later.

And so, the council met. So important was this, that all the High Elders were there, even High Elder Brangwen Binning was there, though she still wore her Wellington boots! High Elder, Govannon Staley of the Elven community who was the only Elf on the council was there as well, neither of these two High Elders normally came in person but normally appeared only in the 'neither here nor there'. But everyone wanted to see the boy and meet the boy! They were all even just a little excited. Though none would admit it.

"Well, now we are all here, what can we do? We can't arrest him, he's only thirteen summers and has committed no crime?" asked Govannon Stealey, of the Elven community.

"Well we could arrest him, he has the ring, or at least we hope he has the ring, and he should have brought it straight here. He's obviously not to be trusted, or worse, a thief," said Brangwen Binnion. She as usual said out loud what others were only thinking.

"Why don't we just invite him to come and meet us, to have a friendly little chat?" Aneta Stepanek said in her thick accent, "he will agree I am sure."

It took them over an hour to discuss, debate and make that one decision.

"The motion of Aneta Stepanek is carried," announced the clerk.

A messenger was sent down into the town where Tom was being closely watched by the castle guard to make sure they didn't lose him again, and Tom was invited to meet the council and have a little chat, a great honour for such a small boy it was explained, they don't invite anyone you know, you must be very special to be invited to meet the council. The messenger fainted and fawned around him trying to impress him and hoping to persuade him to go. He was most surprised when Tom said:

"Yes, of course I'll go, just stop being so creepy."

Tom was guided through the bailey by the sycophantic messenger and then up to the central keep of the castle and shown into the council chamber. The High Elders all looked at him in astonishment. He was so small, they thought, how could he be 'the one'?

As usual, the clerk to the Elder of Elders spoke first.

"Thomas Jones, son of Llewellyn the Brave, welcome to the Council of the High Elders. All rise for the Elder of Elders."

The door behind the 'throne' opened and in swept the Elder of Elders. Dressed all in dark grey with his hood pulled well forward obscuring his face, his long black cloak flowing behind him. No one could see any part of him, not his face, a hand, a finger or even a toe. He was, as usual, hidden from all.

The clerk turned towards Tom and spoke again, but not in his normal formal, high, and mighty voice, but in an altogether softer, friendly, almost warm tone.

"Well young Tom, first things first, how are you? We hope you're enjoying your stay in the Land of Trymyll."

He sounded very awkward as if speaking in a friendly tone was totally alien to him. He was struggling, something Tom noticed at once, much to Tom's amusement.

"Yes, well, it's very different from Wales," he said, "I have seen some very strange sights in my travels. I must ask my father about them when we meet."

'Aha'! He thought, 'that will throw them off the track'.

They were all staring at them, and when he said it, Aneta Stepanek smiled.

"Tell us, young Tom, where have you been these many weeks since you suddenly disappeared into the thin air of Merrick's Wood?" she asked.

Tom remembered what his father had said and repeated what he had told him, almost word for word. What if they asked him who this 'true and powerful wizard 'was? What would he say? To him, it seemed the obvious next question, but for some reason, no one asked it.

There were more questions, questions about his magic training and what he had learnt, they asked about his flying and how that was coming along. All the questions seemed sort of normal and ordinary to him. Why were they not asking any awkward ones?

What they all seemed to be avoiding was the question of the ring. It was almost like it was the elephant in the room, they talked around the subject, everyone knew what the subject was, but for some reason, no one liked to mention it by name. So, Tom asked them.

"Don't you want to ask me about the ring of the elders?"

There was an inaudible gasp in the room. All the elder's immediately broke eye contact with him as if they really didn't want to know.

"How do you know its name?" asked the clerk.

"Llewel the Elder told me," he lied as he didn't want to get Flintock into trouble.

This time there was an audible gasp which went around the room. For some reason, they seemed genuinely shocked that he knew the name.

"Why is everyone looking so weird and angry?" he asked.

"Oh no, young Tom, we, no, they are not angry with you, they are shocked that Llewel told you its name, and just as amazed that you spoke its name, for just by speaking its name while wearing the ring can invoke great magic. So powerful is the ring, that one would not normally name it in the presence of the wearer.

'Weirdos' thought Tom.

"Well, do you want it back or not?" Tom was becoming bored. It had taken them over an hour and a half to avoid the subject.

"Well, yes, if you would be so kind as to remove the ring and place it in this small oaken ring box, one would be most obliged."

The clerk held out a box at arm's length averting his eyes at the same time as if receiving something dirty or dangerous, or as if by looking at the ring he might be turned to stone or a pillar of salt.

Tom took off the ring and placed it in the small casket. The clerk closed the box and handed it to the Elder. Tom felt the atmosphere in the room change. Now there were hostile mumblings all around the chamber. He realised that the ring had been protecting him somehow from questions he could not answer, now he no longer had the ring he could feel anger and resentment in the room, now they wanted explanations, they wanted to know more. Brangwen Binnion was first to her feet.

"May we question the boy more? Where has he been all these months? Who is this 'true and powerful wizard anyway?"

But before he could finish, the Elder rose from his seat and left the room.

"Council of High Elders is now dismissed," said the clerk.

They all looked at each other perplexed and in shock.

"But we haven't had a chance to question the boy properly," several of them shouted.

As if from a preprepared script, the clerk then declared.

"The boy Thomas is a minor of only thirteen summers, we have no power or authority to cross-examine or question him further as he has committed no crime. Council dismissed!" he said firmly.

And that was the end of that. Tom left the chamber, his dad was waiting outside, they hurried away and around the corner out of sight before any of the others came out and apparated away back to the place they called home leaving the elder's to argue amongst themselves.

"Well that was fun," said Tom.

"No awkward questions then?"

"Well, all the time I was wearing the ring it was going really well, but as soon as the ring was off my finger, the whole atmosphere changed. They all became quite agitated and were shouting questions about who you were and where I had been and why I hadn't handed over their precious ring sooner. But as soon as they started, the bloke in the middle just dismissed them and told them they had no authority to question a kid of thirteen."

"That would have been the ring I expect," Llewellyn said to reassure him, "it would protect the wearer from any hostility when required."

"Well, it didn't protect me from that idiot Llewel very much."

"I know that you don't like him, but I've told you before, please don't be rude," Llewellyn said, much to Tom's surprise.

Tom smiled sheepishly, apologised, and then told his dad about the time Llewel had tried to wipe his mind of a conversation they were having about the ring, and the spell bounced back and Llewel couldn't remember what they were talking about at all. They both had to giggle at that one.

The dark wizard they had captured in the Dragonlands was one Arvel Mordecai. A not extraordinarily talented wizard from Tywyll, home of Asmodeus. Llewellyn had deposited him in the dungeons of Castell y Blaenoraid upon their return and destroyed his wand. He was a grumpy little wizard, very badly turned out with no pride in his appearance and a distinct lack of personal hygiene. To put it bluntly, he was a small, dirty, and smelly wizard.

A couple of days after his arrival at Blaenoraid he was brought up for trial. A trial in Blaenoraid would be before three of the High Elders who would act as both judge and jury. Their word was final and there was no right of appeal. The prosecution was presented by the clerk to the court, who just happened to be the clerk to the Elder of Elders as well. There was no defence lawyer, in this court, you had to fend for yourself. More serious crimes, such as murder were heard before the whole of the council, and there, the accused was allowed an intercessor. But although this was a serious crime, it was not serious enough for the whole council. It was held in the council chamber. Today's judge and jury were High Elder Aneta Stepanek, High Elder Traveon Baughan and the newly appointed High Elder of Wrth y Môr, Trevonn Brice, who had already replaced the now-disgraced Llewel, the former High Elder of 'The Castle by the Sea'.

The whole hearing was of course completely pointless, Aneta Stepanek already knew exactly what had gone on by probing the weak, feeble mind of Arvel Mordecai, Aneta Stepanek was after all, from the City of Enlightenment. She could not be lied to as she already knew all she needed to know. But still, the little charade went on. If there are two things Trymyll loves, it is procedures and bureaucracy, and a trial is procedure and bureaucracy at its best.

The only witnesses were, of course, Llewellyn and his two boys.

The clerk to the court asked him first to explain his side of the story.

"Well me Lady," he said addressing Aneta Stepanek who was chairing the trial, "it was just by happenstance that I come across the two dragons in distress, oh it was such a pitiful sight, it tugged at me heartstrings, so I had to do something to help, and it was while I was attempting to free the poor beasts that these two," he nodded towards Jon and Tom, "came along and interfered, messing up my chance to save them."

"And how might you explain how they became trapped and chained?"

"Well, it was them, the two boys, they set a trap for the poor creatures and captured them."

"Surely you do not expect the court to believe that two minors, acolytes aged thirteen and fifteen with little magical power could entrap a Golden Dragon and her whelp?"

"Well, their dad was with 'em, he was the ringleader, obviously," his voice trailed off at the end as if he couldn't believe his story either, "yeah, their dad planned the whole thing."

"But earlier, you said that the two minors arrived after you and interfered with your rescue attempt."

"Did I? Well, I got confused, they were there all the time."

"And what of the three Blue Dragons? Did they also just arrive by happenstance?" she said with a hint of sarcasm.

"Oh no yer honours, he replied sounding the H, "they was theirs. It's obvious," (well obvious to Arvel Mordecai at least), "there was three of them and three Blue Dragons, obviously they owned one each," his voice rising as if a question.

"But it is well known and factual that no wizard was ever owned or aligned with a Blue Dragon, the best you could hope for is a temporary deal, which the Blue Dragons probably wouldn't stick to anyway," quipped the new High Elder Trevonn Brice, "it is further known that Llewellyn the Brave is already affiliated with a Purple Dragon called Howel, and you cannot associate yourself with another unless the bond is broken by death."

"Oh, poor 'owel, is he dead then?"

The clerk looked toward Llewellyn and asked.

"Can you tell us of any malady or concerns over the wellbeing of the Purple Dragon named Howel?"

"Howel is alive and well and sitting at my feet in the guise of a Jack Russell. If the court would allow him to revert from what he considers a most indecorous position, he could reveal his full and healthy self," he said with a wide grin.

"No, that will not be necessary thank you," said the clerk, but without any smile.

Howel jumped up onto the table. He may have been small, but his deep baritone and frightfully posh voice filled the chamber, "It is indeed most incongruous for me, a fine example of a Purple Dragon to be appearing in the guise of a small dog, especially a half breed like a Jack Russell, but I can speak for myself. I am in exceptionally fine fettle; indeed, I am in my prime, and definitely not yet in a state of demise."

"Thank you Howel," the clerk said, sounding a little apprehensive that there was, potentially at least, a sixty-foot dragon in the chamber.

And so, it went on for hour after hour of procedural interruptions and bureaucratic interventions, conventions and precedents, hours, and hours. Everyone, except for the High Elders were now very bored with the whole procedure, even Arvel Mordecai, who then made a most unusual intervention.

"All right, I give up. Before I die of boredom, I confess, it was me, I was trying to capture the whelp to sell on the black market. Golden Dragon whelps sell for a large sack of gold if you find the right buyer."

"But we have so many more questions, and we haven't even

asked the adult witness his side of the story yet," High Elder Traveon Baughan said, almost sadly.

"Well now you don't have to. I confess it was me. Job done."

"The court will retire to consider its verdict. All rise," the clerk barked.

They all stood up and the three High Elders left the council chamber courtroom.

Howel made a hasty exit through the door and bolted out of the castle, POP! He was away, stretching every muscle he could think of while flying off into the distance. His destination involved an ox, but we won't go into the details.

The next morning, they all assembled in court again, all except Howel that is, he had a bad case if indigestion!

"All rise for the High Elders."

In they paraded and sat to give their verdict. High Elder Aneta Stepanek spoke, "This court finds you, Arvel Mordecai guilty by confession of attempting to capture a Golden Dragon whelp with a view to selling on the black market. You are hereby sentenced to ten years in custody with supervised labour in the Sanctuary for Orphaned Dragons. With compliant behaviour, you could apply for release in five years." Aneta banged down her gavel on the bench, "court dismissed!"

"But yer Honour, I'm innocent, it was them," he pleaded pointing at the family Jones.

"The case is closed, yesterday you confessed to your crimes. The court is dismissed," she said firmly.

And that was that. Arvel Mordecai was enclosed in the iron cage which then descended to the dungeons below. The boys hoped that was the last they would see of him for a long, long time. They knew that they too had made an enemy.

CHAPTER 19 - LLEWEL'S REVENGE.

High Elder Llewel, was now just poor old Wizard Llewel. His rise to fame and fortune thwarted by his own incompetence, ineptitude, inability, inadequacy, incapability, incapacity, incompetence, insufficiency, and several other words beginning with 'in'. Unfortunately, that is not the way he viewed matters pertaining to his downfall. The small squeaky-voiced wizard was now even more obnoxious than before. Now he was vengeful, vindictive, spiteful, malicious, mean, resentful, and wanting to get even. He blamed everyone but himself for what had happened. In total denial of his own responsibility, he blamed the Council of the High Elders, he blamed Flintock the Elder, he blamed Llewellyn the Brave, but most of all he blamed Tom. If only he knew his whole and proper name, he could have hexed him by now, but he didn't. Or at least, if he did, he had forgotten it.

Following a short period of incarceration in the castle dungeons, he was released just twenty-four hours later. To him, it was a great injustice, a humiliation, and one which would not be forgotten or forgiven.

Now, just as had been predicted, he went around stirring up trouble for the Jones', especially for Tom and his dad. He would spout off any who would listen, and there were many who would.

"What has changed?" he would say, "the so-called wonder boy has been here for months now, nothing has changed, magic is still draining away from us. I tell you, the boy's a fake. He has no magic of his own, I don't even think he is Tom Jones at all. For a start he's not Llewellyn's firstborn, Jonathan is, and we all know Jonathan knows no magic, not even a cantrip! If you ask me their father is just the same, Llewellyn the Brave? We've only got his word for it, no one ever saw him fighting dwarfs after all. For all we know he might have never even met one!"

"Thomas's appearance before the Council of Elders was a complete sham. He couldn't answer any of their questions in a coherent nature, kept changing his story every time. High Elder Aneta Stepanek knew the truth, but she wasn't allowed to ask questions at all.

"He and his brother went to the Dragonlands, they teamed up with some Blue Dragons and captured a Golden Dragon and her whelp, and then pinned the blame on poor old Arvel Mordecai."

"If he were here now, I could prove my point. The boy has no magic and neither does his brother, firstborn of Llewellyn the coal miner!"

Unfortunately, in their world as in our own, if you say something often enough and with enough passion, people start to believe you. Then they start repeating the story, often adding their own embellishments. One was overheard saying…

"He's been here for six months now and things are now worse than ever. He's not the firstborn like what the prophesy talks about. I've heard he's not Llewellyn's son at all."

"You know he's nowt but a common thief, tried to keep the ring for himself. Took 'em months to find him and then they had to remove the ring by force."

…and another, "I heard he attacked a Golden Dragon with three Blue Dragons and killed her and her whelp. Shame on him, he should be banished for life. But instead, he stitched up poor old Marvin Mordecai, and he got sent down for twenty years hard labour in the quarries."

He couldn't even get Arvel's name correct and the fact the quarries had not been worked for several hundred years was only a minor detail to be ignored!

Within a few weeks, half the land seemed to be turning against Tom and his family. They found it difficult to travel or even go to market, the boys were jostled and abused but as usual, no one said anything directly to Llewellyn because like all bullies, they were also cowards. But things were about to take a turn for the worse.

The two boys were in the city of Dolydd, where High Elder Brangwen Binning was in charge, who should they bump into but their old friend Llewel the loser, as they now called him. Tom was fuming when he saw him.

Oi Llewel!" Tom shouted, "Why are you spreading lies about me and my family you horrid little wizard?"

Llewel remained calm and confident, now was his chance. Revenge at last. There was a good-sized crowd here, quite enough to cause quite a stir, enough to whip up a mob and cause a lot of trouble.

"I am only telling the truth boy," he said disparagingly with his whining sneery voice, "you have no real magic and your brother here is a phobl. Huh! He could hardly muster a cantrip strong enough to light a match.

Jon held his staff aloft and a sheet of flame spread out in every direction above the heads of the crowd, hurting no one, and singeing nothing, but they all felt the heat.

"I think I lit that match quite well," said Jon smugly.

"What is your problem Llewel?" asked Tom.

"My problem is, that since you arrived the magic has not only been slipping away, but it is also now leaving at a faster pace than ever before. Your job was to stop it!" he said jabbing his finger in their direction but as always keeping his distance.

"Well mine is not diminishing, when I arrived in Trymyll I had no magic, didn't even believe in magic," the crowd gasped at such heresy, "my magic is growing daily along with Jon's and several other true and trustworthy wizards. How is your magic?"

"How dare you ask me, a former High Elder, how my magic is doing! I'll show you if you wish."

With that he shot a bolt of energy straight at them, Jon banged his staff on the ground and they, and the immediate crowd were enclosed in a hemisphere of impenetrable reflective shield, Llewel's bolt ricocheted off and up into the air.

"Don't be stupid Llewel, you could hurt or even kill someone doing that in a crowded place," Jon shouted

"Oh, I intend to, but it will be you and your brother who will get hurt."

"No Llewel, you can't tell where a ricocheted shot will go. It won't hit us, but it might hit someone else."

"Then you will be to blame for defecting it won't you."

Even with the threat of imminent death or injury, the crowd was still cheering Llewel on and jeering at the boys.

"In that case, we lay down our staffs, we don't want anyone to get hurt, not even you."

Tom and Jon both laid their staffs on the ground where they turned into wands again. Even Llewel would not attack two unarmed boys, he was tempted, but thought better of it. There is only so far he could carry the crowd.

"Quick, grab them and their wands. We will take them up to the castle and set them before my particularly good friend High Elder Brangwen Binning."

The boys were set upon, jostled, bound, and escorted up to the castle with Llewel leading the triumphant procession.

"You won't get away with this Llewel, we've done nothing

wrong and you know it!" Tom shouted.

"Don't be so cocky boy, you attacked me in broad daylight and everyone here was a witness. Bangers Binning and I go way back, she is both judge and jury in Dolydd. I think I hold all the trump cards this time.

They were indeed taken before High Elder Brangwen Binning, as soon as Tom saw her, he remembered that she was the one who went off on one as soon as he had handed the ring over. So possibly not the best High Elder to be brought before.

After the formal greetings, Llewel started the proceedings.

"High Elder Binning, I was, as usual, minding my own business in the town this morning when I was accosted by these youths, shouting insults, and threatening me. When I tried to reason with them, they unleashed a bolt of energy which I was, of course, able to deflect away from the crowd with my superior magic. Before they could act again, the fine people of Dolydd putting themselves in great personal danger, managed to overpower and disarm them."

High Elder Brangwen Binning eyed the boys up and down, "What do you have to say for yourselves?" she said with a malevolent sneer.

"That's a lie, he attacked us, and we deflected the shot, and when we told him to stop in case someone got hurt, he just laughed and told us that would be our fault not his, so we laid down our wands. And...."

"Silence," said Brangwen Binning, "how dare you call my fine wizard friend a liar. I've heard enough. Take them to the dungeons while I think about what to do with them or how to dispose of them. Attempted murder is a serious matter!"

Tom and Jon didn't like the sound of that, but what could they do. No wands, no magic. They were taken down and down and down to what must have been a hundred feet below the ground and thrown, quite literally, into a cell. There was one candle, no other light as they were so deep below ground. Once that went out, they would be in complete and utter darkness.

Tom started to snivel, small tears falling onto his cheeks.

"If we had our wands, we could be out of here in a flash," Jon said.

"If a wand is taken away unjustly, then it will return to its owner," said Tom. Then in unison, they said it.

"Wand!" and their wands appeared.

"Right, let's get out of here," Jon said, "we'll apparate back to Blaenoraid and tell dad what's happened."

They both visualised the place they called home and envisioned themselves being there, but nothing happened.

"Damn!" exclaimed Tom, "the walls, floor and roof must be run through with cold iron to stop people escaping. Now what?"

"Well, magic works in the cold iron cage, it just can't get out of it. So, here's an idea, only an idea mind you, so don't get too excited. Next time a guard comes to check on us, just before he opens the peaky-hole thing, make ourselves disappear, invisible like, when he can't see us in here, he'll open the door to see where we're hiding. With me so far?

"Yes," replied Tom.

"When he sees the dungeon is empty, he'll run to get help or form a search party or whatever they do when someone escapes. Well, when he does that, we just slip out, find a way to the surface, and skedaddle. Plan or what?"

"Good plan apart from one thing. What if he slams the door shut as he runs out in panic?"

"Good point. Let me think," Jon thought for a while and then..., "the door opens inward and so it is then inside the cold iron cage and within our domain. As soon as the door opens, hex the lock to jam it so it won't lock even if he slams the door."

"Good one. But once we are outside the door, surely we could apparate from there?"

"Worth a try, if we can't, just keep moving until we can," Jon said.

After a couple of hours, a guard came along, "Governor wants you two back upstairs, it's judgement day. Hope your wearing brown underpants...," He stopped mid-sentence, not bothering with the peaky-hole thing, he just swung open the door to be faced with an empty cell. He turned on his heels and ran off shouting.

"Escaped Prisoners! Call out the guard! Escaped Prisoners! Call out the guard!" leaving the door wide open.

"Well, that bit was easy. Let's hope the next bit is as well," Jon quipped.

No such luck, they stepped out, tried to apparate, nothing, "Right, stay visible so we can see each other, wands at the ready, let's see how far we can get."

They hurried off in the same direction they arrived in.

"Footsteps!" Jon whispered, "go invisible and float to the ceiling. Lie as flat as you can."

Six guards ran down the corridor towards the dungeon as if to check that what the first guard had said was true.

"Split up and start searching," the sergeant at arms shouted, "they can't have got far and they ain't got no wands."

"We need a way out, quickly," Tom whispered, and then added as an aside, "got any ideas wand?" he hadn't expected an answer, but he got one anyway. The wands changed to staffs and then flew off at high speed, the two boys hanging on for all they were worth. They flew straight into the guardroom, which fortunately was empty, over to the huge inglenook fireplace and then straight up the chimney. Whoosh, out into the fresh air. It was a dark night, pitch-black dark, they and their staffs were covered in soot, the perfect camouflage. No one saw their leaving or suspected a thing.

As soon as they were clear, there was a small pop as they apparated back to base in the depths of Blaenoraid.

Excitedly they told their dad about all that had happened.

"Revolting little man, and to think I was trying to give him the benefit of the doubt. I think this needs sorting once and for all, I should involve the council, but that would mean involving Bangers Binning. Strange lady, in many ways far too political for a farmer, and yet she puts on her 'Jolly Farmer' facade for all to see. Never thought she would team up with Llewel though," Llewellyn stopped short of addressing him as Llewel the Loser.

"Yet not a word in his defence when Llewel returned to Blaenoraid and was called before the council. I wonder what she's playing at. Surely, she's not after the top job too?" Llewellyn said, mainly to himself.

Llewellyn knew who his main ally was. Aneta Stepanek, nothing was hidden from her.

CHAPTER 20. LLEWEL THE LOSER.

Flintock had returned home to Wrth y Môr. He enjoyed life by the sea, even if there wasn't one there. He was the senior of the seven elders who came under High Elder Trevonn Brice. Trevonn Brice had been elected High Elder following the downfall of Llewel the Loser, although he would not say it out loud, Flintock quite liked the new title that Tom and Jon had given the diminutive wizard. He had himself been nominated for the post of High Elder, but he refused to stand. He had all the power he needed as a very accomplished and gifted wizard, he was far more powerful than any of the High Elders, but he did not want all the politics, bickering and the stupidity of their procedural bureaucracy. He was more than happy being an Elder, he did not want a high office as well.

Wrth y Môr was a peaceful little city, always an abundant supply of fresh fish, Pike, Brown Trout, Perch, Zander, Eels from the freshwater rivers which fed the sea and of course, an abundance of fish from the vast saltwater lake. Flintock liked to eat fish, he liked to catch fish and he liked to mess about in boats, he just liked peace and quiet, he and Trig chose the quiet bachelor life and enjoyed it. Unfortunately, Llewellyn, as usual, had other plans for his friend.

He and Tryg sat quietly in an alehouse garden by the sea watching the little waves splash gently on the pebble beach. He had his ale; he had his long clay pipe and a full stomach. Tryg, like all trygalls, did not take alcohol, so instead sipped on a cool fruit and herb drink of his own design. What more could they want?

"Hail to you Elder Flintock, and hello Tryg."

Llewellyn's voice boomed across the garden. Flintock had half a mind to apparate away but decided that would be very rude, and it would leave poor Tryg there, Tryg, of course, could disappear into a wisp of smoke if he wished, but that would also be rude. So, he stayed sitting there and gave Llewellyn a very world-weary smile and returned the greeting.

"Hail to you too Llewellyn, old friend," he paused for a second and sighed, "don't tell me, let me guess, you have a small favour to ask."

"But yes, how did you know," Llewellyn said with a smile, "am I that obvious?"

"It is normally the only reason you seek me out, otherwise, you leave me to live out my lonely existence here on my own."

The two men hugged, it was only banter, Flintock was as usual, pleased to see his friend, but he had just settled back home after the last adventure and was not ready for another just yet. Llewellyn was tall, just over six feet, he shared the red hair of his boys, Flinty however had a good three inches on him and was much more powerfully built, his black skin shone in the sunshine, especially his shaved head which complimented his short and well trimmed beard.

"It's your ex, he's giving a little trouble to my boys."

"My ex?" I don't have an ex!" he exclaimed.

"I'm talking about your old friend Llewel."

"Oh him? Well he's not my ex as you call him and he's not my old friend either," he then added for good measure, "and he never will be."

Llewellyn set invisible magic boundaries about them and filled them with white noise so no one could eavesdrop on their conversation. It was beautifully quiet and peaceful within the boundary, but anyone trying to eavesdrop in would just hear an indiscernible hissing note. He then told the tale of the two boys and their capture, imprisonment, and subsequent escape from Dolydd Castle.

"I'm as much worried about Bangers Binning as Llewel. She was very complicit in this affair. There was, what can only be called a show trial, with only Bangers as judge and only Llewel being allowed to speak. She then threw two minors into a dungeon which is illegal. She made vague threats about what was to happen to them and put them in fear of their lives. For a legal trial, there should be one High Elder and two elders as a minimum. She had no right to put the boys on trial anyway, not without them having parental representation, so the whole thing was a sham."

"So, what do you want me to do?" Flintock asked.

"I don't actually know. But we need those two closely watched, see if and what they are plotting together. Llewel certainly had the crowd going and he is stirring up dissent amongst townsfolk all over Trymyll. I know you have a good network of trusted people, both elders and wizards. Can you see what you can find out, not only in Dolydd but in all the towns and cities where Llewel has been stirring up trouble."

"Can't the council just bring Llewel in for questioning, even if Binning was at council, she wouldn't show her hand there."

"Well yes, we could ask for that, but I don't think we would find out anything from either of them, Llewel would lie through his teeth and Bangers would back him up whilst denying anything and everything. Let's face it, the lady farmer didn't even speak up or defend Llewel when he was last before the council, so I'm not sure yet what game she is playing. And if someone is controlling their minds, then that could easily obfuscate Aneta from seeing the truth."

"Good point. I'll put out some feelers and see what I can find out. I don't want to go myself as both Llewel and Binning know me too well and I appreciate that you can't go for the same reason."

"No, I can't go because next time I see the little midget wizard, I might end it there and then on the spot."

"Another good point," said Flintock.

Flintock sat there quietly, head bowed, for a good five minutes, his staff resting across his lap, the stone set firmly on the top pulsing light in different colours. If you listened carefully you could hear what sounded like a babble of voices chatting over a bad phone line with all the wires crossed with everyone listening and talking to each other at the same time.

"My team is now alert and tapping into their own little webs for information."

"How's the new boss? Shaping up well I hope as I need a new ally, not another enemy."

"You'll be all right with Bricey, He's one of us. Straight and true as an arrow. Or I wouldn't have let him get the job."

"Excellent" Llewellyn smiled.

Llewellyn knew that what Flintock had said was true, Flintock had in the past always had such a great sway in the 'democratic' decisions of Wrth y Môr, that it was hardly worth going through the process. They should just ask him who will win and save all the bother of an election.

"You'll let me know when you have some news then?"

"Sure will. I'll send you a Jackdaw."

Llewellyn dropped the boundary of sound, finished his beer, said his goodbyes, and disappeared. No one else in the garden was any the wiser.

It was a two days before Llewellyn received news from Flintock.

"News from Flintock the Elder," the Jackdaw announced, "Hight Elder Binning and Llewel had an interesting visitor for afternoon tea today, one Asmodeus, the Dark High Elder! We are attempting to find out why."

Interesting indeed, thought Llewellyn, perhaps I might involve at least some of the council.

On what can only be described as a group conference call using the 'neither here nor there' trick, Llewellyn, Aneta Stepanek, Traveon Baughan and the new High Elder Trevonn Brice conversed. Llewellyn first told them the story of what had happened to his sons when they visited Dolydd. How High Elder, Brangwen Binning had imprisoned the boys and of their escape, but without detailing the actual escape. All three were as shocked and horrified by what had happened, as they should have been. He then disclosed that Llewel and Binning were in conference with Asmodeus. That surprised them even more.

"What do you want us to do Llewellyn?" asked Aneta Stepanek

"Nothing now, I am just making you aware as High Elders of what has happened so that you may use your own good offices to see what you can find out as well. I don't see that we can do anything anyway, it's not illegal to have a meeting with Asmodeus, just unwise. It is illegal to set up a sham court against minors but moving against them now could stop us finding out what is going on between the three of them. They would deny everything and anything anyway."

"Okay, it's agreed then, we keep our heads down until we have more information," Aneta Stepanek said with authority. Llewellyn loved the way that she always assumed the lead role. He was sure that she would one day be the Elder of Elders.

"I have spoken to Aneta Stepanek, Traveon Baughan and Trevonn Brice" Llewellyn told Flintock, "they have agreed, or maybe they were told by Aneta Stepanek, to do nothing until we have more information and some idea what the three of them are up to," reported Llewellyn.

"It is quite out of character for Binning to behave like this, what do you think has happened to her for such a dramatic personality change?" Flintock asked.

"I don't know, but I do know it's beyond Llewel's powers to bend her mind, it may be the work of Asmodeus, but I don't even think he is capable or powerful enough to change Banger's personality."

"Perhaps then there is a force at work here we don't yet know about." concluded Flintock.

"My theory exactly, my friend, my theory exactly," Llewellyn repeated.

Llewellyn returned to the place they called home, and to his boys. Both were now becoming very accomplished wizards, far more powerful than many wizards twice or even three times their age. He was pleased with and proud of them. Jon had really connected with his wand and was able to do some amazing magic. The two boys worked as a team and complimented and balanced each other perfectly. Jon was feisty and ready for a fight, ready to defend themselves and others come what may. Tom was a gentler soul, always trying to find a way out without violence. It's not that he couldn't fight, he could, he could summon fire dragons, and if so controlled, the fire dragons could destroy whole villages and the people in them, not that Tom ever would. He could send mighty bolts of power enough to vaporise solid rock, but Tom was a healer, he liked to repair, restore, rebuild, regrow, and renew. Where Jon was impulsive, Tom was contemplative in character. Both, however, had learnt too the power of a good strategy. Often, they would come up with diametrically opposed ideas on a problem, but sometimes, taking bits from one, and pieces from the other, they were unstoppable.

"Hi boys, sorry to be away so long, busy, busy, lots to do."

"You've only been gone a couple of days, we've been fine, we've been using the training room to hone a few skills. But now you mention it, where have you been?" asked Jon.

Llewellyn told hem of his meeting with Flintock, his virtual meeting with Aneta Stepanek, Traveon Baughan and Trevonn Brice and all they had found out and what had gone on. But they were not going to do anything until they had more information.

"But that scag Binning threw us in a dungeon. Can't you arrest her or something?" remonstrated Jon.

"No, or at least not yet. We need more information first. She may have been acting under duress or have had her mind altered in some way."

"Well she seemed happy enough when she threw us in the dungeon," added Tom.

"Yes, maybe, but I've known Bangers Binning for a long, long time, she's just not malicious, it's not in her nature, she's a happy gentle soul. She does love to get involved in the politics of Trymyll, she is after all, a High Elder, but at heart, she just likes to be a farmer."

"Perhaps we could help, go back to Dolydd cloaked and disguised and see what we can find out?"

"No, bad idea, if you get caught again, Llewel might just let the mob sort you out. Individually, there's a chance he could take you on, especially you Tom, you always try to find a peaceful, non-violent solution. Whereas Jon has good defensive and attacking techniques and is not worried about using them, but Llewel has both the experience and the mob on his side. With you two together, he wouldn't stand a chance. But you might get separated, and that would be just too dangerous."

The boys listened intently, knowing that every word their dad spoke was true, knowing that every word their dad had said was going to be ignored. As soon as Llewellyn left in the morning, they were gone too.

Tom and Jon flew high over the town. To anyone looking up, they would look like a couple of birds circling in the thermal up-currents. Dressed in their light absorbing black, detail was difficult to pick out, so they circled high above looking down on the town unnoticed. Their clothing was such that they could walk quite openly amongst people and if they had their hoods up, not many would even notice them pass. But they didn't rely on it, so they cloaked themselves invisible before descending into the town. It wasn't long before they heard Llewel spouting off in his normal manner.

"Those vile boys who attacked me must have bribed one of the guards and made their escape. I doubt if they can fly or apparate, so they are probably still in the town. I'll give a bag of silver to whoever locates them so they can be locked up again."

How little he knew, the boys thought, they could out fly Llewel any day. Especially as, when Llewel did deign to fly, it was always only a few feet off the ground in case he fell off or suddenly lost the ability. They were tempted to fly past him at speed to see if he would follow and then give him eye-watering aerobatics display just to show off. But decided against it.

They stayed invisible and flew into the castle to see what Binning was up to. Once inside, they dropped the invisibleness, their hooded cloaks made them appear almost invisible anyway, especially in the dim light of the castle farm, so they did not expect to be seen, and like their dad had told them, holding invisibility takes a great deal of concentration. They needed to be one hundred per cent alert and on the lookout, not concentrating on their invisibility. They hunted high and low but couldn't find Binning. She wasn't in her rooms, no sign of her in the great hall or in her offices either. The boys decided to have a look around the farmyard and the farm. Nothing.

"Perhaps she's down in the dungeons trying to work out how we escaped?" said Jon.

"Okay, let's have a peek down below."

They walked silently down towards the dungeons, past the guardroom, which was full of guards, but none of them seemed to either notice or care. Down and down they went until they found the dungeons where they had been incarcerated a couple of days earlier. It was there that they found Binning. She was as they though looking for a way of escape, but not in the way they imagined. Binning was chained hand and foot to the wall with no way out. The boys didn't know what to do. They couldn't leave her here, but they couldn't do anything to help either. They whispered to each other to go retreat, re-group and decide what to do next. But as they turned to leave, Llewel and a couple of guards were walking down the dark corridor towards them. They went invisible and floated to the ceiling, daring not to make a sound or even breath. They were sure that their heartbeats could be heard in the next village, but Llewel just passed underneath, unlocked the door, and entered the dungeon with two guards. The door swung shut, keys still in the lock. It was too good an opportunity, so they floated down, and quietly locked the door. Tom waved his wand a little, muttered and then they flew off down the corridor and out the way they had come flying straight out of the town to a safe distance before restoring visibility and breathing normally again. Then they collapsed with laughter.

What were you doing after we locked the door waving your wand about?" asked Jon.

"Oh, nothing really, just soundproofing the door, so the guards won't hear Llewel's squeaky little screams when he realises what has happened."

They both burst out laughing again.

"Right, now what do we do?" Tom asked.

"Well, we can't just leave Binning there, dad was right, Llewel or someone more powerful is using her and has her under their control. Do you think it's Asmodeus?"

"Possibly or possibly not. I know we'll be in deep poop, but we have to find dad and tell him what's happened," Tom said, knowing what was coming next.

"No, we have to go back and rescue Binning, we can't just leave her there," exclaimed Jon.

"Well, we could have, if we hadn't locked Llewel in the dungeon. Now he knows someone is onto him. We may have made things worse. We really need dad now," Tom said insistently.

After a few more 'buts', Jon reluctantly agreed and they disappeared, reappearing just outside the city wall, and walked in past the guards, who didn't notice them entering. It took them ages, but eventually, they found their dad with Flintock and Tryg in the alehouse deep in discussion. They interrupted.

"You did what?!?!" their father exploded, "what did I tell you only last night! I said you were not to go there under any circumstances!"

Despite being enclosed in one of Llewellyn's sound traps, people on the tables near looked round to see what the commotion was all about.

Once he had quietened down and Flintock had reminded him of what they would have done in the same circumstances and gave a few examples from their youth, Llewellyn settled down and smiled.

"Yes, you're right, tell a teenager they can't do something, then they always will."

"Well we always did," added Flintock, "shall we muster the troops?"

"No, I think we'll sort this one out ourselves. If we go in mob-handed, we may be surprised by what we find. If we go in quietly, we may get away with it."

"What do you mean by that?" asked Tom

"By what?"

"We may get away with it. Mainly the word 'may'."

"Oh, just a turn of phrase. But you can never be sure of success. Now you two have alerted Llewel that someone is onto him, he may set a trap."

"Sorry," Tom said quietly, "so what's the plan?"

"Well, the first part of the plan is that you two don't get involved and stay well away from it, and this time I mean it!"

"Okay," they said sheepishly. 'Yeah right' is what they meant.

They all returned quickly to the place they called home. Llewellyn apparated in Flintock and Tryg as he still had not revealed the whereabouts.

"First, we have to know the layout of the castle. I know where the main rooms are, but I've never had the pleasure of a visit to the dungeons. Jon and Tom," he looked up at the boys, "sketch out everything you can remember about the dungeons, starting right back at the entrance to them, where the guards hang out and all in as much detail as possible. Flinty and I will then discuss how we go about getting Bangers out and hopefully Llewel in for keeps."

The boys sat down with a ballpoint pen and a pad of paper and tried to sketch out the layout. It really wasn't that good. They tried to imagine the layout in their minds so the pen could draw it. But it wouldn't. It was useless. Jon, who was easily frustrated by tiny setbacks swept everything off the table and across the room. The pen smashed against the wall.

"What did you do that for Jon? That was my only pen, not that I ever used it. Now you'll have to use an old dipping pen and paper."

Llewellyn gave him a quill, and ink bottle and some old parchment paper. They tried again, this time the pen zipped across the page drawing the whole layout of the dungeons and castle with incredible detail, even showing secret doors and passages and naming all the guards and others with their current positions right down to Llewel, two guards and Bangers, all still stuck in the cell.

"This is good," said Llewellyn to Flintock, "too good. If they are all still in the cell and we act quickly, we could kill several birds with one stone. And I've changed my mind about you two coming as well. I could use a particular skill which only Tom has."

"Bring the map, it's updating every time someone moves." Flintock added.

"You're not dressed right!" exclaimed Jon.

"Meaning what?" his dad asked.

"Well, we adapted our wardrobes to this light-absorbing black and we walk about unnoticed by most people, you should do the same."

Jon produced his wand and worked on the two grown-up's clothes. Soon they also were hard to see at all. Flintock, with his already ebony complexion, even harder to see. In the dim light of the dungeons, they would be all but invisible.

They apparated in as a group.

"Right," Llewellyn whispered, "meet at the top of the stairs which lead down to the dungeons. I'll lead, Tom with me, Jon take up the rear and keep us covered from the back. Tom, give me the keys."

"What about me?" asked Flintock.

"Can you go to the guardroom and disable all the guards, there are seven of them in there now. But do it quietly and try not to hurt anyone."

"Okay, I'm on to it."

With that, they all disappeared and reappeared at the top of the steps. They moved off silently.

Llewellyn whispered to Tom, "As soon as I unlock the door, freeze everything, then unfreeze me and Jon as soon as you can."

"Yes dad," Tom said with some trepidation. He didn't think he would need Mrs Glyn this time, he was scared already.

Flintock went straight to the guardroom, the door was open and as expected there were seven guards in the room, who were, for some reason, all huddled around an unlit fire. No one noticed his arrival, neither did they notice their departure as they were all apparated away to the far side of Trymyll. Only an incredibly powerful wizard could transport seven people in one go, normally you would need to be touching someone to apparate them, but Flintock was no ordinary wizard. As he once jokingly told Howel when he first met Tom, 'I am a great wizard, I have sight beyond sight, I have powers beyond power and knowledge beyond knowledge', and he meant it.

He then hurried silently along to catch up with the others. As he rounded the last corner Jon let go a bolt of energy which Flintock was only just able to dodge.

"Stop Jon, it's me" he whispered loudly as the bolt ricocheted off the walls taking off chunks of stone as it went before eventually hitting the guardroom and nigh on destroying it.

"Oops, sorry Flintock. You alright? Thought it might be guards."

"Yes, but it was a close one. Good shot by the way," he smiled. Not that anyone could see his mouth in the darkness of their outfits.

"That's probably alerted others that something is amiss in the dungeons. Quick, show me the map, let's see who's where. Oh dear, we seem to have woken up the guard, there are about ten of them heading across the yard towards the main building area and they will discover the empty guardroom, which now also seems to have a wall missing."

"Keep a lookout at the rear and we'll carry on to the cells," Llewellyn could see on the map that Llewel, who had obviously somehow heard the commotion, had moved to behind where the door would open hoping to surprise whoever unlocked the door. Well, the surprise would be his, eventually.

Llewellyn unlocked the door then threw it open with all his strength, knocking Llewel across the room and before he could gather his senses, Tom stepped into the cell and FREEZE! Everything went very still and quiet. Llewel's wand was suspended in mid-air as it flew from his hand when the door crashed into him. Llewel himself was falling and halfway across the room, as soon as he was re-mobilised, he would crash to the ground and probably hurt himself. Tom had no need to free his dad, Jon and Flintock as they were outside the iron enclosed dungeon.

"Why did you rush into the room Tom? That could have been dangerous," his dad asked.

"The room is in a cold iron cage, so I had to be in there for the spell to work."

"Good point."

Llewellyn took Llewel's wand from the mid-air point it hung in and vaporised it completely. Tom then touched Bangers with his wand to free her from the spell, meanwhile, Flintock took off the cold iron chains and reapplied them to Llewel.

"Oh my goodness!" gasped Bangers, "how did you get in here? Why am I here? What happened to Llewel and the guards? They're like statues."

"Stop. Stop," said Llewellyn, "first, we must get you out of here. There are about ten more guards on the way down here, you must tell them to stop and not attack us."

"No, I can't, he's turned them all against me, they won't listen to me anymore."

"Where's your wand?"

She raised her hand, and her wand appeared.

"Good, we may need to fight, but hopefully we can get out of here without anyone getting hurt."

"No, we can't, there's only one way in and out, if guards are in the corridor, we're trapped."

"No we're not, follow me."

They all turned and followed Llewellyn, but instead of turning up the way, he turned and headed further down into the bowels of the earth.

"It's a dead-end, you can't get out this way and we can't apparate because the whole structure is woven with cold iron," Bangers said nervously.

Llewellyn was studying the map, he suddenly stopped, looked at the rough stone wall and with his wand drew the shape of a door. As he did, the blocks of granite all started turning and twisting and a doorway appeared. They all walked through the opening and onto a steep spiral staircase. As the last person stepped through, the stones all folded back and formed a solid impenetrable granite wall again.

"Where did this come from?" Bangers exclaimed, "there are no doors or stairs or anything below the dungeon area. How did you know about that door?"

"I'll explain later, now let's just get out of here and back to Blaenoraid. We can talk then."

Exhausted and panting for breath, they eventually reached the top of the stairs and came across another blank wall. Llewellyn drew a door again with his wand and they all tumbled out into the fresh air right next to the moat which ran around the farmhouse castle. Llewellyn held onto Bangers, and they all apparated away back to Blaenoraid.

CHAPTER 21 - THE PLOT THICKENS.

There was an audible pop as they all appeared back, just outside the city walls of Blaenoraid. They walked to the city gates where the guards at once stood upright and greeted High Elder Brangwen Binning, it was not that they ignored the others, they just didn't see them.

"I must say, your cloaks are quite impressive, one hardly knows you're there unless one is looking for you," Bangers said.

"That's the idea, a little invention of our own," replied Jon.

"Very impressive for one so young. Llewellyn, you must introduce me to your young accomplice, Tom of course I know, we met in the council chamber, but in all the commotion, I have not yet been introduced," she said nodding towards Jon.

"This is my eldest son, Jon."

"But Llewel said they had no magic, he said that Jon couldn't even light a match, he said that Jon was a phobl, and Toms magic was all fake."

"Well I assure you; they are both fine and gifted wizards. They have already slain three Blue Dragons and rescued a Golden Dragon and her whelp from a poacher."

"Llewel and Asmodeus both told me they had none and yet I know they escaped from my dungeon within a couple of hours of being locked up there and returned with you to rescue me from that fool Llewel. The stupid man even managed to lock himself up with me."

"Not him actually," said Tom, "my brother and I locked him in when we came looking for you."

"Came looking for me? Why would you do that? To avenge for what I did to you?"

"No, we had half a hunch that you were not yourself, so we came back to find out why and who was doing it. We found you chained up in your own dungeon but before we could rescue you, Llewel and the two guards came down to see you, I'm afraid we could not resist the temptation and locked him in there with you," said Tom.

"Oh boy, was he mad when he found the door locked, he hollered and screamed in his squeaky little voice, then he got the two guards to do it as well, banging on the door and making such a racket, but for some reason, no one heard the commotion."

"That's because, before we left, I wove a sound-dampening spell around the entire cell, so no one could hear him anyway. In fact, it's still there, so they still can't hear him," Tom laughed as he said it.

"And what about the time freezing spell, for want of a better description? One of yours Llewellyn I expect."

"No, also Tom. As I said, they are both very gifted wizards."

"So, what happened to the Dungeon Guard? I do hope you didn't kill any of them."

"No, luckily they are all safe, just a long way away, I apparated them across to the other side of Trymyll. They should be back in a few days if they walk fast," said Flintock, smiling.

"Why luckily?"

"Sorry," Jon interjected, "I thought we were being attacked and I sent a bolt of energy up the corridor and blew the wall out of the guardroom."

"No matter, walls can be replaced, lives are more precious and harder to replace," she said.

Llewellyn interrupted, "It's late now and the boys must be tired. We'll take you up to the Residency of the High Elders, you can stay there overnight quite safely, and we will talk more on the morrow."

With that, the days business was concluded, Bangers went to the residency, a sort of six-bedroom hotel for visiting High Elders, the boys were sent back to where they were staying to make their own supper and then bed. Llewellyn and Flintock returned to the alehouse where they were interrupted earlier by the boys and continued to talk over another pint of ale and a roast chicken.

Next morning Llewellyn and Flintock went over to the residency to pick up Bangers.

"We are here for High Elder Brangwen Binning," Llewellyn asked the steward, "please tell her that we are here."

"Sorry, you're too late, I'm afraid she's gone."

"Gone? We arranged to pick her up here at 8.00 this morning. When did she leave?"

"About an hour ago, the Elder himself came and collected her, and they left together."

"But that's impossible, are you sure?"

"Oh yes sir, we all know the Elder, it was definitely him."

Llewellyn and Flintock turned and left the same way they came in.

"Why do you think the Elder wanted her? How would he even know she was here?" Flintock asked.

"Simple, it wasn't the Elder who collected her, it was someone else."

"But surely the steward would know?"

"How could he, no one sees his face, not even a finger appears from beneath his cloak. The steward would hardly know his voice as so few have heard him speak. No, our friend Bangers has been escorted out of there by someone just dressed to look like the Elder," Llewellyn said in a very frustrated voice.

"How can you be so sure?"

"Oh, believe me, I know. I was with the Elder at 7.00 this morning."

Flintock didn't pursue the comment but asked, "So, who collected her and where is she now?"

"If we knew that, we would have a lot of answers. Come, I have an idea. Let's find the boys."

The went back to where the family Jones was staying. He still didn't know where they were as Llewellyn apparated him and Tryg in rather than show him the door. Flintock decided that it was not within the city as charms and dweomers had been set around the city walls to prevent apparating. But, he thought, 'I could be wrong because he had already witnessed Llewellyn apparate within the city walls'.

Llewellyn explained what had happened to Bangers to the boys.

"After all we went through to get her out of Dolydd, she's been captured again?" Tom said.

"How do you know it wasn't the Elder who took him?" Asked Jon.

"Trust me, I know, I know exactly where the Elder was at the time he was supposedly picking up Bangers, and it was nowhere near the residency."

Flintock also accepted that as a reasonable explanation, Flintock was not with Llewellyn at the time either, so he presumed that Llewellyn was, as he had said, with the Elder around 7.00 in the morning and as usual was being secretive about it.

"So now what?" the boys said.

"Where's your map of Dolydd Castle?"

"Here in my pocket," Tom pulled it out, "it's a bit screwed up," he flattened it out as best he could and laid it on the table, "now what?"

"Can we see Bangers on the map, back at the castle?"

"No, she's not there, neither is Llewel the Loser," oh, how Tom loved that name!

"Then put the quill on the map and ask it where they are."

"Who?"

"Either of them it probably doesn't matter as I suspect they are together."

Tom laid the quill down and the boys concentrated on Bangers.

The quill leapt from the map and on to a new sheet of parchment.

"Well, that confirms she's not in Dolydd," Llewellyn muttered, more to himself than anyone else.

The quill pen scribbled and scratched to reveal a system of caves, in the caves, were Llewel and Bangers plus seven other named wizards, but they had no idea who they were. At the centre was clearly marked a further presence, but it was unnamed and unidentified.

"Very strange," Llewellyn said to himself, "very strange indeed. Where are these caves.?" he said out loud.

The boys looked at the quill as if to ask the question. The quill wrote a heading on the map, but in very fancy writing...

The Dragonlands of Trymyll.

"So, they have hidden in the Dragonlands. I bet I can guess where as well, The Blue Mountains!"

The quill continued....

The Blue Mountains, by way of a sub-heading.

"Amazing," said Flintock, "how did you teach the boys that bit of magic?"

"I didn't, they worked it out themselves. Don't ask me how."

"And don't ask us, we haven't a clue, we just did!" exclaimed Jon.

Then Flintock added, "Damnation! Not a place for the faint-hearted. I can think of so many places I would rather go."

"Why?" Tom enquired.

"As you may have surmised, Blue Mountains means Blue Dragons. Hundreds of them, hundreds, and hundreds. Not a nice place."

Llewellyn chimed in, "Not only dangerous because of the dragons, but vile and stinking of rotting flesh. I warn you now, you will be sick. It is the vilest place on earth."

"I didn't think we were on earth."

"Well we are, sort of, but in a slightly different dimension."

That's another conversation Tom decided not to pursue for the moment.

###

A Cave in the Blue Mountains

There were six little pops as they all appeared on top of a ridge overlooking the Blue Mountains. Howel had also appeared next to them, though when they left Blaenoraid he was a small dog carried by Tryg. As usual, Tom was still awestruck at the immense size, strength and power that exuded from his shimmering, well-muscled body. Sat on the great beast's neck was Tryg. He had also come to do battle.

"Good morning Llewellyn, Flintock, Jon and Tom," he said in his posh Oxford accent, "I refuse to greet and be civil whilst in the guise of that half-breed dog."

They all returned the greeting to both Howel and Tryg. Tryg, of course, said nothing as usual but did manage a smile, or at least as best he could. It's quite difficult to smile when your mouth is full of hideous looking teeth, sharp like barbed ivory thorns, but you could still see the warmth in his face.

"Why are you here?" asked Tom, not in a rude way, but a curious inquiring sort of way.

"To, if necessary, fight alongside you. A Purple Dragon in his prime, like me, can take on many Blue Dragons and defeat them in a fight to the death, also, of course, I can play mind tricks with some of them, but not all. You see, with their tiny brains I can easily turn them to do my will instead of theirs."

"Cool," said Tom.

"Of course, I prefer the more intellectually challenging game of psychological warfare to fisticuffs," Howel said with a visible grin.

It was soon put to the test. A few moments later four Blue Dragons flew overhead staring down on them from above. Howel looked up at them and launched into the air. Howel flew up to them, through their tight formation and onward into the clouds. The four Blue Dragons followed him upwards. But at a slow pace, not an attacking speed, their throats were not even glowing, they were not, it appeared looking for a fight. A few seconds later, one Blue Dragon fell from the air crashing into the rocks below where its fire chamber burst and the whole dragon seemed to instantly cook in its own combustion. Seconds later a second, then a third, shortly followed by the fourth Blue Dragon all fell from the clouds and were dashed on the jagged rocks below.

Howel swooped down and stood again next to the four wizards,

"Nice work," said Tom, "how did you defeat them so quickly?"

"Simple dear boy, I persuaded three of them that they couldn't fly, so they just plummeted down to the jagged rocks below to their ultimate demise, the forth dragon thought he was smart and above such mind tricks, so I flew straight at him and with one mighty blast, I cooked his head. Blue Dragons are the most stupid of dragons, those were even more stupid than normal, they followed me up into the cloud not looking for a fight, but out of curiosity to see where I was going. I do believe they should not be called dragons at all but instead have some inferior name more suited to their very secondary existence."

Tom loved the poetic way that Howel spoke. He had missed his old dragon friend these past months.

"And I have missed you too young Tom," Howel shot the thought straight into Tom's head without speaking.

As they moved down the mountains, the stench came up to meet them. It wasn't the dragons that had just died, although the smell of the burning flesh of the first to fall was unpalatable, it was the rotting corpses of hundreds of half-eaten ox, cows, pigs, deer and even the odd weird wolf that filled the air. A few minutes later, Tom said hello to his breakfast, as it spilled out and onto the mountain path. That set Jon off and moments later they were both puking until there was nothing left to throw up. Everyone was looking quite green with nausea. Tom then held the stone on top of his staff sending out waves of soothing anti-emetic magic into everyone else. They all felt a lot better, but Tom could not do the same for himself. So, they had to carry on down with Tom feeling worse and worse while the others felt better and better. He liked being a healer but wished he could heal himself.

They looked at the map, the cave entrance was in the hill after next, they needed to be careful now not to be spotted. They pulled up their hoods and then they were all but invisible because of their cloaks, Howel went into 'undignified mode' and reappeared as a small Jack Russell, but this time, not the usual white, black, and tan colour, but a colour to match the rocks and mountain they were walking on. Tryg disappeared into a wisp of smoke which then followed the little party down towards the cave. They arrived at the cave entrance and Tryg reformed out of the smoke. There were still seven wizards, plus Llewel and Binning and the unknown one deep in the cave.

"Tom and Howel, you stay here and guard the entrance, I'll take Jon, Tryg and Flintock and see what we can find in the cave."

Tom agreed readily as he felt safe with Howel and caves were not his favourite place, if it came to a fight, they would be better off with Jon anyway.

They moved into the cave. They had only gone a short distance, when the unknown one disappeared from the map.

Around the mountain a thunder of Blue Dragons emerged from the clouds, this time Tom could see evil intent in their faces, their chests were glowing almost white with the build-up of fire they had worked up in their bellies ready for a fight, someone had obviously tipped them off. Howel reappeared in all his glory and launched off towards them. Five of the Blue Dragons peeled off to go after Howel, the others, about six turned down towards the entrance of the cave. Tom backed into the cave entrance.

The others were now some way into the cave complex. There were torches lit and hanging at regular intervals, Tryg noticed and noted each one as they passed them and as they passed by, each one went out, leaving their escape route in complete and utter pitch-black darkness. As they rounded the last bend, the tunnel opened out into a vast cathedralic cavern with massive stalactites hanging from the ceiling and stalagmites rising to meet them. There in the centre of the cavern stood a group of wizards with one very noticeably short wizard who seemed to have assumed authority, Llewel, and one slightly stout lady wizard who was, of course, High Elder Brangwen Binning. They stayed in the shadows as they moved down towards their prey. Tryg took out all the torches at once, there was a scurrying sound followed by shouting and cursing, a few seconds later all the torches re-lit. In the centre of the cavern stood Tryg with eight now mauled and several unconscious wizards, including Llewel, and an amazed, slightly frightened looking but unharmed Brangwen Binning. Tryg was vicious but effective, he could see perfectly in the complete darkness and completed his task well. It was not the way Llewellyn wanted to handle the situation, but Tryg knew it would be easier to seek forgiveness from Llewellyn than to ask permission.

Meanwhile, back at the surface, the six Blue Dragons flew at speed towards the cave, each intent on a little light supper. Stupid as they are, the crashed into the cave entrance and were unable to move as they were all both tangled together and had their heads and necks jammed in the entrance. There was much snapping of teeth and biting each other as each fought for dominance in the cave, all the time becoming more and more stuck in the tight entrance hole. Tom could see the build-up of fire in their guts, he knew they were going to blow soon, and if he were in the way, he would be roast dinner. He couldn't outrun the fire when it came but he hoped he could block it.

"Staff," he quickly wove an impenetrable and hopefully fireproof shield between him and the Dragons. They all seem to explode their bellies of fire towards him at the same time, he could feel the heat as his shield glowed first red, then yellow, and finally white-hot with the intense heat. He could hear them screaming as the flames were contained and bounced back and directly onto their stupid heads. He was fighting hard to hold it in place and knew he could not hold it for long. But, almost as quickly as it had started, it was over. He dropped the shield and was sick again. The entrance of the cave was filled with the burning flesh of the Blue Dragons. In their stupidity, all had perished, instead of him, it was they who were roast meat. Tom decided at that point that he really hated the smell of burning flesh, even if it was dragon flesh, in fact, especially if it was dragon flesh.

He illuminated the end of his wand and used it as a torch as he ran down into the cave. It was not many minutes before he had reached the others. He hadn't thought about what he was running into, for all he knew there could have been a great battle going on and he could run straight into the firing line. But he just had to get away from the entrance and away from the smell of burning flesh. He was quite horrified by the scene which greeted him, but for a moment he didn't care and ran straight to his father and grabbed him around the neck sobbing.

"Calm down Tom, it's all right, we are all safe and thanks to Tryg, none of us are even hurt. Now tell me what's the matter?"

Tom tried to relate the story in between sobs.

"Six Blue Dragons……stuck in the cave mouth……..massive fireball…….put up shield……..fire bounced back…..cooked them all alive……terrible screams…… terrible screams……, hate the smell……..of burning flesh…….. What happened…….here?"

"Well, not what we had planned, well actually we didn't have a real plan, we were going to decide what to do once we had surveyed the scene. But before we could, Tryg here, a one-man army, put out all the torches, sorted the wizards out quite viciously, and this is what we found once he re-lit the torches a few seconds later. Nor pretty I'm afraid."

Tom composed himself and said, "I must start work immediately."

Tom took his wand and went to each wizard in turn, starting with those who seemed in worse shape but leaving Llewel until last.

"Don't worry about them, look that dreadful trygall has mauled me, quick, come and stop the bleeding, I think I'm going to faint. I am the most important wizard here, so I should be treated first not them," Llewel whined.

Before long, each wizard seemed to be in a cocoon of ever-changing light. Tom even went over to Bendy and cocooned her, as although physically unharmed, she was in a state of high shock and looked terrible, finally he went and attended to Llewel.

"How long will healing take?" asked Flintock.

"No idea, I expect Llewel the Whining Loser will be first as his wounds are superficial. Bangers might be the longest as her wounds are to her emotional wellbeing rather than physical. But some of them are quite gravely injured, so it could be weeks for some," Tom had no idea where the concept of emotional wellbeing came from as it was not a phrase he had ever used, but decided it must be the wisdom of the wand.

"Well we don't have weeks, we need to be out of here and on our way, there may be reinforcements on the way."

"What about them?" Tom nodded towards the prisoners.

"We'll take them with us, all of them. Flintock, are you able to apparate this many people in one shot?"

"Easy-Peasy," he replied, "where to?"

"Back to Blaenoraid and into the dungeons. Jon, take their wands, all of them."

"What if they won't give them over?"

"Ask them if they want another round with a trygall."

Jon quickly produced seven wands and took them to his dad. As they had been taken legally, Llewellyn was able to quickly destroy them.

"Where's the other one?"

Llewel claims he hasn't got one.

"Tryg, come with me, we need a word with Llewel," Llewellyn said this in such a way that he knew Llewel would hear.

"I haven't got a wand; you took it yesterday. Keep him away from me! NO! Keep that animal away!"

"Prove it."

"How do I do that?" he snivelled almost in tears.

"I can extract your wand from you if you have it, and you know I can. If I find a wand the size of a matchstick on you, I'll walk away and just leave my friend Tryg with you."

"No! No! No! Don't do that, I haven't got one, I haven't had time to go back to the wand tree, it's several days journey from here and you know I don't apparate. Please, don't let him near me."

Now he was crying. Tears and sweat ran down his face, washing the grime of years from his matted beard.

"Wand" he whispered in Llewel's ear, "wand of Llewel Mathias Gaynor appear."

Nothing happened.

"Well that's a first, Llewel Mathias Gaynor wasn't lying."

"How do you know my whole name; I have never spoken it to anyone."

"Well Llewel Mathias Gaynor," he said it louder so that everyone could hear, "Well Llewel Mathias Gaynor," he said again "that is for me to know and you to worry about, especially now all your compatriots know your whole given name as well. Quite a big worry I should think."

He turned to Flintock and the boys, "Right, let's be out of here."

They went to apparate.

Nothing happened.

CHAPTER 22 - BETWEEN A ROCK AND A HARD PLACE.

Llewel leered a sardonic smile, "Did you really think it would be that easy? The Master, the new Elder of Elders will return soon with his hoard. Then you may wish the boy had not been so quick to help my compatriots as you called them."

"Shut it Llewel and leave my Tom out of it. Tryg is still here and I think he may be hungry after all the excitement."

Llewel blanched at the thought and stopped grinning.

"Right, we do it the hard way, back to the surface."

They turned and walked up toward the blocked exit of the cave, as they walked the torches before them lit and the torches behind extinguished.

"Are we going the right way," asked Jon, "this seems a lot longer than when we came in?"

"Of course, Tryg knows the way, he set the torches to go out in sequence as he walked down to the cavern and to re-light as we exit. He is a fire master don't forget."

They rounded the last bend. They were back in the cavern; they had somehow gone round in a circle.

"What the...," said Flintock, "how did we do that?"

"A little trick of the Master I expect," said Llewel, animated again and almost giggling with excitement.

"Shut it Llewel, we weren't talking to you!" Llewellyn said firmly, "when we want your opinion, we'll ask for it."

There in the centre of the cavern stood a single figure. Dressed in black, hood up and no visible features to recognise.

"It's the Elder," said Jon, "he's come to rescue us."

"I think not," a voice said, it was a deep disengaged Afro-Caribbean voice which filled the cavern without any discernible direction from where it came from, "I am not the Elder. But you may refer to me as the Master."

"Who are you and where do you come from."

"Good question Llewellyn the Brave, but I will answer neither. My real name does not matter, I am just the Master, you also need not know where I come from, but this I tell you; it is not from this stinking hole of a land you call Trymyll, but from another land. Far away and beyond your reach or knowledge."

"Why are you here?"

"Now that I will answer. I am here to take you over and take you down. This land will bend the knee to me and my will or I will destroy and lay waste to every square inch of it. It will become a barren land where there will be no life, not a blade of grass or even an ant will live."

"Why would you do that?"

"Because it gives me great pleasure to punish those who disobey."

"Llewel said you would return with a hoard, an army. Did you forget something?"

"Llewellyn the Brave, I do like a sense of humour. I need no army. No army can stand against me or ever has. I will rule this land unopposed until I get bored with you, then I will destroy you all and move on to another. I am omnipotent. Nothing and no one can stand against me."

"We will fight you until there is not one of us left standing!" declared Llewellyn.

"Oh, I'm sure you will, and believe me, not one of you will remain standing. Those who do not bow the knee will be utterly and ruthlessly destroyed."

His voice swelled and filled the cavern. As he spoke louder and louder the walls began to shake and small rocks rattled down from the roof of the cave.

He had no staff or wand. He just held out his hand towards Llewellyn and a bolt of power shot out. It was met by one of equal power from Llewellyn's wand. The two streams of pure energy crackled and bent, connected in the middle by a bright ball of light, a solid ball of energy. The Master's power was blue and Llewellyn's pure white. They arced off each other like a massive electrical charge. Llewellyn pushing forward, then the Master gaining a little. Back and forth they went while circling around the floor of the cavern. They rose into the air and began to spin round and round each other like a couple of aircraft having a dogfight. On and on the energy continued to flow. The others had never seen anything like it, such power, such pure raw energy pouring out of the two wizards, meeting between them crackling and sparking as pure energy hit pure energy and sheer power hit sheer power.

"What is this? No one has ever stood against me and lived!"

Then, as suddenly as it started, it ended. Both men disappeared.

"Dad! Dad!" shouted the boys, "where's me dad gone?"

They had barely finished shouting when Llewellyn re-appeared in the same mid-air position he had just left and fell to the floor. He was blackened with soot and he had burns on his hands and face. Tom ran to him and enclosed him in his healing power. He was alive.

"Quick, we have to get dad out of here, let's try for the surface again."

As they turned towards the exit tunnel Howel appeared in his guise of a dog.

"How did you get in?" asked Tom.

"Well it wasn't easy, but I'm in, so let's get us all out again."

They rushed for the surface; Tom noticed that Howel was limping. It must have been quite a fight, this time a proper one, not just mind games.

When they reached the end of the tunnel, it was still blocked by the now dead and roasted Blue Dragons, dried and congealed blood splattered all around and again the putrid stink of burning dragon flesh.

"How do we shift that lot?" asked Flintock to no one in particular.

Without comment, Jon stepped forward and held out his wand towards the blackened remains of the Blue Dragons. He let out a blast of energy which literally vaporised them before their eyes. It definitely shifted them, but the smell was even worse, and now there was a thick red mist from the vapourised blood of the dead dragons. They all stepped out onto the ledge at the entrance to the cave, the ledge was slippery with blood and the air was filled with hundreds of Blue Dragons, attracted by the smell of their burning brothers. They were not above a bit of cannibalism if the opportunity arose.

The prisoners were all bound in magic manacles, not that any of them were capable of escape. Llewel still wanted to defy whatever was coming. He was still proclaiming his innocence and the injustice of all. Flintock huddled them all together, then, just as the Blue Dragons dived down and fell upon them, 'Pop' and they were gone. The boys left next closely followed by Howel and Tryg who were apparated by and with Llewellyn.

The Blue Dragons crashed against the mountain, and as usual began fighting amongst themselves. Trymyll would be no worse off for the loss of a few more Blue Dragons.

The dungeons at Blaenoraid were rarely used, so to have this many 'visitors' was going to cause some inconvenience and not a little work for the guards. They were however clean, well-lit, and free of vermin, not like all the other dungeons in the land which were typically rat-infested hell holes. Most times the guards had so little to do that they cleaned and painted all the cells just to relieve the boredom.

This was good for the injured among the visitors as the hygienic conditions would be better for healing and to ward off infections. A couple were in an induced coma brought on by Tom so that the body's natural healing powers could act more quickly. The walking wounded, for want of a better term, were all housed in single cells and the more gravely injured in a sort of hospital dormitory. Llewel was taken to a special high-security cell on another and lower floor. His cell had no natural light but was still well lit, bulbs were strung across the ceiling with no visible source of power, the cell was clean, and comfortable, which was more than he deserved. Bangers was taken to the Residence with strict instructions that no one, not even the Elder was to visit, and special high wizard guards put in place around her room and in the grounds.

There was an immediate call for a full meeting of the council. Llewellyn, Flintock and the boys were to attend and give an explanation as to what they had found.

Llewellyn decided he was too injured to attend.

"Sorry folks, you go on ahead, I took quite a battering down there and now need to go and rest up for a while. I'm utterly drained and exhausted. I'll brief the Elder before the meeting and see you all later."

Flintock, again speaking to no one in particular, "I wish I knew how your dad did it. He seems to have unfettered access to the Elder. I've never seen him once. Well, of course I've seen him, but never had a conversation or even a single word to pass between us. Yet he and your dad seem the best of mates. He definitely knows how to network and reach the right people."

CHAPTER 23 - LLEWEL AT THE COUNCIL OF BLAENORAID.

The council met in closed session and secret. All were there, even Brangwen Binnion was there despite her ordeal over the last few days and Asmodeus as well.

After the usual preamble by the Clerk to the Elder of Elders, the earnest discussion began, "Today we are here to discuss a dreadful and terrible threat, that of the Master."

There was then some general discussion about points of order, whether they should refer to him by such an exalted title as 'The Master'; and all the other things the council always did to try to put off discussing what they needed to talk about for as long as possible.

"Llewel has thrown his lot in with a wizard who calls himself 'The Master'," High Elder Brangwen Binnion said nervously starting the conversation. She was getting tired of the continual procrastination of the others, "We don't know where he has come from, all he would reveal was that he was from a land far away and that he would destroy us all and lay our land barren if we did not bow the knee to him."

Brangwen continued to tell all she knew. Telling the story of Llewel, of the boys, of their imprisonment and escape, of her imprisonment and rescue, her recapture, and all that had happened in the cave. It was both informative to the others and cathartic to her. Telling it all through again seemed to settle her nerves a little and the more detail she gave, the better she felt.

"Tell us again what happened in the cave when you encountered the Master there," asked High Elder Govannon Stealey of the Elven community, "it is important we hear every detail you can remember."

Bangers went through it again, "....and then they engaged in battle. The Master, as he calls himself does not use a wand or staff, the power comes from his hands, and it was an awesome power, Llewellyn the Brave fought back with equal power. The ball of energy moving back and forth between them, the Master seemed shocked that anyone had the power to withstand him. They battled for only about two minutes, maybe slightly less, but it seemed an eternity. The power had lifted them from the ground where they spun round in a circle, then suddenly they both disappeared. A few seconds later, Llewellyn reappeared in exactly the space he had gone from and fell to the ground. He was burned on his hands and face, probably elsewhere as well, but his cloak hid any other injuries. Tom, his son, then stepped forward and used his amazing healing and restorative powers to revive his father so we could all get out as quickly as possible."

"The Master did not reappear at the same time; can we assume that Llewellyn the Brave defeated him?" Aneta Stepanek asked.

The Elder of Elders then rose and for the first time in years, addressed the council. They had to listen very carefully as he spoke in just a whisper as was his custom.

"My esteemed friends and colleagues, High Elders of the Six cities. I have spoken at length with the sadly injured Llewellyn the Brave about his battle with the Master. No, he did not defeat him, but more importantly, the Master did not defeat Llewellyn. It would seem strange to pick our former colleague Llewel as his partner or gateway into Trymyll, there are possibly others of more power, importance, and even a bent for evil, to whom he could have turned."

He did not mention Asmodeus by name or even nod in his direction, but they all knew who he meant. Asmodeus knew too, but instead of being offended by the suggestion, he felt a small glimmer of pride.

"I believe Llewel summoned him here to Trymyll and opened a gateway for him to enter. Unfortunately, now that gateway is open, the Master may come and go as he pleases. Our priority therefore is to find the portal and close it. So, I suggest we bring Llewel before the council and question him closely."

The Clerk went to adjourn the meeting but before he could the Elder spoke again, "No," he said gently, "we will see him now, not at some future meeting or date....and while I'm in the mood to speak, may we please cut out all the stupid points of order, procrastination, delaying tactics and all the other ploys some of you engage in to avoid what may be an unpleasant discussion. From now on, no more of it. We need some urgent action not a long-winded debate about procedures, policy and practice."

They all sat down again and right on cue the round table at the centre of the council chamber folded to the sides and an iron cage rose into the room Llewel was led from the cage by the eight-foot tall guard in black, the cage then disappeared below and the table folded and moved together, again like the solid looking table that had been there previously.

The Elder, who normally spoke through his Clerk took to the floor, wand in hand, "Llewel Mathias Gaynor you are here today charged with high treason, a charge punishable by sudden death."

As he did it, he poked Llewel with the pointed end of his wand. Llewel winced and whined at the same time

"I really don't know what you are talking about. I have done nothing wrong, ask Binnion."

"She is High Elder Brangwen Binnion, mind your manners or you'll feel more than the pointed end of my wand."

"Oh, I doubt it, no one can use magic in here," he said smugly and stupidly.

A small spark of energy flashed out of the Elders wand and gave a real sting to Llewel's chest and burnt a small hole in his cloak. Llewel looked shocked and scared, he turned as white as a sheet, whimpered a little more and nearly fainted. They had never seen the Elder do such a thing or even thought it was possible. Most of the assembled High Elders also looked stunned, they too believed that no magic was possible in the chamber. They had never seen the Elder do anything that might hurt or harm anyone. They exchanged glances and mumbled to each other. Aneta Stepanek smiled to herself. She was, as usual, loving it!

"Point of order!" Traveon Baughan said standing up as he did.

"I did say to cut out all the stupid point of order rubbish. If you don't like what you see or if I scare you, please feel free to leave and resign your position on the council."

Traveon Baughan sat down again, sheepishly.

"Now Llewel Mathias Gaynor. Tell me what you know of the Master. How did he get here, how did you let him gain access to our world and why?"

"I don't know much, honestly, I received a letter a few days ago, signed simply 'The Master' asking me if I wanted to avenge myself of the wrongdoing of the council and of others."

"And to whom was he referring when he said 'others'?"

"Well, Llewellyn the Brave, and his sons, the phobl, Jonathan and that scheming vile and phony child Thomas," he said with venom in his tone.

"What else did the letter say?"

"I was to go to a particular cave in The Blue Mountains of The Dragonlands and there, deep in the cave there was a door or portal which I had to open by reciting a spell in a language strange to my eyes."

"Can you show us the letter?"

"Well no, as soon as I had read it and memorised the spell the letter burst into flames."

"And how long was this spell? It could not have been that long for you to memorise it," he said sarcastically,

"Just three words," he then opened his mouth to say the spell, a spark flew from the Elder's wand, this time hitting him in the shoulder.

"Don't be so stupid, if you say it, you may summon the Master again. Utter a single word of it and I'll take your head off right here and now."

Traveon Baughan stirred in his seat again but decided against it.

"You have another point of order High Elder Traveon Baughan?"

"No. No. No. No. Well no. No. I was just adjusting my seating position Elder of Elders. These seats can be quite hard."

"Then might I suggest you bring a cushion next time. Right, Llewel Mathias Gaynor. Explain the happenings at Dolydd. Explain the abduction of two minors, explain the so-called trial and the imprisonment, of said minors."

"Well, it started in the town square, I was innocently going about my business when they attacked me."

Another spark shot from the Elder's wand, but this one was hotter, it caught him on the other shoulder and blew a big hole on his cloak. Llewel let out a scream.

"Try again."

"They shouted at me in the town square asking why I was spreading stories about them and their father, so I shot a bolt of energy at them, they deflected the spell, but then laid down their wands so no one else in the crowd might be hurt, so I took them into custody to save them from the mob." he almost shouted the answer, and so quickly there was no discernible punctuation, it was as if he was trying to get the truth out before he received another bolt.

"The mob which you had turned against them in the first place."

"Yes," he said quietly hanging his head low, "I didn't mean to hurt them, I knew they would deflect the spell, I knew they'd be all right."

"And how did you know they would deflect the spell, these were, according to you, these two young acolytes, phobls and frauds had no magic of their own?"

"Well, ...well," Llewel stuttered, "I knew it wasn't true really, I could sense their true power, I just said that to turn the populous against them."

"Did you not goad them into a fight which they refused to enter because of possible harm that would come to the crowd around them, and did you not say that if someone was killed or injured it would be on their heads, not yours?"

"Yes." he said, even quieter, head now in his hands.

"And did you not then organise a sham trial using High Elder Brangwen Binnion as your stooge, somehow under your control? Please tell us, what would have happened to these two minors had they not escaped you, and the incompetent fools you called guards so soon?"

"Yes, yes, yes, I did all those things. I didn't know what would have happened to the boys afterwards, I hadn't thought it through that far. Before I could think about what to do with them, they had escaped. I'm sorry and ashamed, I don't know why I did it. Maybe I was jealous."

"Did you know that it was they who locked you in the dungeon and then returned to rescue Brangwen Binnion later that night?"

"No!" he said, head now up and hate in his eyes, looking directly at the two boys, "The little rats. I blame their father and I notice he's not here. Scared to face me in case I embarrassed him in front of you all. They're nothing more than a couple of trouble making delinquents just like their father was at their age."

"Oh good, now we see your true nature, so all the snivelling look of remorse and the tears we have seen up to now was just an act?"

"Yes, and one day I will get even with him and his revolting offspring."

"Enough! Now tell us what the Master offered you in return for you unlocking the portal into Trymyll?"

"He offered me power, all the power I wanted and needed to get my revenge on you, your sycophantic council, Llewellyn the Bully and the obnoxious vermin he calls sons. As a taster, he gave me the power to manipulate the feeble mind of Binnion and her pathetic guards."

"He's said enough. Take him down. I never wish to set eyes on him again. Take him to the deepest dungeon in the castle put him in cold irons, hand and foot and tell the guards to stop being so nice and to put the rat infestation back in his cell and stop cleaning it every five minutes!"

Again, the round table at the centre of the council chamber folded to the sides and a cold iron cage rose into the room Llewel was led to the cage by the Nephilim of a guard, the cage then disappeared below, down to the very deepest dungeon in the castle. The table refolded and moved together, looking again like the solid table that had always been there.

"What do we do now?" Aneta Stepanek asked.

"We will do nothing at the moment," the Elder said softly.

The council had heard more words today from the Elder than they normally would hear in a hundred meetings.

"Llewellyn the Brave, Flintock the Elder and the two young wizards Jonathan and Thomas together with Tryg the trygall will return to the cave and attempt to close the portal."

They noted that Jon and Tom were no longer referred to as acolytes. For two boys so young to be given the title 'Wizard' was an honour indeed. Some of the council were quite shocked. Normally it would take seven years, seven months and seven days from the time of entering service as an acolyte to be known as 'wizard' Jon had taken a long time, over ten years in fact, but it was only the last few months that he had really blossomed. It was Tom they were amazed about; he had only been an acolyte here in Trymyll for just seven months and seven days.

CHAPTER 24 - WIZARDS ROBES.

Flintock met up with Llewellyn and told him what had happened at council.

Jon and Tom were aghast when their father told them that the Elder had referred to them as Wizards in the council. They of course, were there, but did not realise the significance of the remark at all. Especially Tom who was so young and inexperienced.

"Yeah, we heard him, but it could just have been a slip of the tongue," Jon said, "I know I've been trying for nearly ten years, but it's only the last few months that I've actually been able to do anything."

"And I've only been here a few months, surely he's mistaken?" questioned Tom.

"The Elder does not make mistakes; he speaks slowly and carefully considering every word before he says it. Boys, you are fully-fledged, licenced to thrill wizards. However, make no mistake, there is still a lot for you to learn, you never stop learning, and your magic never stops developing. The Elder is obviously in a hurry, normally a gowning ceremony is only held twice a year at the equinox, but yours is tomorrow and each of you must show your prowess before the assembled Council of High Elders, the forty-nine elders, the three-hundred and forty-three senior wizards plus the assembled crowd." Flintock said.

"How do we do that?" asked Tom.

"That's for you two to work out, no help from your teacher. That's the rules!" dad joined in.

"But you always said that the rules were meant to be broken." Tom replied.

"Not this one," he laughed, "I'm so proud of you two, my heart could burst with joy."

"Me too," said Flintock, "you've both done amazingly well these past few months. I'm just as proud as your dad."

The boys retired to their room to discuss their plan for the morrow.

"Shall we apparate in just as the ceremony is about to begin? Straight onto the stage? In the build-up to the ceremony everyone will be looking out for us and wondering where we are. Let's keep them guessing," said Jon.

"No, we shouldn't be able to apparate inside the city walls. Shall we fly high up above the clouds and streak in at just below the speed of sound," Tom exaggerated, "over the heads of the crowd and then stop dead on the stage?"

"Decide later, what we must work out is an amazing display of magic that will wow the crowd."

"I could produce a fire dragon and fly it all around the castle just above their heads," Tom said excitedly.

"And I could vaporise a tree to show my awesome firepower," added Jon.

"Okay, let's do it."

Each of them chatting away excitedly and thinking of more difficult and awe-inspiring magic they could do, but in the end, they settled on the two they had thought of first. The fire dragon and the tree.

Next day, a huge stage appeared in the castle grounds just outside the bailey, decked with all the colours of the seven cities, their flags and banners gently wafting in the cool autumn breeze. On the stage were seven daises each draped with the colours of the seven cities and on each dais a throne like chair, one large one set centre stage for the Elder and three on either side for the six High Elders. Behind them, their seven elders sat on raised platforms so that they could also see the ceremony, and behind them, the forty-nine senior wizards. Even Asmodeus had had been invited and he sat proudly at the end of the row with his seven elders behind him. Unlike the other elders, they did not smile a lot, and his forty-nine senior wizards, who were placed behind the elders, didn't seem to smile at all! The boys were there as well but dressed in their light-absorbing black robes they were able to mingle unseen by the crowds of people. They couldn't see their dad or Flintock, but they knew they were there somewhere. They too had adopted the boy's style of dress, so it was difficult to find them anyway. But they could sense that they were there.

The ceremony was about to begin, they could see the look of consternation on the faces of the High Elders and of their elders. They were concerned because they had no idea where the boys were. It was normal for Acolytes to prepare for the ceremony in advance and to be very visible in the run-up. The only one who seemed unconcerned was the Elder, mainly because no one could see his face. He wasn't anyway and in any way, even slightly concerned.

The Clerk to the Elder stood, looking nervously around to see if he could see the boys. the Elder signalled to him to get on with it.

"Elder of Elders, High Elders, Elders, Senior Wizards, assembled wizards, mystics and phobls. Today is the gowning ceremony of Jonathan, first son of Llewellyn the Brave and Thomas, second son of Llewellyn the Brave. I present to you the wizards, Thomas, and Jonathan," he made a flourish with his hands, hoping the boys would appear.

With that, the two boys apparated centre stage. This was a

shock to both the High Elders and the assembled crowd as apparating should not be possible within the city walls. They then launched vertically upwards until they were two small dots in the sky, then turned vertically downward and shot down at absolute breakneck speed towards the crowd. There were cries of "They're falling!" "They're going too fast!" "They won't be able to stop!" "They'll crash!" and the crowd became agitated and started to try to get out of the way as they came flying down. Just inches from crowd, they shot horizontally across their heads, around the castle in opposite directions and heading straight towards each other, and with the crowd gasping for breath stopped dead and facing each other in the very place they had left a few moments earlier, stepped down from their staffs and faced the crowd.

Tom then threw his staff into the air, it transformed as it flew and grew into a forty-foot-long fire dragon which then flew all around the castle and city walls, twisting and turning in a spectacular display of aerobatics. It then flew out over the crowd and then straight back towards Tom, it then stopped, hovering in mid-air. Tom looked perplexed. That was not the thought pattern which he had formed in his mind for his flying display. Why was his fire dragon not obeying him now? He waved his hand, at which point the fire dragon should have just disappeared like someone had turned off the gas. But it didn't, it just hovered for another second, then solidified into a real Golden Dragon right before their eyes.

"Thomas, son of Llewellyn the Brave and Jonathan, son of Llewellyn the Brave," her voice penetrating into every corner of the city, "I am Máthair, Queen of the Golden Dragons, Queen of all Dragons and Mother of Dragons. I am here to honour you on this your cloaking day. In your bravery, you fought and defeated three Blue Dragons and defeated the poacher Arvel Mordecai while still only acolytes."

The crowd and many of the assembled elders gasped at this news. Llewel had told a completely different story about how the boys had attacked the Golden Dragon and whelp.

"That Golden Dragon you rescued is my own daughter Morcan, and the whelp my grandson, Bryn. Morcan told you then, that your bravery would not be forgotten and indeed, it will be spoken of for millennia to come. After this ceremony, Thomas, son of Llewellyn you are commanded to attend my royal household in the far mountains of the Dragonlands and there you will receive your reward. You, Thomas, son of Llewellyn the Brave will receive a companion male Golden Dragon called Ren, Ren will teach you and you will teach Ren. Ren is both wise and magical, barely an adult he is just one hundred years of age. He will become a great and powerful dragon and you will become a great and even more powerful wizard. You already hold more power in your wand than many of those assembled here. Use that power wisely and for good, for with great power you also have a great responsibility. So be wise, compassionate, and brave," she then turned slightly to face Jon.

"Jonathan son of Llewellyn will attend the valley of the Red Dragons and there receive a gift from my kinswoman and friend Aelwyd, Queen of the Red Dragons. You will receive a companion called Bevon, a Red Dragon of one and a half centuries. He will teach you and you will teach Him. Red Dragons have great power, are fearless in battle, and are faithful and trustworthy. Treat Bevon with the respect he deserves and Bevon will return that respect. You are already brave; you have only a little wisdom and lack compassion. Build on those weaknesses and you too will be one of the greatest wizards of the age and will be known as a Dragonmaster."

That brought a gasp from the assembled crowd as well.

With that, Máthair vanished and Tom's staff floated down and into his hand. The boys both looked stunned. The High Elders looked astonished; the whole assembly looked surprised; everyone was speechless. The Clerk to the Elder however continued as if nothing had happened.

"Jonathan Jones, first son of Llewellyn the Brave, receive your cloak as a wizard. May the Maker go with you, may you become a great and powerful wizard, and may you use your power only for good and never for evil."

With that, he removed Jon's acolyte cloak, which was now back to its drab and dirty green colour and placed on his shoulders a rather boring looking grey cloak. As soon as it was placed upon him it changed, flashing through all the colours and hues imaginable to man, but after a few seconds turned to into the deep red of an autumn sunset, trimmed in fur and embroidered with dragons. His face turned into a smile which almost outshone the beauty of his wizard's cloak.

"Thomas Jones, second son of Llewellyn the Brave, receive your cloak as a wizard. May the Maker go with you, may you become a great and powerful wizard, and may you use your power only for good and never for evil."

He then removed Tom's acolyte cloak, which Tom had returned to its normal green colour. A drab grey cloak was placed on his shoulders. Then the same happened to Tom's, it began its transformation, flashed every colour in the rainbow and more, settling finally into a brilliant gold colour, again trimmed in fur but with a single golden dragon emblem centred on the back. His cloak shone as bright as the sun. He looked magnificent.

They both looked splendid, they both looked proud, they looked around for their father, they still could not see him but could sense his presence. A voice spoke to them in their heads.

'You my sons have made me the proudest father ever to walk the earth.'

Which was a bit odd, as they weren't on earth now. But they understood the sentiment.

The Elder stood, the High Elders stood, the forty-nine Senior Elders stood; the robing ceremony was over, and they all solemnly paraded off the stage following the Elder back into the castle bailey.

Now it was all at an end. The appearance of the Golden Dragon had rather overshadowed the formal part of the ceremony. Jon didn't have his chance to vaporise a tree to show his awesome power. But on reflection, he thought it was just as well. He needed to work on his compassion and wisdom and destroying a beautiful tree and any birds or wildlife that resided within it, just to show off, was neither compassionate nor wise.

There then followed an afternoon of celebration, partying, and general enjoyment for all the gathered crowd. There was a hog roast in every corner of the town square, there was ale, lots of ale, wine and mead for the ladies, there were meat pies, fruit pies, cakes, and fancies galore. Dancing and singing, mummers and jugglers, entertainers, clowns, and fools. Such a party had not been seen for many a year. For the council to lay on this much food and fun, these boys must be special, incredibly special.

Jon and Tom, however, attended a slightly more formal and boring affair in the main castle, the food was good, fine wine was served to the grown-ups, but the entertainment was rubbish. Every Elder in the land was there except the Elder of Elders, who never joined in such celebrations, Flintock, Tryg and their dad was there, so that made the whole thing a little more bearable, but hardly fun. All five of them would have preferred to have been outside with all the other wizards and phobls. They were sure that the others were having much more fun than they were.

And yes, they were.

CHAPTER 25 - RETURN TO THE DRAGONLANDS.

Next morning, it was business as usual. They put on what they called their 'working cloaks' the light-absorbing black 'uniform' as did their dad and Flintock. The boys of the Black Hood were back! But now they were four. Tryg didn't want to play their little game, so, Tryg remained Tryg. He didn't need to really, he could disappear into a swirl of smoke whenever he needed to, Tryg didn't need their silly cloaks. He thought to himself.

Breakfast was only a light one, toast and jam with a mug of warm oat milk and was completed in about two minutes,

"Why can't we have a nice cup of tea in this place?" asked Tom, "me mam always made us tea in the morning."

"Because we don't have tea in Trymyll, well no one except the Cadwaladers, I tried bringing it in once or twice, but there was no market for it. Folks here thought it was weird and didn't like the taste," Llewellyn replied, "now, off with you. To the Dragonlands."

Tom picked up Howl, they all held hands and apparated away. They did it this way because with only one person initiating the spell, they would all arrive at the same place at the same time. They also apparated back to base the same way, they did it as a group because Llewellyn still hadn't revealed the exact location of 'home' to Flintock and Tryg.

They appeared at the entrance of the cave where they had last met the Master.

"I thought we were supposed to be collecting our new companion dragons, not coming back here," complained Jon with Tom nodding in agreement. There was still a strong smell of burnt dragon hanging in the air which immediately made Tom feel queasy. Most of the congealed blood was gone now, cleared away by an infestation of a million maggots and other vermin.

"All in good time, but first the Elder has set us the task of closing the portal through to wherever the so-called Master comes from. Shouldn't take long. We know it's in the main chamber somewhere, we just need to locate it and seal it."

"Okay da, but let's be quick. We don't want to meet him again down there."

"Neither do I Tom, neither do I," Llewellyn held up a still bandaged wand hand.

They headed down into the cave, Howel trotting along beside them, following the familiar pattern of torches lighting before them, and going out behind them. This time were always three lit torches in front and three lit behind. Deeper and deeper they went until they finally came to the vast cavern. Torches magically lit all around the cavern, but even in their light, it was difficult to see Llewellyn, Flintock and the two new wizards Tom and Jon in their 'working clothes'.

"Wands out and stay alert. We need to head down to the area where we both disappeared, the portal must be there or thereabout."

"But what are we actually looking for?" asked Tom.

"Not a clue," said his dad, "but hopefully we'll know it when we find it."

"So, we're looking for an invisible needle in a massive haystack?" Tom replied

"That just about sums it up. Yes."

"Great," he said with a sigh.

"Flintock, Tom and Tryg, you circle that way round, Jon, Howel and I will go this way."

He said indicated the direction he wanted everyone to go. They then went around in ever increasing circles until they met up again at the exit tunnel. They stood there staring at each other and shrugged their shoulders.

"Well that is strange, we didn't know what we are looking for and we didn't know where to find it, and yet somehow, we haven't."

Once they had worked out what he had just said, they all smiled, breaking the tension.

"Let's try another tack. Perhaps me disappearing was nothing to do with the portal. Let's check the walls of the cavern, see if we can find anything."

The two teams split again and went their separate ways. Llewellyn and Flintock tapping the walls as they went around with their wands to see if anything opened. Finally, they all met up again and stood there staring at each other as if looking for inspiration.

Tom spoke, "If we do find this door or whatever it is, and presumably to find it we have to open it, what if we all get sucked in and disappear off to another dimension?"

Jon added, "Or what if, when we open it, we release the hounds of hell or something?"

Llewellyn thought carefully for a moment.

"Oh, that's simple. If either of those things happens, we're in deep do-do! Except that, when I was dragged through the portal there was nothing, just a bare and barren land. I could see nothing that lived, not even a blade of grass. the Master has devastated that land and now he's coming for ours."

"Great!" they both said, "no one's actually thought it through then," continued Tom.

"No, not really. But when you don't know what you're looking for and you don't know how to find it, planning is a little difficult."

"Then let's retreat back to the surface, go away and come back when we have a plan," Flintock suggested

"WELL, WHEN YOU DO, LET ME KNOW AND I'LL TELL YOU IF IT WILL WORK!" The voice of the Master echoed around the chamber.

Jon instinctively tapped his staff down and threw up a force field around them, as he did an almighty bolt of energy hit it and whistled off into the distance. Rocks rained down all around them and a huge chunk of the cavern ceiling crashed to the floor narrowly missing the Master. Fortunately, Jon's defensive shields were just as powerful as his offensive firepower and that was better than any of the others. Jon immediately shot one off towards the Master, but he was gone, he was not going to hang around to be shot at by them. 'Coward' thought Jon.

They retreated to the surface and apparated away to a safe distance.

"That was close, too close in fact," Llewellyn said, stating the obvious, "next time I think we go with a proper plan and strategy, try not to make it up as we go along."

They all agreed with that idea, although none of them knew what the plan might look like.

"Can we go and get our dragons now? You never know, they might come in handy," Tom said, with an air of excited expectancy.

"Good idea," his dad replied, and they all disappeared again.

"Máthair, Queen of the Golden Dragons, I come as you have bid me," announced Tom.

He stood amid the canyon and caves where the Golden Dragons lived, loved, and learnt. Somehow Tom had expected some sort of royal palace, but instead, it looked like rocks, rubble, and ruin. This was a quest he had to undertake on his own, the others stood waiting at the head of the valley which led down to the canyon. A Golden Dragon magically apparated next to him, giving Tom quite a start.

"Thomas, youngest son of Llewellyn the Brave, I will escort you to Máthair, Queen of all Dragons," he spoke very formally.

Tom was then led off to the entrance of a cave. As they entered his eyes quickly adjusted to the gloom, it took Tom's breath away. It was beautiful, gold ornaments everywhere, jewels encrusted the walls, golden statues and a solid gold pathway which led into the most fabulous cavern he had ever seen. Statues of full-size dragons made from pure solid gold, gems, and stones of every description; gold chandeliers hung from the ceiling lit with dragon light giving a soft glow to all around. At the far end was a massive chaise-longue sixty or seventy feet long with twenty or more gilded legs all along the front of it. Reclining on the chaise-longue was Máthair, Queen of them all, and this was her throne.

"Thomas, son of Llewellyn the Brave, welcome. You have come today to receive a companion dragon, Ren. Ren, appear before me."

A most beautiful Golden Dragon flew across and hovered next to the Queen.

"Ren, son of Heulwen, daughter of Máthair, Queen of all dragons, may I present to you a young wizard, Thomas, son of Llewellyn the Brave. For his courage, and maturity in the face of great danger, you are to be companion wizard and companion Golden Dragon. This binding is made by solemn oath and cannot be unbound except by death. You will both learn from each other, together you will have great power, possibly greater than any who may have gone before you. However, do not speak of this to anyone lest it is thought of as boastful. Your powers will increase with your years and with your learning. Go now into the world, show compassion, wisdom and judgement all your long lives."

Thomas didn't know quite what to say so he just quietly said, "Thank you."

Then 'POP' and they were outside again back in the valley. Ren looked magnificent in the sunlight; his scales looked like plates of solid gold. Next to him was a huge chest that looks just like the sort you would expect a pirate to have. Tom thought it must be Ren's things as he was leaving home. They both apparated to the head of the valley with the chest.

Tom introduced him to all his family and friends, including a rather sniffy and snooty Howel.

"Tom, the box is a little gift from Máthair to you. A little extra for your bravery in defeating the three Blue Dragons."

Tom opened the lid, he struggled because it was so massive and heavy, but inside was just stuffed with gold coins, silver coins, diamonds, rubies, emeralds and every precious stone you could think of, the case itself was lined with gold, the hinges and the clasp were solid gold. He was now incredibly wealthy. Rich beyond his wildest dreams, he had more wealth now than he would have ever thought possible.

"Dad," he said quietly, "I don't need all of this, hardly any of it in fact. Can't I send it to mum?"

"Oh my," said Ren, "what a son you have Llewellyn the Brave. You must be so proud. But in answer to your question. No, you can't. But next time she digs potatoes in her garden, she will unearth a new pot of gold and she will know that it is your gift to her."

"Wow! You would do that for our mum? How?"

"Well Golden Dragons are the most magical of all creatures, so if we can't do it, who can?" Ren replied, "Meanwhile I'll transport this little lot back to your lodgings for safekeeping."

"But you don't know where we live, even I don't know exactly."

"Tut, tut. You really have not been listening. I know more about you than even you know yourself."

And with that, the cask disappeared and hopefully reappeared back at their hideout in Blaenoraid.

Howel looked as if his nose was out of joint. He had one of his superior, looking down his nose looks on.

"Well," he started, "that is all very well, but gold and precious gems are a most unsuitable gift for a thirteen-year-old boy."

"True," Ren retorted sarcastically with an equally snooty look on his face, "but what were you expecting? A train set. He will not be thirteen for long and one day, when he is a man, he will make good use of his wealth, I assure you he will not use it foolishly or gloat over his fortune but use it for the good of others."

Llewellyn stepped in, "Now lads, you two must all get along together. We are a team," he said waving his hands towards Flintock, Tryg and the boys, "You two, and soon to be three, are members of the Black Hood Gang or whatever Tom calls us."

Ren laughed at the name, Howel just looked snooty still.

"It's Boys of the Black Hood, and we're not a gang," Tom said.

Now it was Jon's turn. They stood at the head of the valley which led down into the home of the Red Dragons. He too thought it was a rubbish place to live, just rocks and caves. If Aelwyd was really a queen, she should have something better than this he thought.

"Aelwyd, Queen of the Red Dragons, I come as commanded by Máthair, Queen of all dragons," Jon announced in just the same way as Tom had done. This time a Red Dragon swooped down and landed beside him.

"Jonathan, son of Llewellyn the Brave, we bid you welcome to the palace of Queen Aelwyd, Queen of the Red Dragons!"

He announced with the same pomp. 'Palace'? Thought Jon. Looks more like a caveman's house. The dragon led Jon into a narrow cave which opened out into another magnificent cavern. The floor was made of red rubies, the walls were hung with silk tapestries and encrusted with rubies, there were piles of gold coins and silver coins, diamonds, sapphires, emeralds and rubies just dumped in piles around the cavern, everywhere had a red glow and everywhere glistened under the light of a thousand candles floating in the air. Jon was gob-smacked.

Again, just like in Máthair's cave, at the end was a massive golden chaise-longue, upholstered in rich red velvet, with the Queen lying along its length.

Jon couldn't believe his eyes. There was a flutter and a large red cockerel appeared at his side.

Queen Aelwyd spoke, "Jonathan, son of Llewellyn the Brave, welcome to my humble home," with that, she visibly smiled, "I know, bit over the top really, far too much bling, but that's what you get when you're the queen. Now down to business. You are here to receive a great reward for your bravery and courage in assisting in the rescue of a Golden Dragon, Morcan and her whelp Bryn. Queen Máthair, mother of dragons and queen of all dragons has bid me offer a companion for life in the form of Bevon, an almost mature Red Dragon having a span of one hundred and fifty of your years. May I present to you your lifelong companion Bevon, not quite fully grown, but very accomplished at both magic and warfare. He is a lifelong companion because you cannot leave a dragon and a dragon cannot leave you. That is why every care has been taken in picking you as the ideal companion for Bevon. Blah, blah, blah, blah!" as she spoke, her tone changed from one of great pomp to a slightly higher pitched maniacal voice.

" So, it's to have and to hold, from this day forward, for better, for worse, for richer, for poorer, in sickness and in health, to love and to cherish, till death do you part, I pronounce you companion wizard and companion dragon. You may now kiss the bride."

Jon stepped forward, lips puckered.

"Stop! Only joking. Well, you can kiss him if you want, but I don't advise it. His breath probably stinks!" she then laughed out loud, little puffs of smoke and small flames running down her nose. Bevon himself was not looking at all amused.

"Yes well, sorry about that, I've always wanted to say that little speech, you know it's from your human wedding ceremony, but it makes me laugh so much," and she was off again laughing, "I mean, what does it mean! They all say it, but hardly any of them stick to it."

Jon was laughing too, "I'm sorry your majesty," laughed Jon, "I didn't mean to laugh."

"Oh, don't worry my dear, and please don't call me majesty, just call me Aelwyd, or Queenie or something."

"Sorry, but I thought that dragons were always serious and dignified in the way they spoke and the way they conducted themselves."

"Oh no, that's just an act we put on for the council and Phobls and people like that. Actually, we are quite fun but don't tell anyone, it's our little secret my dear," and with that, she burst out laughing again.

"Okay, that's it, off you go and don't forget to take Bev with you."

"That's it? Sorry, I was expecting a ceremony of some sort, solemn vows and stuff like that," said Jon.

"Well I just married you, didn't I? What more do you want! A wedding breakfast with after dinner speeches?" and she was off again, laughing so much that she nearly fell off the throne. All the other dragons in the great hall were laughing so much that the ground was shaking. All except for Bevon.

Jon and Bevon exited the cave, there was a 'pop' as the red cockerel morphed into a Red Dragon, about fifty-foot long with ruby iridescent scales which shimmered and changed to every hue of red and crimson possible, and a huge case of rubies, gold and silver coins and other jewellery

"I'm so sorry about that, please don't mention mum's behaviour to anyone, she can be so uncouth sometimes," he said in a very haughty tone and sounding just as bad as Howel.

That's more like it, thought Jon, that's how a dragon should be, snobbish, cultured and slightly pompous sounding.

Bevon, of course, caught the thought.

"I may be cultured, but I am not snobbish or pompous," he declared.

"Sorry," said Jon, remembering that dragons can catch your thoughts, "I'll introduce you to my little group in a bit. There are four of us plus a trygall, a Purple Dragon called Howel who's me dad's and a Golden Dragon called Ren I think, only just met him, he's with my brother Tom."

"Oh goody," Bevon said with a bored and 'do I care' sort of attitude, "I'm so looking forward to that."

"So why did Queen Aelwyd choose you and not one of the others?" asked Jon.

"She wants rid of me; seems to think I have attitude problems and lack respect."

"Ooh, I never noticed," said Jon with more than a hint of sarcasm.

"Really," said Bevon with a hint of mock shock, "there is no need for sarcasm!"

"Well, I think your mother matched me as your companion for the same reason."

"And what is that dear boy?"

"She probably thinks that I also have attitude problems and lack respect."

"Oh," said Bevon, "in that case, I think we are going to get on just fine."

CHAPTER 26 - GET TO KNOW YOUR DRAGON.

Back at Blaenoraid, the three of them sat around the table. In one corner of the room was Tom's treasure chest, diagonally opposite was Jon's chest. They must be worth millions of pounds if not trillions. Well they would be back home, but they had absolutely no idea what they were worth here.

"So, da, all those jewels, all that gold, silver, diamonds and stuff. Are we now rich? I know we would be back home, but are we rich here as well?" Jon asked.

"Yes boys, you are both very wealthy here as well. One of the small gold coins in those casks is about six months wages in Trymyll, a large silver coin is a months' worth and you have thousands of gold and silver coins plus all the gemstones and other pieces of jewellery. You both have so much, you will never have to earn another copper coin for as long as you live and still have plenty over."

"Where do we keep it? We can't just leave it lying around here can we?" Jon added.

"Well actually yes, we don't have banks as such here in Trymyll. But I'll make you both a secret room where you can store your treasures, no doors, or windows and only accessible by you and me," he said, tapping the side of his nose and winking.

"Awesome!" they both said in unison.

"We've got an hour before I fetch the others, so I'll set to work on it straight after breakfast."

Minutes later, the two little rooms were ready, they were not large, they didn't need to be, inside they were about six foot in every direction. The walls, floor and ceiling were three feet thick and made of solid granite reinforced with cold iron rods which went every which way through the structure. They thought their dad had somehow made two twelve-foot hollowed out cubes of granite to the side of the room with cold iron rods for reinforcement out of thin air, and the twelve-foot cube of stone and earth which was there, was now nowhere to be seen. And all without leaving the room.

"How did you do that da?" asked Tom.

"Simple really, the rooms were already there when I set up the hideaway. There are several arranged around the perimeter of the structure. That's where I keep my gold and silver. There was a couple of spare rooms, so I just opened them up for you two!" he said as he laughed, "You didn't think I just made those two rooms in a few seconds do you?"

"No, obviously not," Tom fibbed, "but how many rooms are there with your money in?"

"I have three, but there are six in total, so now there's one spare just in case I get rich all of a sudden!"

"THREE! You must be well rich!" exclaimed Jon.

"Oh no, I am a wizard of most modest means really."

"What?"

"Oh, alright then, yes I am quite wealthy actually, but I live modestly and never flaunt my wealth. And neither should you two," he said looking straight at the boys.

"So why haven't you sent any of your gold back to me mum?" asked Tom, "she's as poor as a church mouse"

"Prudent would be a better word to describe your ma."

"Meaning?"

"She has plenty, probably the richest woman in Wales, and now with your two caskets, she'll have even more. But she keeps herself to herself and discreetly helps others without making a fuss and without anyone knowing where the help comes from."

"She gives it all away?"

No, not exactly all, she has far too much to just give it all away. She helps those in need but only to the extent that they need help, that way she will always have more than enough. It's all in the bank. She basically just lives and gives from the interest and investments."

"But she's on benefits," Tom said indignantly.

"No, she's not, she just pretends to be and lives modestly so it would appear like she is. It's her choice. I've often told her that she could afford far more and far better but she's quite stubborn about it. She was born in a miner's cottage and that's where she's staying. Anyway, enough of this, I'll go and get the others."

Llewellyn disappeared and two seconds later he was back with Flintock and Tryg.

Flintock looked around as if looking for something, eyeing the room from side to side and from floor to ceiling, "You're going to need a bigger place now you've three dragons to keep."

"Not really. I have come to an arrangement with them all, Howel can sleep in the dog basket over there, Ren has a perch over that side and Bevon can roost over there in that coup," he nodded over to a non-existent dog bed, perch, and roosting box.

"Yes, that will work," Flintock said laughing.

"Of course not, they are nearby but not yet together. I think they need to get to know each other a little better before they all move in together. They are close by, so they will be able to come when needed and quickly if required."

"So, spent all your money yet boys?" Flintock asked with a smile.

"Of course not. Do you want some, we have plenty?" Tom offered on behalf of them both.

"Thanks for the offer boys, but I also have plenty. Safely locked away in my home in Wrth y Môr I have a fortune to almost match your fathers, so thanks, I'm touched by the offer, but no thanks."

"How come all you wizards are so rich but dress like...." Tom paused while he thought of a word..., "Worzel Gummidge?"

"Worzel who? Who's Worzel Gummidge?

"Excuse my sons. Worzel Gummidge is a fictional character back in their former world. He's actually...," then Llewellyn had to think about how to phrase it without insult, "it's a book of stories about a scarecrow who comes to life. He's very jolly and kind to people, but he .... dresses differently!"

They all laughed at that most awkward of descriptions.

"Right all, let's get down to business," Llewellyn said to bring order back into the room.

"First, if you and your dragons are going to be any good to anyone, you two need to get to know them and they need to get to know you. If we want to fight effectively, then you must be in each other's minds. Easy for a dragon, but not so easy for humans. So, go learn."

"What if they don't let us?"

"Don't worry, they will."

The boys disappeared and went to where they had left their respective companion dragons. Jon arrived at where Bevon was lodged.

"Hi Bevon,"

"Oh. Hi to you too Jonny boy," came the reply.

"Me da says that I've got to come down and get to know you a bit so that we can be effective in battles and stuff. But I've been worrying about that. Can you fight? I mean a proper fight, or is it like slapping or handbags at dawn? Not wishing to be rude or anything, but you don't sound like a fighter."

"Oh! What terrible stereotyping! Of course, I can fight! I have already fought and won many an affray. Just because I'm cultured does not mean I cannot fight."

"Well then, let's go to my dad's training room, he can conjure up some worthy opponents so we can have a sort of mock battle. I need to understand how you fight and you've got to understand how I fight. If we work together, we could be invincible."

"I already am invincible. Don't you doubt it."

"Alright, forget the training room, let's go to the quarries and test out our power there."

"Okay, if you insist," Bevon sighed the sigh of a bored teenager and turned into a rather handsome cockerel. Jon picked him up and they apparated away to the quarries.

'Pop' and Bevon returned to his normal form of a ferocious looking Red Dragon.

"Okay Jonny, what do you want me to do out here in this wasteland?"

"Well, I don't know how magical you are as a dragon. I know a lot about Howel...

"Oh! Don't speak to me about Howel, isn't he just such a snob?"

Jon was a little taken aback by Bevon's little outburst, but he stuck with it.

"Howel is exceptionally good at mind-bending, spell weaving and incantational magic. What specifically are you best at then?"

"Well, I can't pull rabbits out of hats or card tricks, don't really have the hands for it. Can't apparate, but you know that. Only Golden Dragons can apparate. We have the ignominy of being carried like pets by our human hangers-on. Oops, did I say that out loud? Of course, I meant, our human friends," he said with a mocking bow of fake respect.

"Never mind what you can't do. What the hell can you do?" Jon was getting irritated; he knew they had a battle on their hands soon and Bevon was not taking things very seriously.

"Ooh, tetchy, Well, like you I can send out an energy blast which will blow most things apart, especially humans, they are so soft and squishy. Go on, pick a rock, any rock, any size, and I'll show you."

"What about that one over there?" Jon pointed to a rock about the size of a small car.

"Hmmm. Maybe something a little smaller? How about that one over there." he said indicating toward a boulder the size of a large watermelon.

"No, I'll demonstrate," Jon's staff appeared, a bolt of energy flashed out towards the quarry face and he blew a hole in it the size of a house, not a little miner's cottage sized house but a large four bedroomed detached, two reception, double garage, with study and two en-suite bathrooms house. At the same time, he tapped his staff down and enclosed them in a force field as tonnes of rock and stone rained down around them from the blast.

"Ooh, impressive. Would not want to be on the receiving end of one of those. But can you do this?"

He belched out a long flame of fire which melted the huge pile of rock and rubble into a white-hot granite pool which then flowed down the quarry forming a stream of lava. The flames seemed to go on forever, even after about a minute, they were still coming out. This guy might be weird, but he sure could throw a flame when he wanted to.

"Ooh, impressive," Jon said in his most pompous accent, "would not like to be on the receiving end of one of those," he said, imitating Bevon.

Bevon was highly amused and laughed out loud, "Oh, very good, I almost thought it was me then."

"Now watch this," said Jon, water fell from nowhere, quenching the stone, sending up billows of steam forming huge clouds in what had been the bluest of cloudless skies.

Bevon pretended not to be impressed.

"How about some flying? Bevon suggested. Jon had not seen Bevon fly yet, but they launched off together. Bev was exceptionally fast, far faster than Howel and Jon thought he was fast. Jon was easily able to keep up with him. They then went into some aerobatics with all the normal loop the loops, barrel rolls and stall turns, they even flew at high speed towards each other narrowly missing just like the Red Arrows do on their displays. They both had the same idea at once and "Smoke on,"

Up they went and formed a huge heart in the sky made from the smoke before landing and falling about laughing.

"Oh boy Jon, are we going to have fun. I was dreading being 'sold into slavery' as I used to call it because I knew the old witch Aelwyd was going to get rid of me at the first opportunity, but this is really not what I envisaged sitting all alone in my little cave, ostracised by the other dragons just because I was different. No, we are going to be the absolute best of partners, BFF in fact."

He had hardly finished speaking when in the distance they could see a thunder of Blue Dragons heading their way. They had spotted all the antics of the explosions, the instant cloud formations and maybe even the aerobatic display.

"Quick," said Jon, "rooster mode, then we can apparate out of here."

"Not on your Nelly. You wanted to see if I could fight, let's go fight."

He launched up towards them. Jon hard on his heels, well maybe not heels exactly, but you know what I mean.

"No stop, there's about twelve of them, don't be stupid."

"Oh dear, well if you're going all scaredy-cat, you can apparate off. I'm going for the kill."

They sped off together heading straight for the thunder of dragons, they could easily outrun them if necessary as Blue Dragons are not the fastest of beasts, they could outmanoeuvre them as they are not that agile either, but they couldn't outnumber them. It was two against twelve. Jon had an idea suddenly form in his head. He conjured up a fire dragon, now it was twelve against three. The fire dragon sped on ahead of them straight into their flight path and then looped around them in a tight loop come barrel role manoeuvre. The Blue Dragons were completely disoriented, and their formation fell apart. One of them fell out of the sky in surprise and it was a thousand or more feet down before he found his wings again. They were scattered all over the sky. The fire dragon had done its work and disappeared into little wisps of flame. Jon struck first; a massive bolt of energy literally vaporised the lead dragon. Bevon belched out a massive lick of flame which burnt the patagium off the wings of the next beast and he plummeted down, no longer able to fly. Two dragons came at Bevon, both shooting huge plumes of fire. Bevon seemed to wallow in the heat, it did nothing, he then took one down while Jon blasted the other out of existence. 'Teamwork!' he heard in his head. Bevon was communicating with him telepathically. They both looped around the now reforming pack and took two more out from behind. One dragon managed to tailgate Jon and was just about to belch out his fire when Jon sent a few cubic metres of water from his emerald right into the throat of the dragon, his flame went out and the weight of a couple of tonnes of water sent him spinning towards the ground. 'Three more to go for a full set', he heard in his head. 'Let's get them', he thought back, not knowing whether it was one or two-way communication. The one that had plummeted down after the fire dragon startled him was now almost back up with the others. He then attacked another Blue Dragon, sinking his massive teeth into his neck and they both fell, ungracefully down, locked in a fight which would end in them both dead. 'What the...?' thought Jon. 'Simple mind games, I suggested to him telepathically that we were his friends, so he turned on them. Stupid creatures really. I'll let you have the honour of number twelve. Though you'll have to be quick, he's vamoosing it out of here fast'. Tom turned, accelerated to his maximum speed, and blasted him out of the sky.

Back down on the ground, they sat for a while to catch their breath. Jon was curious about one aspect of the fight that they had just had.

"How come when the two Blue Dragons blasted you with fire, you seemed to just absorb it and the flames had no effect on you?"

"I have all the magic of a trygall, so I am also a fire-master. I can absorb the fire back into my body and release it at will."

"Mmmm. Best if I don't ask how you acquired those skills'" Jon quipped.

"I hope you don't think I ate a trygall do you?" Bevon said feigning shock.

"No. I wasn't suggesting......"

"Well, actually I did, and in case you're wondering. They taste of sushi."

"Yukky!"

"No, Sushi."

CHAPTER 26½ - TOM AND REN.

Meanwhile, Tom had met up with Ren, his magnificent Golden Dragon.

"Hi Ren, dad said that I need to get to know you better, get inside your head and you get inside my head so we can act as one. Any idea what he's on about?"

"Yes, dear boy, we need to be as one, to fight as one, to think as one, to act as one. That way we will be an invincible team."

"How do we do that then.?"

"For a Golden Dragon, it is simple. For a small boy, it is not quite so simple," he said condescendingly, "but not impossible. Come sit in front of me and look me straight in the eyes, relax and try to make your mind still."

Tom sat cross-legged on the floor in front of Ren, Ren prostrated himself full length on the floor in front of Tom and they stared into each other's eyes, meditatively.

"My, my, young Tom, yours is not an open mind at all. Even I am having great difficulty in penetrating into your thought patterns. This is a fantastic ability you have. It means that you are difficult if not impossible to influence and control by thought and mind power, a trait which I am sure will stand you in good stead in the future."

"I know that, Howel had the same problem before I came to Trymyll. He had difficulty weaving incantations into my head. But I'm not doing it on purpose, it's just me, it's just the way I am."

"Oh, I know that, but it is a great gift, a great gift indeed. Now, try to relax a little more. Look into my eyes, concentrate on me and try to imagine you are reading my mind."

They tried again and again and again. Tom was just getting fed up and thinking it would never happen, when suddenly they connected.

Tom felt like he was falling into another world. When he stopped falling, although he knew he wasn't, he looked around. He could see through Ren's eyes, He could see himself sitting there in front of him, cross-legged on the floor, staring back at Ren; it was as if he were inside Ren's head. Tom could see all of Ren's thoughts, he could see all his one hundred years stretching back, right back to when he fought his way out of the egg his mother had guarded day and night for nearly a year. He could see the love in his mother's eyes as he took his first hesitant steps and stepped out of the last piece of shell. He could almost taste the richness of Morcan's milk as Ren suckled for that first year. He watched his childhood, his learning, his magic being formed as he matured. He saw his battles, he saw his sadness's, his joys, his laughter, his devastations, his mourning at the loss of a loved one. He saw everything, his most intimate of thoughts and Ren also was seeing them all again as well.

Tom also knew that Ren had the same access, Ren had seen his hopes and fears as well. Tom could now see Howel weaving thoughts into his mind, he could feel and remember how the Hadleigh-Smythes were imagined and created into existence, while at the same time, not existing at all. He could see the mountainside as seen by others and he could see it as it was spell woven by Howel, the cave entrance and the path and stile which led up to it. He could see his school days flash before him, and he could not only see Mrs Glyn, but understand her, he could see how passionate she was as a teacher and how she only wanted the best for them all, even if she had to be a little hard on them at times. Tom could now remember right back to his earliest days, Tom could see his father weeping bitterly as he left him and his mother behind, he could remember, see and feel the trauma for Jon as he was taken from his mother at just a couple of years old. He remembered every part of his life right back to when he first opened his eyes and looked on the loving gaze of his mother and father. He watched and winced as his father cut his umbilical cord at his birth.

They released each other but still sat staring at each other. Tom had tears in his eyes at what he had seen, not only in his own life, but in Ren's life as well. Ren had lost his brother; his brother had died, but Tom still had a brother even though he had not seen him in all those years, at least now Jon and he were again united. He was filled with so many emotions that he started to weep. He looked up at Ren, he also was weeping, huge tears making puddles on the dry ground below. Tom had never thought that a dragon could cry, but he was wrong.

Such an encounter is both thrilling and revealing. It lays bare the emotions. Neither would forget it, neither could forget it, for now, they were forever connected.

Jon looked at Bevon and Bevon looked at Jon, now they too were connected. Not in the same intimate, soul piercing way Tom and Ren were, but in a very understanding, knowing the next move type of connection, they were like a couple of twins who always knew what the other was doing wherever they were in the world. They could feel each other's pain.

"What next?" asked Jon.

"Flying lessons!" was the unexpected answer.

"But I can already fly."

"Yes, on your own, but not on the back of a Red Dragon!"

"Why would I need to do that?" Jon said, a little nervously.

"When we fight, we fight as one. You with your incredibly

powerful energy bolts, and me with my strength and fire. Together we will be invincible," Bevon declared, "here, sit just at the back of my neck and hold on. You won't fall, in fact, you can't fall. If you come off, just fly back on again. Don't forget, you don't need a staff to fly. When you fly with me, I am your staff."

Jon gingerly mounted the neck of the Dragon, his gangly legs hanging either side. Bevon pushed off. Jon wobbled but kept his place holding on to one of the spikes that stuck out at the base of the neck, and up they went, weaving, ducking, swooping, and cheering all around the quarries.

"Blast a few rocks, let see how it works, but be careful you don't blow my head off!" Bevon laughed and Jon heard it in his head.

Jon released bolts of energy from the end of his wand, smashing huge boulders into a thousand pebbles. He envisioned a cave right through the wall of one quarry and into the next, closing it back up as soon as they had passed through it.

'Good move if we were being tailgated', he felt Bevon think. And so, it went on until they were both bored, then Bevon took on some height on and they winged their way back to Blaenoraid and home.

Tom's encounter was far less physically energetic, but mentally exhausting. They had not had to leave the clearing where Llewellyn had 'parked' Ren when they arrived. You don't ride a Golden Dragon anyway, you fly with it and almost become part of it. Taking on all its skills and powers as you do so. Tom was surprised to find, that like Ren, he could now pick up the thoughts of others, the only mind he could read directly was Ren's, but now he had the same power that Howel had, he could catch the thoughts and intentions of others and also project his own thoughts into their minds. Ren had taught him, in those few moments that their minds were connected as one. He now knew how to weave thoughts into another's mind, how to bend the will of another, subtly and without them noticing.

"I see you have focused on the mind weaving young Tom. Be careful with it. It is a great power and with great power comes great responsibility."

"You dragons really like that phrase don't you," interrupted Jon.

"Which phrase?"

"With great power comes great responsibility!" Tom said laughing.

"But it's true, so do not use it just to get your own way, tempting as that might be. Use it only in situations where it is necessary. Yours was the first mind I could not see straight into as soon as I wished. Your sub-conscious blocking of my attempt to get into your mind was outstanding. Having been in your head I know that this is a latent, not a learnt skill. Make sure you keep it honed. From now on you will know when someone or some thing is trying to influence you through your mind. Find that block and keep it engaged. It may save you and others in the future."

"Why do people keep saying someone or some thing? I don't like the idea of a some thing."

"I know, I have seen that in your memories. But do not fear little one, your mind is strong, the strongest I have met. You have little to fear except fear itself. So be brave, be fearless."

With that said, Ren disappeared. Tom heard in his head, 'When you need of me, I will return in an instant. I have apparated away home now, but we are as one, so should you want me, you only have to think, and I will return.'

Tom smiled happily and walked back into the city. With Ren, they would be a formidable team. He couldn't wait to tell the others.

CHAPTER 27 - HOW TO GET YOUR MAGIC BACK.

Tom and Jon arrived back at their hideout at the same time. Both excitedly telling the other about their day and their dragons.

Both experiences were so different. Tom's had been a meeting of minds, Jon's a battle Royale!

Tom told of how Ren had had difficulty in breaking through his barriers, he told of how he could see right back to the moment Ren had broken out of his mother's egg and how he could see all the way back to when he opened his eyes and first saw his mother and father and watched his father cut his umbilical cord. He fell silent for a few moments as he said this, welling up a little, but he soon settled down again and continued his story. He completely left out about the mind-bending bit. He didn't want the others to know that. He decided he would tell his dad when he was ready and alone. He would tell Jon only if he had to, but he wouldn't tell any of the others. He would also know when Howel was 'eavesdropping' and how to block him. But he told them all that he wanted them to know for now.

Jon told of the fun they had had in the quarries, how when Bevon told him to pick a boulder for him to blast.

"I picked him one the size of a small car, but Bev looked around and picked another that was no bigger than a watermelon!"

He told them how Bevon melted the rocks into a pool of white hot liquid granite with a mighty and long blast from his chest. He told them of the flying lesson and how they moved as one around the quarries blasting out tonnes of granite and the cave he envisioned, flying through it, closing it up again behind them. He told them that Bevon was a firemaster, but without the detail of how he acquired the skill. He told them how they could communicate with each other just by thinking. Not forgetting, of course, their battle with the twelve, no fifteen, no, maybe as many as twenty Blue Dragons and how they had defeated them. He particularly relished the battle part of his story and told every detail, twist and turn, plus a few extra bits to make the story more interesting!

The two boys told their stories, each trying to outshine the other until at the finish, they both ended with the same words, "Together we will be invincible!"

"I think," said Llewellyn, "that together, you two brothers would be invincible, with or without dragons."

Tom then stood up and said nervously.

"I need to talk to the council. Can you get them together tomorrow for me da?"

"What? You can't just call the council in on a whim. They run a great bureaucracy and have long and drawn out procedures, it really is not that simple. It is highly unlikely they would assemble tomorrow even if a war were declared, let alone at the request of a thirteen-year-old, still green behind the ears wizard."

"Well call them anyway. Just tell them it's important."

"What do you want them for anyway?"

"It's not that simple. Ren has a message from Máthair, but I'm only allowed to tell the council and no one else."

"Not even me?" he said with some dismay.

"Not even you. Her message was quite specific."

"Well at least give me a clue."

"No, I can't. I can only tell only the council."

Llewellyn shook his head in disbelief but said he would go and see the Elder tomorrow and request an audience.

"But don't get your hopes up. I doubt very much if he will acquiesce."

Next day, after breakfast Llewellyn left the hideaway. He apparated out and then returned about half an hour later.

"the Elder says he will not at this stage ask for a full council meeting but will grant you an audience to discuss the matter with him. If after that, he thought it necessary, then he would call them together."

"But Máthair said only the council."

"Well, the only way to get a full council meeting is by either telling the Elder about it first or killing someone."

"Will you come with me da? That bloke gives me the willies."

"Unfortunately, no. When the Elder grants an audience, it is only with the person whom he has called. Not his family or his mates. I will take you to the chamber, but you have to see him alone."

"Okay, I suppose I'll have to man up and see the creepy old man on my own. When will it be then?"

"Now," his dad replied.

"What now? Okay, let's do it."

The two of them apparated out and reappeared outside the castle walls. They then walked in unchallenged right to the council chamber where he would meet the Elder.

"Are you sure that you can't come in with me? I'm scared. Don't you think he's a creepy old man as well?"

"No, I don't, now in you go and good luck," Llewellyn said.

Tom walked into the chamber and looked around. It was completely empty, spooky, and cold. A few moments later a door opened behind the biggest chair and in glided the Elder and stood before him.

Tom tried to see under the hood, but it was all darkness. He tried to look inside the Elders mind to see if he could get any thoughts from him.

The Elder spoke, "Thomas Jones, son of Llewellyn the Brave. Before we start, there are a few things you need to know. One," he said sharply, "do not try to probe my mind or try any mind weaving tricks on me or you will be the worse for it. And two, I am not a creepy old man," he made the second point with a small giggle, "thirdly, this had better be good. What do you want that is so important that you can't even tell your own father and you need the whole council for? Please explain."

"It's Máthair, Queen of the Golden Dragons and Queen of all Dragons. She has sent a message for the council concerning why magic is fading and failing in Trymyll."

"And this news is such that you could not tell your own father? Could he not have brought me the message?"

"No, it was too upsetting, I couldn't tell him. On my journey to the city, Llewel the Elder..."

"Llewel is no longer worthy of that title. Do not use it again!"

"Sorry, Llewel said that it was probably my father who was responsible for the magic disappearing and I hated Llewel for it."

"So, what is the message?"

"Well, it might be my dad after all, which is why I couldn't tell him first."

Tom could feel the Elder stiffen up as he said that.

"You won't be hard on him, I'm sure he didn't do it on purpose, he didn't know," Tom began to snivel a little.

"What did he not know?"

"When he visited me and my mum he would take things back from the other side and had quite a trade going in things like trainers, watches, keyrings, souvenirs and stuff like that, even mobile phones, but I don't know why, they don't even work here."

"They were a status symbol. No use at all but for showing off," the Elder explained.

"Even silly little things like ballpoint pens and pencil sharpeners. None of them necessary, but wizards, elders and even High Elders used to buy them from him and pay good money for some things. But bringing in things from the non-magical world was ruining your world just as science and a lack of belief have ruined my world."

"And how did Máthair, Queen of all Dragons come to this conclusion?"

"She is very old and very wise I suppose."

"She is incredibly old, so old that she might have lost a few marbles. No. Sorry. If I call the council for this, they will laugh at you and think me a fool for calling them in. Where is your evidence?"

"I know two things which Máthair made me understand. One. Llewel would not or more likely could not fly because he had lost the ability as his powers had faded, though actually, I saw little evidence that he had much magic at all in the time I was with him, the only thing I ever saw him do was set a bush on fire and then set fire to half the countryside. Obviously, he never admitted it to anyone, but once he was rid of his trainers even I could feel his power growing, and then I heard that he was able to fly to Blaenoraid after he dumped Flintock."

"How can you prove this?"

"Ask him, he is in your keeping, bring him in and ask him. Even if he won't tell you, I know that you can get into his weak little mind and find it yourself."

"How do you know that?"

"You just told me."

"When?"

"By asking me how I knew."

"You, young man are too clever by half. You should be a lawyer, not a wizard."

the Elder turned and rang a small hand bell which was on the central table. In came his clerk. the Elder explained what he wanted and a few seconds later there was sliding of stone and up popped the cage with Llewel inside. His eyes looked wild, mad even, and a look of pure hate when he saw Tom in the chamber.

"What do you want with me Elder of the stupid Elders? Whatever it is, I won't tell you anything. Because I don't know anything!" Llewel literally spat the words out.

"My question is a simple one. After you abandoned your ridiculous trainers, did your power return?"

"What do you mean? How dare you suggest I ever lacked or lost any of my power. My beautiful trainers were nothing to do with it."

"To do with what?"

"No comment!" Llewel knew he had said too much.

"No comment necessary. You have told us what we needed to know."

the Elder waved his hand as if to dismiss him. With that, there was a sliding of stone as the central table opened and folded back, Llewel then disappeared back to the dungeons below.

"What did he tell us?"

"Well, listening is a great skill which few master. When he said that his beautiful trainers were nothing to do with it. He inadvertently told us that he had a problem. Also, I was inside his head, so I could see everything he was trying not to say. But what else have you for me?"

Tom related the story of the map and produced the crumpled-up piece of paper out of his pocket. The guards were still moving around, and everything was still as they left it except that there were now builders repairing the hole in the guardroom wall.

"When Jon and I tried to draw a plan of the castle using a ball-point pen and paper, we got nowhere, Jon accidentally broke the pen and all we had left was a quill and ink. The quill took over and produced this amazing map for us."

"Why are there builders repairing the guardroom wall and chimney?" the Elder asked.

"Well Jon accidentally blew a hole in the wall while we were there rescuing High Elder Brangwen Binning."

"Accidentally? Your Jon must be very clumsy," Tom couldn't see the smile, but he felt it coming through the dark hooded cloak.

"Can anyone collaborate what you have told me?"

"Well, Jon and dad can tell you about the map. But why are you being so awkward about this? You know the truth; you can see inside my mind just as you saw inside Llewel's."

"No, I can't actually, your mind is quite closed and impenetrable. I need collaborative evidence. Send in your father, I will talk with him," the Elder turned to leave but before he did......

"I can't."

He turned slowly back.

"Tell me child, why can't you? It is a simple request; he is waiting outside."

Tom was sweating by now and breathing extremely fast.

"Because he's already here. You are my father."

the Elder turned again and left. Moments later Llewellyn entered the chamber

"How'd it go then, what did he say?"

"Oh, come on da, don't play the innocent, you were here, you know what happened."

"Sorry, I don't know what you're on about."

"You are the Elder. You two, you're never in the same place together. When I was questioned by the council, you had urgent business elsewhere, at Arvel Mordecai's trial, you were there but the Elder wasn't. the Elder looks and smells the same as the figure I met when you called me in my dreams, and when I saw you in the neither here nor there. At our robing ceremony, the Elder was there but you were nowhere to be seen and after, at the celebration, you were there, the Elder was not. Shall I go on? Also, as pointed out by Flintock, no one else seems to have the access to the Elder apart from you. No one else knows where to find him but you. He doesn't have an Elder of Elders palace or mansion, or a little blue plaque on the wall of his house saying 'Here lives the Elder' does he? Apart from when he appears at council, no one except you ever sees him."

"But the Elder is hundreds of years old, he shuffles about like an old man...."

"No dad, their minds have been made to believe he is hundreds of years old. No one really hears him speak, no one knows his name. If that is true, how was he chosen as the Elder of Elders? You can't exactly vote for someone without knowing their name. Come on dad, tell me what's going on, I'm not as stupid as you think. Please."

"Sit down and calm down, I'll tell you the truth. Yes, I am the Elder. No one knows apart from Aneta Stepanek, she can not only be trusted, but is probably the only person apart from you and Jon that I do trust."

"What about Flintock?"

"Well yes, I do trust Flintock, up to a point, but not with everything."

"You haven't had a fling with this Sputnik woman, have you?"

"No, I have not. Don't be so rude, you're not too old not to get a clip round the ear. And her name is Stepanek."

"The reason that Aneta knows is that nothing is hidden from her, just as nothing is hidden from Máthair, Queen of all Dragons."

"But you said Máthair was losing her marbles."

"Yes, well, that may be a slight exaggeration, but Aelwyd, Queen of the Red Dragons, she really is as daft as a brush, but still wise though."

"But I just grassed you up to the Elder, to you. Sorry da, I hope you don't get into trouble," Tom spouted out before he thought it through.

"Oh, don't worry about that. If I don't tell anyone, the Elder promises not to tell anyone as well. Anyway, back to the story. The council was becoming very corrupt, they were all power hungry and only interested in themselves and in looking after their rich and powerful friends. The ordinary wizard or the phobls of the land were of no concern of theirs. We organised a little coup. One by one, the High Elders vanished and were replaced by more trusted people. Even Llewel was trusted in those days, but the power, no, not the power, the prestige went to his head and he became too self-important. One or two of the others are now also getting a bit pompous now, Traveon Baughan, Brangwen Binnion for example, so we may be due for a reshuffle again soon. I was never elected as Elder of Elders. The new council were just made to believe that I was the Elder, that I had been there for centuries and that no one could remember or pronounce my name."

"So, what happened to the old High Elders? You didn't kill them, did you?"

"By the Makers name, no! They were sent into exile, forbidden to return."

"What happened to the old Elder of Elders then?"

"There never was one. Again, that was all part of the deception. I became the Elder of Elders of the new council and they all thought that it had always been that way."

"But everyone in Trymyll believes the same thing, you can't bend that many minds all at the same time."

"You don't have to, people believe what they want to believe, they wanted a strong, straight and honest council under an incorruptible leadership. So that's what we delivered."

"Who's we?"

"Aneta Stepanek, Máthair and me. With a little help from a few dozen Golden Dragons to help change the minds of those who weren't quite following what was happening. If you get my meaning."

"But that's terrible, bending the will of the people to suit your own ends. Even if those ends are noble, it hardly makes it right, it's brainwashing."

"I know, I know, wise words from one so young, and slowly they are being released from the spells we have woven, and they too understand that life is now better than it was."

"But what about the stuff you brought in from home which is now affecting the magic?"

"Simple, we will announce a purge of all such items, declare them illegal and burn them in the city squares."

"But that will cast a bad light on you, dad you that is, not Elder you."

"I will humbly regret all that I have done, admit that it was wrong and ask the people to understand that I did not know it would leach power from the land."

"So, you believe me then."

"Yes."

"You already knew didn't you?"

"I probably did know all along, but I was in denial as I could not, or would not see a connection. Máthair did warn me a couple of years back, but again, I didn't want to believe her, so I just dismissed it."

"So, what's next?"

"I will convene a council tomorrow and you must again present your evidence and they will pass it through into law."

"Is it really that simple?"

"Yes, if the Elder recommends a course of action, they never vote against it. Especially if Aneta helps a little. Now, all that you have heard and all that you have worked out for yourself today must be a close secret. No one is to know, not even Jon. Promise?"

"Of course I promise," replied Tom.

"All rise for the Elder of Elders" the Clerk to the Elder barked. The full Council of High Elders stood as did everyone else in the chamber. This was a three line whip meeting, and everyone was there in person.

the Elder shuffled into the chamber and took his seat. The High Elders took their seats, High Elder Traveon Baughan made a point of bringing a cushion and making sure the Elder had seen it. Then, once Traveon Baughan had arranged himself and his cushion, the others all took their seats as well.

"We are here today to hear evidence from Thomas, son of Llewellyn the Brave concerning the disappearance of certain magic from the Land of Trymyll. Thomas, son of Llewellyn the Brave, please take the floor."

Tom told the council exactly what he had told the Elder, the council wanted more evidence and moved to call Llewel to the floor, but the Clerk intervened and related the story of his confrontation with the Elder, so they settled down again. They then heard about the map and how that had been made. Some were quite impressed, others less so.

"What do we do about Llewellyn the Brave, we can't let him get off scot-free," stated Traveon Baughan.

"That's my dad you're talking about. Don't forget, he didn't know and still doesn't know because I was told by Máthair to tell you lot about the problem, not him," Tom said hoping they would believe him.

"I am sure that Llewellyn the Brave knew nothing of the effects his little bit of trading were having, or he would have stopped it himself. He is a man of great integrity," said Aneta Stepanek in her strong Eastern European accent. Sending out thought waves of compliance at the same time.

The Elder stood, "Is it not more important at this time to sort the solution or is it more important to apportion blame? Who of you has not had a trinket or two from the other world courtesy of Llewellyn the Brave?"

There was an embarrassed silence to the question. Most if not all had had something from Llewellyn even if it was just a plastic dragon on a plinth marked 'A Gift from Wales.'

"So, I suggest that first, we live by example and all turn in our little bits and pieces from the other place. We will sit again tomorrow to seek a way forward. Don't forget to bring your little knickknacks," the Elder said with a hint of amusement.

As he turned to leave, he threw a 'We (heart) Wales' keyring on to the clerk's table.

"There's a start anyway."

Next day, the council sat again. This time joined by Tom, Jon and Flintock. All of them and all the High Elders had a bag full of stuff which they had bought from Llewellyn, all except High Elder Traveon Baughan of Gwir, who held no truck with such trinkets. Even the Elder had a small bag of contraband. Tom thought it would look better if even he had 'sinned' also.

"I'll be wanting my money back of course," stated Trevonn Brice.

"You'll expect no such thing," said the Elder, his own bag under his arm, "we all bought this rubbish in good faith and Llewellyn sold it to us in the same good faith and now we forfeit the money as a penance for doing so."

'Nice one da,' thought Tom.

"Council in session," called the clerk. The Elder sat, The High Elders sat and then everyone else sat. There was quite a large pile in the centre of the chamber, piled up to the height of the central table and several feet in width.

"What do we do with it now?" Flintock asked the council.

"Speak only when asked," barked the clerk, "Flintock has the floor."

"What do we do with it now?" he asked again to the same audience.

"We must take it to the city square, build a pyre, read a declaration that you have passed into law and tell all the other wizards to bring out their stuff and add to it. We must then go city by city and do the same," Tom said.

"Speak only when asked," barked the clerk, "Thomas, son of Llewellyn the Brave has the floor."

The Elder stood up, "Right, that's enough. Just do what the boy says, and will you stop all these stupid time-wasting points of order and procedural protocols for crying out loud," he said softly but with much irritation. He turned to leave.

"What do we do about Llewellyn the Brave, we can't let him get off scot-free," asked Traveon Baughan the same as he did the day before.

"I will talk to Llewellyn the Brave, give him a severe ticking off and banish him from Trymyll for six months;" the Elder said, and then he left just before Llewellyn entered the chamber.

"Oh, sorry, am I too late? Did I miss anything?"

"You were supposed to be here at ten o'clock precisely, it's now ten past, you missed everything," said the clerk, "Elder Flintock, please fill your friend in on the details. Thank you."

The council dispersed, most of them giving bad, angry looks towards Llewellyn, and some even towards Tom.

"What's up with them?" he asked.

"Well da, they've all got to give up the stuff you sold them without you having to pay them back," said Jon, "it's all got to be burnt in the city square."

"Well, winner, winner, chicken dinner," Llewellyn said, then they all laughed and left the chamber last.

"I'd better bring up my stock to add to the pile on the pyre then," he said with a smirk.

And so, a declaration was made, and all the people were made to bring out their souvenirs and trinkets from Wales to add to the pyre. In Blaenoraid, Tryg was on hand to set the fire going and to make sure that everything was completely consumed. There was surprisingly little resistance, a few people grumbled, but none of the stuff had cost them much, apart from the few High Elders and elders who had bought the useless mobile phones not even knowing what they were for.

The High Elders returned to their cities and in each city, the declaration was read, and the fires were had. Even in Castell yr Tywyll where Asmodeus held court the directive was rigorously adhered to. In fact, probably even more so as Asmodeus needed to return to his full power so he could suppress the little lightning bolts which had turned him from Asmodeus the Dark into Asmodeus the bright!

Magic quickly flowed back into the wands and lives of all the wizards in the land.

Now, this could be our happy ever after ending. But the Master was still to be dealt with. The Master was still in Trymyll. His threat still hung over them all. As usual, the council was doing all it could to ignore the situation.

CHAPTER 28. THE MASTER RETURNS.

"The council is now in session," announced the clerk. The Elder swept in, but this time did not sit down. Instead, he motioned for all the others to sit and he took the floor. He paced up and down the chamber, no movement beneath his garments, no sign of hands or face or feet. He was almost like a ghost in his movement, slow and gracefully he continued to pace up and down, all without saying a word. Then, after some seconds, he spoke.

"High Elders of Trymyll. You have spent these last few days dealing with the inconvenience of trinkets from another land when a dark and powerful wizard from another dimension walks our land freely. You have done all you can to ignore this situation hoping it will go away or that it never happened. Tell me, what plans do you have if this wizard who calls himself the Master should come to your city and wreak havoc and bloodshed among you? A rhetorical question, so no need to answer, I know that not one of you has faced up to this situation save High Elder Govannon Stealey of the Elven Community who has mobilised his massive army of elven warriors, archers horsemen and women to oppose any attack by an army of whatever nature that may descend upon them. Valiant as his men and women warriors may be, they will be no match for the power of the Master. He fights not with the weapons of war, but with magic and sorcery of power unimaginable to most of you. We cannot wait for the Master to bring the battle to us. We must take the battle to him. We must, as High Elders be willing to fight until not one among us is left standing, male, or female. We have some strong allies in the form of Flintock, and the sons of Llewellyn the Brave. We leave at dawn tomorrow for the Blue Mountains. You may bring your weapons, but I fear they will be of little comfort to you. We need your magic. Now our powers are restored, and Llewellyn has been temporarily banished for his mistake, we must unite against this terror and bring it down."

The Elder then sat down.

"High Elder Brangwen Binnion has the floor," the clerk barked.

"Elder of Elders, and High Elders present. It is harvest time and I really should be reaping and garnering my crops."

"If we do not defeat the Master, there will be no crops to bring in and no mouths to feed. Remember his threat. He will lay waste the land and not a single living thing will be left, not even a blade of grass or an ant will remain alive. Once he is defeated, then you can worry about your precious crops. Any more questions or dissenters?" no one stirred, "right, dawn at the city gate. All of you."

"One small question," asked High Elder Aneta Stepanek, "without wishing to sound at all rude oh Elder of the Elders, but are you not just a little too old and frail for such a battle. Would it not be better to bring back Llewellyn The Brave to lead the attack? He is, younger and more agile, plus he has already experienced the power and magic of this so-called Master and knows more than any what we are dealing with."

The others in the chamber all nodded in agreement. Little murmurs of, "here, here," and "she has a point," echoed around the chamber.

"I may be a little old, but I am strong, my magic is undiminished, and I am not a coward."

"No one would ever suggest such a thing. But we may lose an advantage if we must wait for you or defend you in the fray. I think we should have a binding vote of the council on the matter," Aneta added.

"The motion is that the Elder of Elders should remain at Blaenoraid and that Llewellyn the Brave should be called to lead the attack on the Master," announced the clerk, "all in favour say, aye."

"Aye!" the cry went up.

"Any against say nay," there was silence.

"The aye's have it," announced the clerk, "council dismissed."

And so, the council was dismissed. All departed except Aneta Stepanek who lingered until the others had gone and the chamber was empty. Llewellyn emerged from behind the Elder's chair.

"Thanks, Aneta, now let's hope I don't get killed, or you'll be short of an Elder of Elders!"

"My dear Llewellyn, if you are killed, then we will all be killed and there is no hope for anyone. I don't think we really need to worry about a vacancy at the top."

Next morning, five-thirty came and the High Elders, Llewellyn, Tom, Jon, Flintock, Tryg, Howel, Ren and Bevon all assembled at the city gate. News of their venture had leaked out and they were heartened to see that a small crowd had gathered to see them off, wish them well and cheer them on. The dragons were in their alter-egos of small dog, sparrow-hawk, and cockerel. Llewellyn and the boys lifted their dragons, the whole party then apparated away to the Blue Mountains as one powered by Flintock who was an absolute master at mass apparation. They appeared on top of the ridge; the sun was just rising over the opposite escarpment. Rocks, boulders, and small craggy outcrops threw huge shadows along the valley, stretched out by the low trajectory of the sun. The light poured into the entrance of the cave; the outer rim still blackened by the burnt dragons which had perished a few days earlier. As they approached, the stink of burning flesh still hung in the air and a little of the dried blood from when Jon vaporised their remains stuck to the edge of the cliff face running down the steep walls red, brown and black streaks of a jelly like substance which still hung heavy with maggots, feasting. Tom was sick, again.

They entered the cave, Tryg lit the torches as they approached each one with just a flick from his eyes. Ren morphed into his true self and flew down the cave into the cavern. He needed no light to see where he was going. As he entered the cavern he cloaked himself in invisibility and circled around the vast circumference sniffing the air as if looking for something. He spoke to Tom. Tom could see, feel, and hear everything that Ren could see in the back of his mind.

"Here is the portal door, it is, as you can see, closed," Tom could see it through Ren's eyes even though they were still some distance from the cavern.

"Ren has found the portal door. It is currently closed" he said to his dad.

Llewellyn passed the information onto the others. They whispered amongst themselves.

"If the door is closed, we should seal it up from this side, then the Master cannot come through again."

"Good theory," said Llewellyn, "but if the master is through the door and in our world, then we just sealed up his exit. No. We must make sure we know where he is before we seal up the portal. At least we now know the position."

They all entered the cavern. Both the other dragons now reverted to form but cloaked in invisibility. Ren and Bevon were completely invisible but Howel still had a slight purple glow about him and again looked like the cartoon character Tom had first met in the hidden cave. The thought made Tom smile to himself. In the event of a fight, all dragons would make themselves visible again so that they might not get hit by any stray spells. The Dragons were big, very big, but the cavern was vast, many hundreds of feet across, possibly a thousand, and high, two or three hundred feet high. In the centre, hanging about one hundred feet up was an exceedingly small swirling disk, set horizontally in the air, not more than the size of a penny across, visible only in the infra-red light thrown up by Ren.

"No wonder we couldn't find it, it's tiny, right up high and outside of the spectrum the human eye can see, clever," Llewellyn muttered to no one in particular.

The small disk suddenly expanded to about three feet in diameter and up from the disk rose the Master. As he rose, his deep Afro-Caribbean voice boomed across the cavern.

"Oh my, I am honoured, the whole Council of High Elders has come to pay homage to me. I do hope that you are all here to bend the knee to me. If you do, you may find me an especially useful friend. If you don't, you may find yourselves dead."

Tom noticed that Trevonn Brice was separating himself slightly from the rest of the High Elders. Tom decided to quietly summon Ren to assist with a little but gentle probe inside his mind to see what he was thinking and why he was moving away. Ren silently communicated with Bevon for back up. Bevon sent a thought to Jon about what was just about to happen. Jon threw up a force shield around the group just as the Master was about to make his move. Jon then sent a stinging shot across the crowd and Trevonn fell to the ground. Wounded, unconscious, but not dead.

"What the..," shouted Llewellyn. The Master disappeared and the floating disk closed back to the size of a penny.

Tom quickly announced, "He was just about to take you down da, we had to act fast."

"Why do say that, he's a High Elder."

"Ren probed his mind when I saw he was moving away. The Master knew we would throw up a defensive shield if he started to fight, but then he would have had a stooge inside the force field to take us out, starting with you and Flintock."

"It is true," Aneta said, "I too saw him moving away and read his intentions."

"Anyone see where the Master went? Is he here or in his own domain?"

"They all shook their heads."

"When the commotion started, we all turned away to look. No one saw where the Master went."

"Rubber necks, all of you," snorted Llewellyn

Tom started to probe the minds of all the others in the room. All except one, Flintock. His mind was blocked and solid. Despite his mighty gift, he could not get in. Even Aneta, who was supposed to have the strongest mind-probing abilities and best block in the land of Trymyll was open to Tom. Then Tom felt Flintock send him a thought.

'I don't know what you're looking for Tom, but don't. Now is not the time or place,' Tom was flabbergasted, surely not Flintock. He was dad's oldest friend. He must be on our side.

"Next time we see him, don't lose sight of him. Whatever is happening around you, you must keep an eye on the Master," Llewellyn barked it out like a sergeant major.

The circle opened and up rose the Master again.

"Ladies and Gentlemen, boys and girls, you disappoint me. So, you have found the first of my stooges. But will you find them all in time to save yourselves?"

Tom quickly gathered his thoughts. He knew that all the other High Elders were clean, perhaps this was just a bit of psychological warfare by the Master, trying to put distrust between allies. He was obviously on the right side as was Jon and his dad. The only one he didn't know about was Flintock. He sent a thought to his dad, 'We've had a quick look inside the minds of everyone here except one and they are all on our side.'

The reply came quick enough. 'When did you learn thought control? Never mind, who's not on our side?'

'I don't know, but Flintlock's put up a massive mental block which I can't get through, and he's warned me not to try.'

'Interesting,' his dad thought, 'But he may have his reasons.'

"So why do you run and hide at the start of any trouble oh great Master," Llewellyn said with a big hint of sarcasm.

"Llewellyn the Brave, I do not run or hide, I merely went to get my pet."

The portal widened even further and out slid a massive three-headed serpent dragon. He must have been one hundred feet long and each head was the size of a small car. It thrashed its tail around throwing tonnes of boulders and stones up into the air as it did so. The three dragons uncloaked and prepared for battle. Jon ran across to Bevon and jumped on his neck.

"No Jon!" shouted Llewellyn and Tom in unison. But it was too late, they were away. Ren and Bevon were straight into the fray, Howel kept his distance a little, but each of them was spilling out immense quantities of flame, it was so hot that rock was melting in the chamber. The assembled High Elders and wizards backed up the cave a little to keep out of the way. Tryg rushed forward, taking the fire out of one of the heads and into himself to protect the entrance of the cavern There was an almighty crack as Jon let go of what must be his biggest surge of pure energy ever. The head nearest him simply vanished and the long neck now hung down like a piece of meat in a butcher's window. Bevon reared up taking an almighty blast of fire into himself, he then expended all that energy and all his own fire in one mighty firestorm which literally cooked the second head all the way down to the end of the neck. At the same time, Ren appeared out of nowhere with what looked like a massive golden sword which sliced through the third neck as if it were butter. All went quiet as the massive beast just fell to the floor of the cavern. Dead.

"Impossible!" shouted the Master, his magnified voice bouncing around the cavern and breaking off pieces of rock. With that he launched his own attack, first against Bevon and Jon, a powerful bolt flung from his hand and bounced off Jon's impenetrable shield ricocheting back and nearly hitting the Master. He then started throwing random bolts of energy at anyone and anything. Ren was unaffected, a Golden Dragon has its own defensive shield which is more than enough for the Master's energy bolts. Howel was not so well protected and took a couple of hits which wounded him quite badly. Two of the High Elders were down, and he even sent a bolt into Trevonn Brice, finishing off what Jon had started. Howel summoned his strength and let the Master have a full blast of from his firebox. He was momentarily disoriented, and Tom managed a powerful and accurate blast which took off one of the Master's hands. The Master was visibly shocked, he had never seen such power before. He had never met with real resistance ever. All other worlds had just crumbled before him. He made a hasty retreat through the portal and the disk slammed shut.

At that moment, the Elder of Elders appeared in the cavern just below the portal. He floated up to the spinning disk. Cupped it in his hands and muttered an incantation. The portal disappeared. The door was shut. Trymyll was safe. For the time being anyway. The Elder floated gently down again to the floor of the cavern and disappeared again. Once the smoke had cleared and the torches were re-lit they could assess the damage. Three High Elders were dead. Traveon Baughan, Brangwen Binnion and of course Trevonn Brice who may or may not have been a traitor, finished off by his own Master. Llewellyn looked round. Flintock was missing, this was not good.

Tom was attending to Howel, his wounds were bad, but not life threatening. One wing was broken and hung at his side and he had a bad wound which was bleeding profusely. Tom seemed to pour healing into the wounds, and they were soon healed enough for Howel to be moved back to the surface if he morphed back into a dog so he could be carried. He had just enough energy and strength left to morph. So, Tom picked up the small limp Jack Russell dog and gave him to his dad.

He looked down at the bodies of the three High Elders, he wanted to be sick, he wanted to cry, he wanted to shout out loud in anger. He looked at the remaining High Elders.

"Well, thanks for all your help. Why not just stand there and let a couple of teenagers with their dragons take on the most powerful wizard you've ever seen. Thanks for nothing!"

Tom then stormed past them and up the slope to the cave entrance, a sparrow hawk on his shoulder. Jon followed him, cockerel under his arm and smoke still rising from his scorched cloak, glaring at the fine bunch of wizards just standing there, gawping. When they hit the surface, they didn't wait for the others, they apparated away back to the hideout without speaking.

Back in the cave, the others gathered up the bodies on makeshift stretchers which they magicked up by combining staffs. They had no wheels; they just floated and were easily pushed up the steep slope to the surface. Once they were out and everyone except Flintock was accounted for Llewellyn send a mighty bolt of energy into the cave, collapsing the roof as half the mountain fell in on itself. No one or no thing was using this cave again as a portal from anywhere.

CHAPTER 29 - ORDER IS RESTORED.

The whole team, minus Flintock and the boys apparated back to the city gates. A large crowd had already assembled awaiting their return. There was shock and anguish at the sight of the three bodies. They all noticed that three others were missing as well. Rumours started at once about the fate of Flintock and the two boys. It mainly focused on the boys, and not all good.

"Oh, those poor wee boys, blasted into nothing by the Master. Not old enough to have lived or loved," "I heard that they disappeared when the Master did a runner. If you know what I mean," "I heard they were eaten by dragons in the cave," said another.

Llewellyn waved for some silence from the crowd and climbing up on a mounting block, he addressed them.

"Fellow citizens of Trymyll, we have returned today form a terrible fight which was both led and won by my two sons and their dragons," he felt a dig in his side, "and of course, by my own dragon Howel who has sustained life changing injuries in the fray. The main casualties where High Elders Traveon Baughan, Brangwen Binnion and Trevonn Brice. We will all mourn their loss."

Llewellyn didn't mention that Trevonn Brice may had been on the losing side or that Flintock, who he knew would have been instrumental in his appointment as a High Elder was missing.

"The Master was beaten but not destroyed. He made his escape back to his previous world and the Elder sealed the portal himself," there was a murmur of disquiet that the Elder was involved at his great age and frailty, "now if you would excuse us all, we are, as you can see, covered in dust, dirt and blood from the affray, we have the dead to attend to and we need to report back to our families and friends to let them know that we, at least, are safe."

He waved his hand and the crowd dispersed. Llewellyn stepped down from the block, made his excuses to the High Elders and disappeared back to the hideout.

He returned to two very hyper and angry teenagers.

"They're useless that lot, not one of them lifted a wand in there, they just watched like it was a sideshow at the circus. Three people dead, poor little Howel injured. In fact, you didn't do much yourself until the end when you stepped up to close the stupid portal," Tom said angrily.

"Well, thanks for the welcome. As it happens, I was doing a lot in there. I was not only protecting the High Elders, well at least trying to, it would have been easier if they hadn't kept running about like scalded cats, but my main effort was stopping any of them from killing you. And it was the Elder who stepped at the last moment to seal the portal!" he said angrily towards Tom.

"What?" said Jon.

"Yes, you heard. Killing you. Except for Aneta, they are in the majority a load of numpties when it comes to a fight, if they had got their wands out there would be bolts flying everywhere, they could have brought the roof down on top of both of you. I wouldn't trust them and their wands at a coconut stall in the fair, let alone in a battle. They would have killed you and probably each other before the battle was done. You however all did exceptionally well, brave, foolhardy, but powerful. Jon has more firepower in his wand than all the High Elders put together, and Tom, not quite the firepower, but a superbly accurate shot taking off the Masters hand. As usual, you didn't go for the kill but taking his hand off was pure genius. No hand, fifty per cent less firepower. Your dragons," he felt the dig in his side again, "and Howel were exceptional as well. Between you all, you took down a hundred foot of three headed serpent dragon and drove the Master into retreat. The very sight of that serpent dragon would frighten the poop out of most wizards, and I think did for a few of the High Elders judging by the smell. So, stop sulking and start celebrating a great victory which will go down in the history books of Trymyll and be retold for centuries to come. Right, speech over, I'm starving, and I expect you are also. I'm going for a quick wash off in the river and then back for some supper. In fact, we'll go out and eat at a local hostelry. Anyone with me?"

They all disappeared in silence from there and reappeared by the riverbank, quickly undressed, and dived into the cold clear water. They quickly forgot their angst and they swam, splashed, ducked, screamed, and laughed the grime and dirt away. As they turned to go back to the bank, there stood Flintock. Wands instantly appeared in their hands.

"Don't! My wand is away, it will not be coming out. I know it looked bad back in the cave but let me explain. It will be difficult, but at least let me try. Their wands disappeared, they left the water and dried instantly with the use of a little energy, dressed, and stood in silence.

"Well?" opened Llewellyn.

"Not here, please, somewhere more private."

"Okay, you can come with us back to the hideout."

They disappeared and all reappeared back in the hideout, Flintock still could not place it, so as usual had to be guided by Llewellyn. Tryg ran across and grabbed Flintock's hand and held it for a few seconds with affection in his eyes. They had only been apart for a few hours, but Tryg new that Flintock might be in trouble, so he was concerned for him.

"First of all, let's get Trevonn Brice out of the way. Yes, I was instrumental in rigging his election. But I have known him for decades, he showed no sign of lusting for power. I don't believe that he was acting under his own free will but being manipulated by the Master. He was a good guy, kind and of the highest morals. Now I must go and tell his widow that he was taken in the battle. I can't tell her the whole story; it would destroy her and his family."

"I will explain to the council, or what remains of it as soon as I can and hope that the rumour mill has not yet leaked out any of the details of the battle. To be honest, Tom only connected to me, so they may not have even realised why Jon had a shot at him and are probably blaming Jon. But I'll smooth that over anyway," Llewellyn said.

"How?" asked Jon.

"I'll tell them that Trevonn was being controlled by the Master and was about to take us out and that you had to stop him from before he stopped us, Aneta will back us up on that. I will also point out that you only wounded him; it was the Master who finished him off. They will understand. Anyway, I'll massage their thoughts a little beforehand. Now Flintock, why the mind block?"

"Two reasons, firstly, with a total mind block up, and I mean total, the Master could not influence me in any way so if I were last man standing, I might have still been able to take him down. Secondly, and this will be difficult for me to say and probably even more difficult for you to understand. So, I won't tell you, but let down my block and let you in, only you Llewellyn, not the boy. He is not old enough to understand."

Tom so wanted to know, but out of respect for his father and the little respect he had left for Flintock, he did not argue. Flintock let down his guard and let Llewellyn into the deeper recesses of his mind. They sat there for a few minutes and then he spoke.

"So, how long have you known I am the Elder?"

"What!" said Jon, "wow, that explains a few things."

"A couple of months, to my shame, I was curious and followed you to one of your meetings, of course, you met no one, just returned with news of what had, or rather hadn't gone on. At first, I thought you were pretending to be a confidant of the Elder and I was laughing at you behind your back. But everything you told me happened or came true, so after a while, I put two and two together. I also noticed that whenever the council was in full session, Llewellyn was nowhere to be seen. The rest was easy. So, who else knows?"

"Just Aneta Stepanek, there is little you can hide from her, Tom, who also worked it out and now Jon, who we just told. Listen boys, this must be a secret between us. Please don't tell another living soul."

"Or even a dead one!" added Flintock.

"And?" asked Tom

"And what?" his dad replied.

"Well, that's not exactly devastating news, what's the rest of the story?

"That I'm afraid is very privileged information, perhaps, when Flintock is ready, he may tell you, he may tell you both or he may not tell you at all. But for now. You have all you need to know. He is still our dearest and trusted friend, and you have nothing at all to fear from him."

"What now?" asked Jon.

"Celebrate. We all go and eat now and tomorrow; we go and visit your mum."

THE END – OR IS IT?

Thank you very much for reading this book. I hope you have enjoyed reading it as much as I have enjoyed writing it. The story however is not yet over. Book 2, Jonathan, Dragonmaster is on the way and will be available as soon as I can write it.

There should be several more books in the series. Each one a story on its own but following on from the previous novel.

I also have in my mind a prequel, Llewellyn, and the Dwarf Wars.

Follow me on Facebook: https://www.facebook.com/Joseph-MasonAuthor

Follow me on Twitter: https://twitter.com/KirkyAuthor

Joe.

November 2020

GLOSSARY OF NAMES, PLACES, AND MAGICAL THINGS.

Aelwyd, Queen of the Red Dragons.

Asmodeus – High Elder Asmodeus, A dark high elder, banished from the council of elders.

Blemonpuss – a mythical creature which looked like a cross between a cat and a demon. Not an animal to be trifled with.

Caer - A Welsh castle, usually built into a mountainside or a large hill for greater protection.

Cantrip - A very minor spell, taught to a beginning apprentice to build his confidence. Any human can perform a cantrip. These include cooling water, lighting a candle, or calling a pet over without speaking.

Cold iron - The one bane of all magic. It prevents magical energy from flowing, and locks spells in place. A magician chained by cold iron is powerless, and cold iron edged steel weapons can kill most supernatural creatures. Magic swords are made by setting the dweomer while the iron is still hot from the forge; once the metal has cooled, the enchantment is locked in place.

Dark magic - (also called Black Magic or the Forbidden Arts.) Use of the powers of darkness, or the taking of life for magic power. Its use is shunned by most wizards.

Dragons Blue - Blue Dragons are the most dangerous, they have no scruples and will eat you as soon as look at you. They normally disguise as black cats, so never trust a Blue Dragon, and never trust a black cat. They are not very magical and can only hold their shapes for a few minutes before reverting to dragon again, the little magic they have is dark, very dark. They also tend to be very stupid.

Dragons Golden - Golden dragons are the most magically powerful and if you can align yourself with a Golden dragon, you will share their powers. Golden Dragons are always for good and never evil. They can change their size and shape, their normal 'disguise' is a sparrow-hawk.

Dragons Purple - Purple dragons are of course the most cultured, intelligent, good looking and modest of all dragons. Our alternative shape is of a small dog of indeterminate breed"

Dragons Red - Red dragons are to be sought; they are very magical, faithful, trustworthy and have longer lives than any other dragons. Their metamorphic other is a hen or cock according to their gender.

Dweomer -The permanent spell set into an object by a wizard.

Elder of Elders – Also called The Elder. Head of the Seven Elders of Trymyll. The most powerful wizard in the land. No one knows his name, no one knows his face, and few have heard him speak. He is just, The Elder.

Enchanter - A magician who specializes in INCANTATION. Most wizards are enchanters.

Familiar - A psychic bond between a human magician and a creature. Familiars share each other's feelings, powers, and traits.

Flintock the Elder – A full and powerful wizard, just below the seven, but has never risen to the top rank purely because he is not political and has no wish to do so. As a wizard he can out magic most of the senior elders but remains modest and caring.

Gate - A spell used for getting from one place to another quickly. Used by wizards who cannot apparate.

Howel – A purple dragon

Hadley-Smythes – An incantational couple created by Howell to 'foster' Tom for the last two months he was at home.

High Elder Aneta Stepanek - Goleuedigaeth, the city of enlightenment.

High Elder Asmodeus - The dark wizard of Castell yr Tywyll.

High Elder Brangwen Binning - from Dolydd, the farm castle.

High Elder Govannon Staley - of the Elven community, Castle Mynydd.

High Elder Llewel Gaynor - from Wrth y Môr, or castle on the sea. One of the seven most powerful (in his own mind) wizards in the land of Trymyll. A short and grumpy wizard with small angry man syndrome.

High Elder Traveon Baughan - of Gwir, Castle of Truth.

Incantation - One of the two major Arts of Magic, in which a long spell is recited and/or runes are drawn out, precisely using the NAME of an object to affect it.

Kraken - a cephalopod-like sea monster of giant size, capable of dragging a ship down to the depths of the ocean.

Llewelyn the Brave – Father of Tom and Jon.

Manticore – A legendary creature like the Egyptian sphinx. It has the head of a human, body of a lion and a tail of venomous spines similar to porcupine quills, if necessary the spines can be shot like arrows, thus making the Manticore a lethal predator. It eats its victims whole, using its triple rows of teeth, and leaves no bones behind.

Máthair - Queen of the Golden Dragons.

Nephilim - Giants, reputably fallen angels. Mentioned in the Bible before the flood of Noah, see Genesis 6 vs 1-4.

Phobl – Someone with few magical powers.

Spellweaver - A magician who specialises in spell weaving. One of the two Mystic Arts, the other being Incantation. A spellweaver uses telekinesis to move THREADS of force into new patterns, which in turn redefine reality.

Trygall – hideous looking beast with scales like a fish, flaming red hair and terrible looking teeth, brown and sharp like barbed ivory thorns, long claw like nails at the end of sinuous fingers and a look of cold hate on its face. However, trygalls are benign and befriend humans, trygalls are firemasters and happen to be particularly good cooks.

Trymyll - Trymyll is a land of seven cities. Each city has a castle or fortified house at its centre.

Printed in Great Britain
by Amazon